A Little Taste of Poison

Also by

R. J. Anderson

A Pocket Full of Murder

A Little Taste of Poison

R. J. Anderson

Atheneum Books for Young Readers
New York London Toronto Sydney New Delhi

ATHENEUM BOOKS FOR YOUNG READERS
An imprint of Simon & Schuster Children's Publishing Division
1230 Avenue of the Americas, New York, New York 10020

For information about special discounts for bulk purchases,
please contact Simon & Schuster Special Sales at 1-866-506-1949
or business@simonandschuster.com.
The Simon & Schuster Speakers Bureau can bring authors to your live event. For more information or to book an event, contact the Simon & Schuster Speakers Bureau at 1-866-248-3049 or visit our website at www.simonspeakers.com.
Book design by Sonia Chaghatzbanian
The text for this book was set in ITC Garamond Std, Akron Handscript, and Oneleigh Pro.
Manufactured in the United States of America
0816 FFG
First Edition
10 9 8 7 6 5 4 3 2 1
Library of Congress Cataloging-in-Publication Data
Names: Anderson, R. J. (Rebecca J.), author.
Title: A little taste of poison / R. J. Anderson.
Description: First edition. | New York : Atheneum Books for Young Readers, 2016. | Summary: Twelve-year-old Isaveth eagerly accepts an opportunity to study at the most exclusive magical school in the city but her scholarship might prove be more a trap than a gift.
Identifiers: LCCN 2015049932
ISBN 978-1-4814-3774-5 (hc)
ISBN 978-1-4814-3776-9 (eBook)
Subjects: | CYAC: Schools—Fiction. | Social classes—Fiction. | Magic—Fiction. | Murder—Fiction. | Fantasy. | Mystery and detective stories. | BISAC: JUVENILE FICTION / Fantasy & Magic. | JUVENILE FICTION / Mysteries & Detective Stories. | JUVENILE FICTION / Social Issues / Friendship.
Classification: LCC PZ7.A54885 Lit 2016 | DDC [Fic]--dc23 LC record available at https://lccn.loc.gov/2015049932

TO DLS, WITH LOVE AND GRATITUDE

Chapter One

ISAVETH SAT STIFFLY in the leather chair, hands clenched on the brim of her hat and heart pounding in her throat. The reception room was hot and smelled of baccy; a clump of snow melted off her boot and plopped onto the diamond-patterned carpet. She longed to take off her coat, but the wool was too damp to lay it on her lap, and she could see nowhere else to put it.

On the opposite wall, a brass plate trumpeted the name of the man Isaveth had come to see: J. J. WREGGET, PRESIDENT. Meanwhile his personal secretary, lean and elegant in a brown suit that nearly matched his skin, shuffled papers while speaking to the call box on his desk: "I'm sorry, Mister Wregget is in a meeting. . . . Pardon? . . . No, he's booked until next Mendday."

Isaveth shifted uncomfortably. This sumptuous ultra-modern office, the inner sanctum of the Glow-Mor Light and Fire Company, was no place for a stonemason's daughter from Cabbage Street. Especially one barely thirteen years old. What could the president of the biggest spell-factory in Tarreton want with her?

True, she'd invented a magic-resistant paper that was perfect for wrapping spell-tablets, and once Mister Wregget had seen it he'd been eager to buy the recipe. But that was months ago, and Isaveth had nothing more to offer him. Even the five imperials he'd paid her—half a year's wages for poor folk like herself—was spent now, gone to pay off old debts and buy her family warm clothes, boots without holes in them, and other long-overdue necessities. In fact, if Papa couldn't find better work than the odd jobs he'd been doing, they'd soon have to apply for relief again.

Dread clutched at Isaveth's chest. What if the president wasn't pleased with her invention? What if he'd called her here to demand his money back?

Perhaps she'd been reckless, coming all the way to the Glow-Mor office by herself. But Papa hadn't been home when the message boy delivered Mister Wregget's summons, and Isaveth hadn't felt comfortable showing it to her older sister, Annagail—let alone the younger girls, Lilet and Mimmi. After all the troubles they'd been through since their mother died, she hated to tell them anything until she was certain it was good news.

Right now, though, she'd settle for it not being too crushingly bad. Sweat prickled beneath her collar and she fumbled open the top button of her coat, but it didn't help. She felt ready to faint by the time the outer door swung open at last, and a balding, ruddy-faced man in a striped waistcoat strode in.

"Miss Breck!" he enthused, engulfing her hand in his big pink one. "What a pleasure. Tambor, take the young lady's coat."

Isaveth struggled out of her winter things and piled them on the secretary, then hurried to catch up as Mister Wregget marched into his office. He sat down, gesturing her to the chair in front of his desk.

"I'm a straightforward man, Miss Breck," he said as the privacy door swung shut, "so I won't bore you with a lot of preamble. How would you like to go to Tarreton College?"

Isaveth goggled at him. Tarreton College was the most exclusive upper-grade school in the city, where the children of the nobility and wealthy merchant families received the finest education—general and magical—that money could provide. He might as well have asked Isaveth how she'd like to fly. "I—I've never dreamed of such a thing, sir."

"Then you need to dream bigger, young lady! Because I'd like to offer you this year's Glow-Mor scholarship." He leaned back, smiling beatifically. "I know it's a mite unusual to start partway through the year, but you're a bright girl, and I'm sure you'll soon catch up. And if you make it through fallowtime and planting terms with good marks, we'll renew the offer next harvest: full tuition, with all books and materials included. What do you say?"

He couldn't be serious. Or if he was, he must be losing his mind. The magic taught at Tarreton College was Sagery, an ancient craft very different from the spellbaking Isaveth had learned from her mother. Instead of recipes using magewort, binding powder, and other cheap ingredients, Sagery relied on precise formulations of precious metals and gemstones to create the kinds of charms only wealthy folk could afford. Its secrets had been jealously guarded for centuries, and some even considered it sacred; it was no craft for a commoner, as the proud masters and mistresses of the college would surely agree.

"Sir," said Isaveth faintly, "I'd be honored, but they'll never—"

"I know what you're thinking," interrupted the president, wagging a finger at her. "Don't worry, Miss Breck, I wouldn't be making this offer if the college wasn't willing to accept you. I know you come from humble stock and your family's had more than its share of troubles, but to my mind that just proves what a resourceful young lady you are. That's the sort of brain I want working for my company, the kind of boldness and sharp thinking that will give Glow-Mor the edge!"

His confidence was buoyant, and Isaveth's hopes rose with it. Maybe this wasn't a mistake after all. Maybe this was what she'd been praying for ever since Mama died and Papa lost his business, a chance to make something of herself and lift her family out of poverty. . . .

Except for one hard fact, dragging her back to earth like an iron anchor. If she'd merely been poor, then Mister Wregget's offer might be seen as an act of charity, a way to enhance his company's good name. But as far as most people in Tarreton were concerned, Isaveth was much worse off than that.

"It's kind of you to say so," she said, forcing the words past the lump in her throat. "Only you don't seem to realize . . . I'm Moshite."

Even as she spoke, she braced herself for his reaction: the hiss of breath, the lowering brows, the frown. But to her surprise, Wregget threw back his head and laughed.

"Honest to a fault, Miss Breck! I see I haven't misjudged you." He folded his hands across his belly, still smiling. "True enough, your . . . er . . . religious background did raise a few eyebrows among the masters. But as Spellmistress Anandri pointed out, there's nothing in the college charter to prevent Moshites from attending. As long as you work hard, obey school rules, and pass your exams, they've got no right to turn you away."

Isaveth had only met Spellmistress Anandri once, and only because her friend Quiz—otherwise known as Esmond Lilord, youngest son of the Sagelord himself—introduced them. Still, the woman had seemed impressed with Isaveth's skill at Common Magic, and even helped bring her magic-resistant paper to Wregget's attention. With such a respected member of the college on her side, perhaps Isaveth's acceptance wasn't as unlikely as she'd thought.

Still, just because the school had no grounds to refuse her didn't mean Isaveth belonged there. She might not even be safe, if anyone recognized her from her last visit, when she'd posed as a cleaning maid to investigate the old governor's murder. . . .

Especially since the current governor of the school, Hexter Buldage, had been part of the conspiracy to kill him.

"I can see you have doubts," said Wregget, "and I can't say I blame you. I'm sure it all sounds a bit too good to be true. But I'll tell you a secret." He leaned closer, voice dropping to a confidential rumble. "Buying that recipe of yours was the best decision I've ever made. Thanks to Resisto-Paper, we've become the leading spell-tablet manufacturer in the city, and orders are pouring in from all over Colonia. You've *earned* that scholarship, is what I say, and anyone who thinks otherwise will have to deal with me!" His hand smacked the desk, making Isaveth jump. "So what's your answer, young lady?"

Isaveth twisted her hands together. Yes, going to Tarreton College would be risky. There were plenty of people, including Esmond's villainous older brother, Eryx Lording, who wouldn't want her to succeed. If Isaveth failed, she'd not only bring disgrace on her family, she'd be confirming what most Arcan and Uniting folk already believed—that Moshites were worthless troublemakers, and everything bad that happened to them was their own fault.

Yet she wouldn't be alone at the college: Esmond would be there too. Isaveth still wasn't sure how to feel about the charming rogue of a street-boy she'd befriended four months ago turning out to be a noble in disguise, especially since they couldn't spend time together anymore without causing a scandal. But at least she'd be able to see him now and then, instead of only writing letters.

Besides, she wanted this. Inside her, beneath the worries and doubts, lay a simmering excitement ready to bubble over at any moment. To face the odds and defy them, to bravely march into danger instead of shying away—wasn't that what her favorite talkie-play heroine, Auradia Champion, would do? There was no guarantee Isaveth would succeed at the college, but if she didn't at least try, she'd regret it for the rest of her life.

Isaveth took a deep breath and smiled at Wregget. "Thank you, sir. I'd love to accept."

Dear Isaveth, I'm afraid I've got bad news. . . .

Esmond rubbed his forehead, staring at the freshly penned words. How was he going to tell her? He was still struggling to get over the shock and disappointment himself. All those weeks spent hunting for the evidence that would prove Eryx guilty of murder, and now . . .

A throat cleared behind him, and Esmond jumped. He flipped the paper over, though he had a sick feeling Eryx had already seen it, and twisted in his chair. "What do you want?" he snapped.

"Mother sent me to call you to supper." As always, his older brother's voice was rich, mellow, and maddeningly calm. "The bell rang five minutes ago, but it seems you were . . . distracted."

He'd come up on Esmond's blind side, and not by mistake: the illusion-charmed lens Esmond usually wore lay unheeded beside the ink blotter, and the scar that ran from brow to cheekbone was plain to see. Not that Eryx would be likely to forget which eye had been injured, seeing as he was the one who'd done it.

Inwardly Esmond seethed, but he kept his expression neutral as he studied the young man who'd made himself the most trusted politician in the city, even as he secretly bribed, blackmailed, and—if necessary—murdered anyone who dared to get in his way. Eryx Lording, Sagelord Arvis's favorite son . . . and for all that they both pretended otherwise, Esmond's most bitter enemy.

"I'm not hungry," he said.

Eryx's brows arched. "Considering your usual rampaging appetite, I find that difficult to believe. To whom were you writing, may I ask? Surely not that Breck girl. I thought we had an agreement."

He hadn't read the letter, then. Or maybe he had, and he was just toying with Esmond. With Eryx, you could never tell.

"Well, you know," said Esmond, "I've been thinking about that. You already burned my street clothes, and Father made me charm-swear not to dress up like a commoner or sneak out of the house again. Then you warned me that if I tried to see Isaveth, you'd have your thugs pay her family a visit—"

"Thugs?" Eryx gave him a pitying look. "Really, Esmond, you sound like that ridiculous *Auradia* show you love so much. I merely remarked that after all Urias Breck had been through since he was arrested, and how hard young Isaveth had worked to clear his name, it would be a shame if they had to endure any further misfortunes."

"Yes, quite," said Esmond. "I'm sure you've lost whole seconds of sleep worrying over it. But it's occurred to me that you could have kept me in line more easily by telling Father about Isaveth, instead of making vague remarks about me 'keeping low company' and 'disgracing the family name.'"

He cocked his head to one side, studying Eryx through his good eye. "Only you don't want to tell him, do you? Because that would mean admitting you botched up, and Urias Breck's daughter caught you framing her papa for a murder *you* helped commit."

Eryx sighed. "We've talked about these delusions of yours before, Esmond. Is there a point to this?"

"Maybe not," said Esmond. "But it's an interesting thought. After all, if I'm not allowed to talk to Isaveth anyway, what's to keep *me* from telling Father the whole story?"

Eryx regarded him steadily for a moment. Then he snatched up Esmond's sheet of writing paper, crumpled it, and tossed it into the fire. "I think you'd find that less satisfying than you imagine," he said coolly. "Remember what happened the last time you accused me in front of Father?"

A dull heat spread beneath Esmond's collarbones. He wouldn't soon forget the agony of Eryx's fencing sword lashing his eye, or the keener torment when Esmond realized that no one—not his mother, not the Sagelord, not even his sister Civilla—was prepared to believe it had been anything more than an accident.

That was the curse of having a silver-tongued demon for a brother. If it came to his word against Esmond's, Eryx would always win.

"In any case," Eryx went on, "if you want to sulk over missing your girlfriend, that's your business. But you know how Mother feels about family dinners. You wouldn't want to upset Mother, would you?"

Esmond was tempted to treat that question with the scorn it deserved. Lady Nessa's fragile nerves were notorious: She'd always be anxious about something, whether her youngest son came to dinner or not. But Lord Arvis was also waiting, and defying him was another matter.

Grudgingly Esmond picked up his half glass, hooked it into place, and rose. He was taller than his brother when they stood side by side, but Eryx didn't allow him that satisfaction; he turned and strode out, leaving Esmond to trail after him like a servant—or a dog.

Dear Isaveth:

I'm afraid I'm a stinking failure as a detective, which means the men who killed Governor Orien and nearly got your papa hanged for it are never going to pay. Also, Eryx caught me writing to you, and if he tells Father I've been "fraternizing with commoners" again I won't have to worry about his dodgy liver—he'll die of apoplexy instead.

But that was black humor, and self-pitying besides, and Isaveth wouldn't think much of either. She'd watched her mother die of a wasting illness and her father get dragged off to jail, and it had only made her more determined to stand up for justice and protect the people she loved. Esmond's family might not need him—or even care about him—the way that Isaveth's did, but he could do better than that.

Dear Isaveth:

I'm afraid we've had a bit of a setback, and by "a bit" I mean "I just found the only evidence we had against Eryx burned and smashed to bits," which is the opposite of what I'd hoped to tell you. But I haven't forgotten what my brother did to your family, and I promise that somehow, I'll make him pay for it. Don't lose heart.

P.S. Have you decided if I can kiss you yet?

That was better. More like Quiz, the jaunty street-boy he'd pretended to be when he first met Isaveth, the bold and funny part of him that she liked best. Even if the last thing he'd said to her had been so embarrassing that he could only recover by turning it into a joke, they were still friends and he hoped to keep it that way.

For now, though, writing Isaveth was out of the question. It could be weeks before Esmond's brother stopped watching him, and if one of Eryx's spies found their secret letter drop it would be disastrous. He could only hope she'd be patient, and not worry too much that he hadn't replied.

"What do you mean, boy, keeping us all waiting on you?" demanded Lord Arvis as Esmond came into the dining room. His father sat at the head of the long table, a big man whose muscles had long ago turned to fat, eyes deep-set in a sallow and blotchy face. Esmond's mother had once remarked wistfully that in his youth the Sagelord had been handsome, even dashing. But that was hard to imagine now.

"I apologize, sir," Esmond answered, chin up and voice strong. The Sagelord hated slouching, mumbling, and all other hints of cowardice. He also despised excuses, so Esmond added, "I should have been paying attention."

"I'll say you should," growled his father. "Sit down and let's get on with it."

He snapped his fingers and the footmen leaped to attend him, filling his wineglass and whisking a cloth napkin into the scant space between his belly and the table. A platter of bread, pickled vegetables, and cheese was set before him—Lord Arvis would have nothing to do with soup, though his wife ate little else—and the evening meal began.

"My darling," Lady Nessa murmured as her husband raised the glass to his lips. "Your liver . . . ?"

Lord Arvis slammed down his wineglass, sloshing red onto the damask tablecloth. "Take this away," he barked at the servant. "Are you trying to poison me?"

Stammering apologies, the footman rushed to obey. Esmond pitied the man; if he hadn't poured the wine, the Sagelord would have lambasted him for forgetting it. Lord Arvis's healers had warned him not to drink alcohol, but whether he chose to heed them depended on his mood, who else was drinking, and how well he happened to be feeling that day.

The healers had also recommended a strict diet, but as Lord Arvis slathered his bread with butter and helped himself to two kinds of cheese and a pickled egg, it was plain that he had no use for their opinion. "And I don't need you fussing over me either," he told his wife, who shrank back and said no more.

"So," the Sagelord went on when the silence around the table had grown unbearable. "What did *you* do with yourself today? Something useful for a change, I hope."

Esmond froze with his soup spoon halfway to his mouth, but for once his father's glare wasn't leveled at him. He was looking at Civilla, who cleared her throat and patted her lips with her napkin before answering.

"Of course, Daddy. I met some friends for tea at the Women's League this morning, and in the afternoon Mother helped me pick out the invitations for my ball. They're the prettiest shade of ice blue, and I was thinking—"

The Sagelord stopped her with an upraised hand. "None of that. I'm paying enough for this party of yours without having to listen to a lot of fluff-headed talk about decorating as well. Did you hear anything I might actually *care* about?"

Civilla's smile thinned. She was undoubtedly the

family expert on gossip these days, with plenty of social engagements and visits to the leading families of the city. But though she was usually quick to share any rumors that would interest Lord Arvis, she had her pride, and he'd ruffled it.

"Well," she said, "I don't know. Have you heard that J. J. Wregget's finally handed out this year's Glow-Mor scholarship?"

Eryx frowned. "What, now? Harvest term's nearly over. Why would he wait so long?"

"Seems he wasn't impressed with any of the students who applied, so he went out and found his own candidate. But he won't say who she is, only that she's a 'deserving young lady' who prefers to remain anonymous." Civilla gave a little shrug. "No doubt her family was ashamed to admit they needed the money."

Esmond watched Lord Arvis out of his good eye. His father's face was set and the corners of his mouth turned down, but he said nothing until Eryx asked, "Father?"

"I don't meddle in Wregget's business," snapped the Sagelord, stabbing a forkful of pickled beetroot onto his plate. "It's bad policy."

Which made sense, because Wregget's wife, Perline, was a close friend of Lady Nessa's, and Glow-Mor's recent "discovery" of Resisto-Paper had made it one of the most successful spell-factories in the city. Of course Esmond's father would want to keep such a valuable acquaintance happy—with unrest still brewing among Tarreton's workers, and a string of disastrous political blunders making the merchants and even some of his own nobles restless, Lord Arvis needed all the powerful allies he could get.

"Even so, you must know who his choice was," Eryx persisted. "As chief patron of Tarreton College, you would have received a copy of the masters' decision." But the Sagelord only snorted and waved the topic aside.

Esmond could guess why. The notice must have arrived on one of his father's bad days, when he was too busy groaning and dosing himself with stomach powder to care about paperwork. He probably couldn't remember the name of Wregget's candidate and didn't want to admit it.

"Perline says," Lady Nessa spoke up hesitantly, "that the girl's a commoner. It sounds like Wregget found her selling homemade spell-tablets on the street."

Esmond's heart did a triple somersault and dropped into his belly. There couldn't be more than two or three girls in the city who fit that description, and only one that J. J. Wregget knew well enough to reward. . . .

"Agh!" Lord Arvis doubled over, and the Sagelady

leaped up in panic. She whisked off her napkin and began dabbing his sweat-beaded face.

"I'm so sorry, darling, I didn't mean to upset you. We must get you lying down at once—"

"Upset?" Even through clenched teeth, his father's voice was loud enough to echo across the room. "I'm not one of your wilting lilies! Bring me some Propo-Seltzer. I'll be fine in a few minutes." Gripping his abdomen, he lurched upright, and the footmen helped him out of the room.

"A commoner!" exclaimed Civilla when they were gone. The Sagelady hovered in the doorway, gazing anxiously after her husband, but Lord Arvis had been having these attacks for weeks and the rest of the family no longer worried about them. "That should please you, Eryx. You're the one always making speeches about equality and better opportunities for the poor."

Eryx said nothing. He took a roll from the basket and began slowly tearing it to pieces, while Esmond bit the inside of his cheek and resisted the urge to whoop and dance around the table. Whether by accident or the Sagelord's grudging permission, Isaveth Breck was about to become a student at Tarreton College. Soon Esmond would be seeing her, maybe even talking to her, every day. . . .

And this time, Eryx couldn't do a thing about it.

Chapter Two

"OW!" ISAVETH FLINCHED as the comb snagged in her hair. Annagail was doing her best to be gentle, but after a restless night with her head covered in pinch pins, Isaveth had ended up with a few tangles.

"Your hair's so thick, I can't help it," said her older sister. "But I promise it'll look beautiful when I'm done. Turn around and let me do the other side."

Isaveth had never bothered to style her cropped hair before; she'd just had Anna trim it when it got too close to her shoulders. But that wouldn't do at a place like Tarreton College, so she sat meekly and endured her sister's tugging as the two younger girls bustled around the tiny kitchen, making breakfast.

"Stop elbowing me!" complained Mimmi, giving Lilet a shove. "You're making me spill."

"Stop standing on my feet, then!"

"Enough of that," Papa called as he came down the creaking staircase. "It's a bad day that starts with a quarrel. You don't want to spoil Vettie's first day at the college, do you?"

"No, Papa," they chorused, though Lilet rolled her eyes as she said it, and Isaveth had to smile. After the shock of Mister Wregget's offer and all the challenges that came with accepting it, there was something comforting about listening to her little sisters squabble: It reminded her that no matter what else changed, the people she loved best would stay the same.

Once she'd eaten her fill of the grainy porridge Mimmi called "birdseed" and Anna had coaxed her pin curls into glossy waves, it was time for Isaveth to leave. Shivering in the chill of the front hallway, she laced up her boots, donned her red knitted hat and matching scarf—a Fallowfeast gift from Lilet and Mimmi—and turned in place while Anna inspected her coat, brushing out the salt stains and touching up a few faded patches with shoe-blacking. "There," she said, straightening up. "I think you're ready."

"I don't *feel* ready," Isaveth admitted, with a glance at the freckled mirror. She'd found it lying in a rubbish heap last harvest and it had been hanging by the coat rack ever since, but now it only reminded her how poor she was compared to everyone else at the college. "I feel sick."

Annagail took her hand. "You can still change your mind. If you're not sure you want to go. . . ."

"I am sure. I'm just . . . a bit nervous."

"Is it Meggery that worries you?" Anna moved closer, lowering her voice so Papa and their younger sisters wouldn't hear. "She can't hurt you, Vettie. All she can do is tell the masters you're Moshite, and they know that already."

"She could also tell the *students* that I'm Moshite." Not that Isaveth planned to deny it if anyone asked: She'd learned that lying about her faith could be worse than admitting the truth. But while Annagail had worn a prayer scarf about her neck ever since their mother died, Isaveth wore hers only at temple or when saying the supper blessing. That was what the scarf was for, after all, and why should she make it easy for people to despise her?

"Maybe, but a housekeeper is still a servant," Anna told her, "and that means Meggery's expected to keep quiet and stay out of sight. She probably won't even know you're at the college, let alone make any—"

"Is that my Vettie?" Papa's broad shoulders filled the doorframe as he stepped out of the kitchen, wiping his beard with the back of his hand. "Look at you, all dressed up and beautiful!" He seized Isaveth by the shoulders, beaming. "That boyfriend of yours won't know what hit him."

Isaveth cringed. "Papa, he's not . . ."

"Don't tease her, Papa," said Annagail. "She's nervous enough already." Stooping to kiss Isaveth's cheek, she whispered, "I'll be praying for you." Then she slipped back to the kitchen.

"Don't worry, sweetling." The twinkle in her father's eye softened to tenderness. "You'll do fine. Especially with Mistress Anandri and the Sagelord's own son looking out for you."

Isaveth couldn't deny it, not when she'd used those same words to convince Papa three weeks ago. But he had no idea that Governor Buldage was a murderer, let alone that Eryx Lording had put him up to it.

Yet how could she tell Papa the truth without confessing all the risks she'd taken to save him from the gallows? If he knew what powerful enemies she'd made, he wouldn't just refuse to let Isaveth go to the college, he probably wouldn't let her out of the house.

"Yes, Papa," said Isaveth, hugging him. Then she scooped up her school bag and ran out to catch her tram.

When Isaveth arrived at Tarreton College, the snow was falling in fat flakes, soft and fluttery as goose down. She stepped off the tram, gazing at her new school in silent awe.

The main gate loomed above her, its square pillars engraved with the college crest on one side and two lines of cryptic runes on the other. Before her lay a cobbled avenue lined with spell-powered lampposts, still glowing faintly in the gray morning light, and past them, at the end of the long drive, rose the steep-angled roofs and pointed archways of Founders' Hall.

The last time Isaveth had walked these grounds was in the heat of fairweather season, when the buildings had stood all but empty, awaiting the rush of harvest term. But she'd been so caught up in her mission back then, so desperate to investigate the scene of Governor Orien's murder and prove her father's innocence, that she'd barely noticed what the college looked like. Only now, with those dark days behind her, could she truly appreciate the school that was about to become her own—and it was beautiful. Even with icicles dripping off every roof edge and grimy salt trails sprinkling each snowy path and stair, the grandeur of the college buildings took Isaveth's breath away. Who could look up at those soaring gray-gold towers, those arched doors and jewel-glass windows, and not feel humbled by their magnificence? Even after a month of preparation, Isaveth couldn't quite believe she was here and not at the dreary little school back in Gardentown.

"Chin up, Isaveth," she murmured, gripping the strap of her school bag. She'd taken an early tram, wanting plenty of time to collect her schedule and other essentials before class started. But her fellow students were beginning to arrive now, climbing out of spell-carriages and taxis, or strolling up the sidewalk with their friends. Most of the girls wore the slim, tailored coats and fur-trimmed carriage boots that were the height of fashion, and Isaveth had to fight the urge to hide behind the gatepost as they approached her.

Mister Wregget had agreed to keep Isaveth's identity a secret, so no one but the masters of the college—and Esmond, of course—would know who she was or where she'd come from. With her new hairstyle, a smidge of lip tint, and her olive cheeks dusted rose for a healthy glow, she'd hoped to pass for the daughter of some lesser merchant family—her father wasn't the only Breck in the city, after all. But despite all Anna had done to help her look the part, Isaveth still felt like the word "commoner" was branded across her face.

Yet the girls swept by without a pause, too busy chatting to notice her. The boys also ignored Isaveth as they slouched past, hands deep in their pockets and collars turned up against the snow. Relieved, Isaveth stood straighter and set off along the path to Founders' Hall.

"Morning, miss," said the porter, and Isaveth stiffened. She'd spoken to this man when she was last here, disguised as a cleaning maid—what if he recognized her? But when she dared to meet his eye, he only smiled and nodded at her to go on.

The corridor ended by the main staircase, where a sign pointed left to the registrar's office. Isaveth was turning toward it when applause rippled out of a room nearby, followed by a voice so familiar it stopped her heart: "Thank you. Are there any questions?"

It couldn't be—her ears must be playing tricks on her. Yet there was only one way to find out. Isaveth followed the sound to a small auditorium, whose door bore a sign reading CLUB MEETING IN PROGRESS. Inside sat several rows of students, from stiff-collared boys her own age to a cluster of fourth-year girls as old as Anna. And at the front stood Eryx Lording, surveying them all.

What a fool she'd been, to mistake his voice for Esmond's! Isaveth ducked out of the doorway, hoping he hadn't spotted her. But Eryx spoke: "We have a latecomer. I'm afraid we're almost finished, miss, but don't be shy."

Fifty heads swiveled toward her, and Isaveth's heart sank. She crept in and sat down in the first empty seat she could find.

"I have a question, milord," said a girl in the second row. "You said you'd been urging city council to increase relief payments to needy families. Does that mean raising taxes for the rest of us?"

"An excellent question." Eryx gave her a dazzling smile, and the girl blushed red as her hair. "Happily, the answer is no. My plan is to ensure that only citizens who are deserving—honest, loyal folk left unemployed through no fault of their own—receive financial help from the city, while those who use poverty as an excuse for crime and rebellion"—his gaze flicked to Isaveth—"do not. There will be plenty of relief for people who need it, if we weed out the lawbreakers first."

Uneasiness squirmed inside Isaveth. The Lord Justice had declared Papa innocent, so he had no criminal record. But Urias Breck had long been a member of the Workers' Club, a political group known for its fiery protests against the Sagelord's rule. Was Eryx hinting that if Papa applied for relief in a month or two, he'd be rejected? If so, how would Isaveth and her family survive?

A brown hand shot up among the students, and a stocky boy in spectacles rose to speak. "Does the Sagelord intend to continue his ban against political meetings and demonstrations in the city?"

"Well, clearly *meetings* are not the problem," said Eryx, "or we'd all be under arrest right now." He waited for the laughter to subside, then went on. "Personally, I believe that free and open discourse is vital to a healthy society. That's why I've been urging my father to lift the ban for any group that agrees to expel all members with criminal or antisocial tendencies"—his eyes flicked to Isaveth again—"and to hold only peaceful protests from now on."

"Antisocial, my lord?" asked a girl in the row next to Isaveth. "What do you mean?"

Eryx gazed at the vaulted ceiling, fingers steepled in thought. "As I'm sure you're aware, there are people in our city with a history of lawless behavior, the kind of folk who stir up trouble wherever they go. They despise the sacred traditions that bind all good citizens together, and promote their own radical beliefs instead. . . ."

He spoke delicately, but Isaveth knew what he meant: words like "lawless" and "radical" had been used to condemn Moshites for centuries. She sat rigid, trembling with the urge to leap up and denounce him—but how could she? Nobody here knew her, or had any reason to care what she thought. Especially since she was one of the very people Eryx was slandering.

"Of course," Eryx continued, "any enlightened society must tolerate some disagreement, however—er—disagreeable. But I think we should draw the line at endorsing bad behavior, much less rewarding it. Thus my plan to reform our relief system, which I hope all of you will urge your local council members to support. Thank you."

With another burst of applause the students rose, many pressing forward to greet the Lording and shake his hand. Isaveth hid her face in her handkerchief, pretending to wipe her nose while she calmed herself, then got up and hurried out the door.

"You'll need a robe," said the registrar, a stoop-shouldered man with a voice as bland as the rest of him. Opening a drawer, he pulled out a square of gray cloth and handed it to Isaveth. "And your timetable . . ." He glanced under the counter. "Hmm. Wait here, please."

He vanished into the adjoining office, while Isaveth shook out the robe and examined it. Unlike the masters' robes it was sleeveless, so she could wear it over her coat as easily as under—and since her first class might be anywhere on the grounds, that seemed like a sensible idea. She draped it around her shoulders and smoothed it, waiting for the registrar to return.

She couldn't think too much about what Eryx had said or she'd start to panic. He'd spoken of treating Isaveth's father and other politically-minded Moshites as undesirables, denying them financial support and encouraging their fellow workers to shun them—and the students in the club had applauded as though it were a splendid idea. As though her family deserved nothing better than starvation, which was what it would come to if Papa couldn't find a proper job soon.

Her only hope was that she'd leaped to the wrong conclusion, and Eryx hadn't been talking about Papa at all. But the Lording hadn't seemed surprised to see Isaveth, and she couldn't forget how his cold eyes had lingered on her as he spoke. . . .

"Miss Breck?"

The greeting came from behind her, so unexpected it made her jump. Isaveth whirled and found herself staring into the lean, sallow face of Hexter Buldage, the new governor of the school.

"Oh," she said, but it came out as a squeak, and she couldn't think of anything else to say.

Buldage smiled. His expression was kindly, his eyes mild as harvest fog; if she hadn't known otherwise, she'd never have guessed him for a murderer. "Welcome to Tarreton College. I hope you'll be happy here."

Mute with fear, Isaveth could only nod. How much had Eryx Lording told him about her? Did Buldage realize she knew his most terrible secret?

"I hear great things about your talent for Common Magic," the governor continued. "If you show a similar aptitude for Sagery, your classmates will have to work hard to keep up with you."

There was no stiffness in his posture, no sinister undertone to his words. If her presence here troubled him, he was doing an excellent job of hiding it.

"It's . . . an honor to be here, sir," said Isaveth, recovering at last. "Thank you for giving me—uh—this chance."

"My pleasure. If there is anything I can do to assist you, let me know." Still smiling, he stepped back, turned in a swirl of midnight robes, and walked out.

Isaveth stared after him, heart drumming in her chest. The governor's office was two floors up, on the far side of the building; there was no way Buldage could have passed this way by chance. What did it mean, that he'd come down especially to meet her?

And why would he welcome Isaveth to the college when Eryx, his master, didn't want her here at all?

Chapter Three

ISAVETH WALKED DOWN the snow-covered steps, studying her new timetable. Her first and only magical course this term was Introduction to Common Magic—which shouldn't have surprised her, since all first-year students had to take that class. But it was frustrating to have to spend a whole term reviewing spells she already knew, instead of starting Sagery right away.

Still, Mistress Anandri liked her, so it should be an easy pass. As the bell in the great tower began to toll, Isaveth stuffed the schedule into her bag and set off toward the spell-kitchen.

Chayla Anandri stood inside the doorway marking attendance, a tall dark-skinned woman with a queenly bearing and a skullcap of pepper-gray hair. "Good morning, mistress," said Isaveth, smiling at her. But the teacher merely ticked off Isaveth's name before striding through the ring of students and calling them to attention.

"Undermaster Yarton will show each of you to a station." She nodded to a gawky young man in an indigo robe, who straightened up importantly. "There you will find ingredients and all the instructions you need to bake light-tablets. At the end of class your results will be graded for purity, consistency, and effectiveness. Any questions?"

The students glanced at one another, and a pert-nosed girl with hair the color of milky tea stepped forward. "Why do we have to learn Common Magic before we can start Sagery? It's so . . ."

"Common?" asked Mistress Anandri crisply. "No doubt you are accustomed to having fire- and light-tablets baked by your servants, or bought for you ready-made. You consider the making of such spells beneath you, much as a fieldlord's daughter might consider it an insult to be asked to pick apples or milk the cows. Correct?"

She arched an eyebrow at the girl, who colored but kept her head high. "Yes, mistress."

"Which is precisely why you need to learn more about it," said the spellmistress. "Common Magic may have a lesser reputation than Sagery, but it is far more practical for everyday purposes, and our city's future may well depend on the manufacture and export of tablets like these."

Her gaze swept over the students, and Isaveth tried once more to catch her eye, but the woman looked through her. "I have business elsewhere, so I must leave for a little while. Undermaster Yarton is in charge until I return."

Grumbles rose from Isaveth's classmates, but when the undermaster gestured for them to spread out along the counter, they obeyed. Isaveth stepped eagerly to her own station, close to one of the two enormous ovens and well lit by the windows high above.

"This is ridiculous," muttered the prim-looking girl, stomping up next to her. "We're supposed to be learning real magic, not *cookery*." She grabbed the nearest canister and began scooping out flour, not even bothering to measure it before dumping it into her bowl.

"That's too much," Isaveth protested, but a scowl from the other girl silenced her. Wincing at the sight of good flour wasted, she turned to her own work.

After weeks of baking light-tablets to sell on the street, Isaveth knew her mother's recipe by heart. She leveled and sifted each cup of flour, then measured out the magewort and other magical ingredients. There were two eggs in her basket, which seemed extravagant, so she cracked one and set the other aside. She whisked the batter together until it ran creamy-smooth, then filled the pan that had been set out for her and carried it to the oven.

As she returned to her station, stares and whispers followed her. One of the girls gave a nervous titter, turning it into a cough as Isaveth glanced her way. The clank of spoons and the clatter of bowls grew louder, and the girl who had used too much flour shot Isaveth a poisonous glare.

"Someone's been taking lessons," she sniffed as she scraped at her lumpy, powder-streaked dough. "I suppose you think you're going to make the rest of us look like fools."

Isaveth hadn't meant to show off. But she couldn't pretend not to know what she was doing. "Not at all," she said politely, and set to tidying up her workspace.

One by one the students brought their pans to Yarton, who inspected them with approving nods or slight grimaces before adding them to the oven. Soon both ovens were full, and her classmates drifted into groups while they waited for the tablets to bake. Isaveth stood alone, watching the clock until she could bear it no longer. She crossed to Yarton and tugged his sleeve.

"Sir, may I take mine out now?"

She kept her voice low, trying not to draw attention, and was relieved when the undermaster nodded. He pulled her pan from the rack, handed her the hot-glove, and let her carry it away.

Isaveth had cut the cooked batter into tablets and was shaking binding powder over them when a creak from the doorway made her turn. Mistress Anandri strode into the kitchen, robe swirling, and beckoned Yarton over for a brief, murmured discussion. Then she walked into the adjoining room and shut the door.

Yarton cleared his throat. "Time's up now. When your name is called, take your tablets to the sunroom and show them to Mistress Anandri. Mister Ableman"—he bent to pull a pan from the oven—"you're first."

As Yarton passed out the remaining pans, Isaveth backed against the worktop, shielding her perfect tablets from view. But when her neighbor slammed her own half-cooked pan onto the counter and glowered at her, Isaveth knew she'd moved too late. She was glad to hear her name called so she could escape—if only as far as the glass-walled room beside the kitchen, where Mistress Anandri awaited her.

"Shut the door, Miss Breck," she said, and Isaveth obeyed before setting her light-tablets down on the table. But instead of taking out her charm-glass and appraising them, Mistress Anandri pushed the pan aside.

"There has been a mistake," she said. "You do not

belong in this class, and I do not wish to see you here again."

A chill rippled through Isaveth. This couldn't be happening. Not with the one teacher she'd thought she could trust. "M—mistress? Did I do something wrong?"

"Nothing whatsoever, which is the point. Your presence here is a distraction to the other students, and a waste of everyone's time. Starting tomorrow, you will join Mistress Corto's class in the old charmery. Collect your belongings and go."

Cheeks burning, Isaveth left the sunroom, avoiding her classmates' curious eyes. But as she pulled on her coat she heard a whisper, "Guess someone got caught cheating," and her face grew hotter still.

At least they didn't suspect she was a commoner—they thought she'd made a special effort to learn spell-baking, rather than doing it as a matter of course. But right now Isaveth was too hurt and bewildered to care. If she'd done nothing wrong, why had Mistress Anandri ignored her in front of the other students? Why had she spoken so coldly even when the two of them were alone?

Perhaps the spellmistress had heard something bad about Isaveth and decided to distance herself. But it was hard to imagine what—or who—could have changed her attitude so completely.

Still, Isaveth had one consolation: She wouldn't have to spend the next ten weeks making spell-tablets. Starting tomorrow, she'd be learning Sagery at last.

Isaveth's second class of the morning was Uropian History, which should have delighted her; after all, it was hard to make tales of queens and kings and great battles dull, even with a teacher who spoke in a hoarse monotone and blew his nose every two minutes. But her thoughts kept straying to Eryx's speech, Buldage's strange welcome, and Mistress Anandri's unexpected rebuff, and she scarcely heard a word of Master Eddicot's lecture. All she could think was that she had to find Esmond and talk to him.

When the bell rang, her fellow students dashed out ahead of her, heading for the dining hall. But Isaveth's scholarship did not include meals, and all she had to eat was a cheese biscuit left over from supper last night. Even if she could find a seat, it would be obvious that she couldn't afford to eat like the others. So she hung back, leaning over the window-lit staircase of the Antiquities Building and gazing at the snowy courtyard below, until the halls fell silent. Then she found a bench on one of the landings and sat down to eat.

As Isaveth chewed her biscuit and sipped her flask of lukewarm tea, she pondered her next course of action.

Even if Esmond hadn't received her letter telling him about the scholarship, he must know that Isaveth was here. If she went to the dining hall while he was eating, perhaps she could signal him somehow. . . .

"Well, miss," said a tart voice, and Isaveth choked on her biscuit as the chief housekeeper climbed the stair toward her.

"So this is where you've been skulking." Meggery's harsh tone was strangely at odds with her apple-cheeked, motherly face. "I heard you were starting at the college today."

Isaveth swallowed. It wasn't surprising that Eryx had known; he had spies all over the city. But if this woman had heard the news of her scholarship as well . . .

"Oh, you needn't look frightened. I've been told my opinion of you isn't wanted, so you've nothing to fear from me." Meggery clambered onto the landing and planted her hands on her hips. "But I won't forget how you tricked me, with your lies and cunning ways. I'll be watching, and if I catch you making mischief . . ." She snapped her fingers in front of Isaveth, close enough to make her flinch. "I won't be the one who pays for it. Not this time."

It wasn't hard to guess why Meggery was so angry. Hiring a Moshite girl without her employers' knowledge could have cost the woman her job, and she'd only done it because Isaveth had pretended she and Annagail were Unifying instead. "I'm sorry I lied to you," she said hoarsely. "But I was trying to save my Papa—"

Meggery sniffed. "I'm sure," she said. "A right little heroine, you are. You won't fool *me* again." She turned her back on Isaveth, then paused and looked over her shoulder. "And take your lunch to the dining hall. I'll not have vermin nibbling about everywhere, if you please."

To anyone else that request might have sounded reasonable; crumbs would attract mice, after all. But the way Meggery looked at Isaveth when she said "vermin" left no doubt what she really meant. Burning with humiliation, Isaveth snatched up her flask, shoved the remnants of her biscuit into her pocket, and fled.

She'd nearly reached the steps of the dining hall when a paper dart soared down from an upper window and bounced off her head. "Ow!" she exclaimed, swatting it away. It dropped to the ground and began buzzing in circles, like a fly with an injured wing.

There was no sign of who had launched it, but they'd clearly used magic to make sure it hit the mark. Angry, Isaveth snatched up the dart to crumple it, charm and all, and throw it away. But when she touched the paper, it unfolded to reveal a secret message:

Meet me at the bell tower after school.

It bore no signature, but she didn't need one. After weeks of trading secret letters, she knew Esmond's handwriting as well as she knew her own.

Relief spread through Isaveth, loosening the knots inside. Whatever Mistress Anandri or anyone else thought of her, there was at least one person at the college who still cared. She smiled up at the window, tucked the paper into her pocket, and walked on.

Compared to the drama of that morning, Isaveth's afternoon was almost pleasant—except when she discovered that Betinda Callender, the girl who'd accused her of showing off in Common Magic, also sat behind her in Calculation. She pretended not to notice, but she could feel that hostile stare drilling into her, and when the bell rang she was glad to get away.

In the shadow of the bell tower, with the wind whipping past and little eddies of snow whirling about her boots, it was bitterly cold. Isaveth rubbed her arms and hopped from one foot to the other, wishing Esmond had picked a warmer place to meet. Where was he, anyway?

"Psst!" The voice came from above, like the dart that had summoned her. Startled, Isaveth looked up—and saw him leaning out of the tower window, a lanky blond boy with a glittering lens over his left eye. "In here," he said. "Quick!"

Sure enough, the door at the base of the tower was unlocked. Isaveth glanced about to make sure no one was watching, then opened it and slipped in.

It was dim inside, and almost as chilly as the open air. But when Esmond came bounding down the wooden staircase and seized Isaveth's hands in welcome, joy warmed her from head to toe. She hadn't realized, until now, how much she'd missed him.

"How did you get in here?" she asked. "You aren't one of the ringers, are you?"

If he'd really been Quiz she wouldn't have bothered asking; she'd assume he'd picked the lock or a ringer's pocket. But she was still learning what this new boy, the Sagelord's son, would do.

"No," said Esmond, his blue eyes—one real, the other glass-framed illusion—wickedly bright. "But I'm glad to see you again. May I kiss you now?"

She should have known it was coming; he'd made the same joke in every letter he'd written her, after all. Once she'd got over being shocked, flabbergasted, then embarrassed as she realized that he must have been teasing her all along, she'd worked up the courage to fire back.

Sorry, I'm taking a dogsled to Borealis, she'd replied

in her first letter, and since then she'd thought of several more witty comebacks so he'd never catch her unprepared. *Not today, I've got the Antipodean lip flu. Maybe, if you bring me the moon in a teacup.*

It was different hearing him ask her in person, though, and she had to look away as she replied. "Not until you've grown a beard," she told him. "A long woolly one, like Father Frost. And you still haven't answered my question."

"Filched the spare key from the porter's office." Esmond started up the staircase, beckoning her to follow. "Thought it would be a good place to talk without Eryx's telltales spotting us."

Of course Eryx had spies at the college. With her luck, Meggery was one of them, and Isaveth would have to be even more wary of the housekeeper than before. "I saw Eryx this morning," Isaveth said. "He was giving a speech in Founders' Hall."

Esmond glanced back at her, surprised. "Really? What about?"

Isaveth told him.

"So that's his plan, is it?" His eyes narrowed angrily, all whimsy gone. "He's still trying to punish you for finding out the truth about him. Well, he can talk all he likes about his precious relief scheme, but he isn't Sagelord yet."

Esmond stalked up onto the landing, and Isaveth climbed after him. The place was far from cozy: just a bare wooden platform stretching the width of the tower, with the bell rope dangling above. But he'd built a rough bench out of crates, sacking, and his own bundled-up greatcoat, while the snapped halves of a sage-charm—a warming-charm, by the balmy feel of the air—lay on the floor beside it.

"Maybe not," Isaveth said as they sat down, "but he's got plenty of support on the city council, and your father listens to him more often than not. We can't just hope for the best, Esmond. We have to stop him."

Esmond sighed. "Which makes what I have to tell you even more rotten. Remember that charm-band I was wearing when Eryx caught us searching his study?"

How could Isaveth forget? The magical recording device was their only proof that the Lording had arranged Master Orien's murder. Unfortunately, Eryx had confiscated it before they could turn it over to the Lawkeepers, and they'd been trying to get it back ever since.

"Well, I found it," said Esmond, pressing something cold into Isaveth's hand. A black, lumpen ring that had once been silver, with a few broken shards of sound-crystal clinging to its surface. "I'm sorry, Isaveth. I didn't think he'd guess what it was for, but he must have."

Isaveth closed her eyes, the tightness in her chest returning. For four months she'd waited, praying for a miracle . . . and now this.

"It doesn't matter," she said, too loudly. "We'll get him some other way."

"I'd like nothing better," Esmond said, "but how? Nobody's going to believe my brother's a murderer just on our say-so. Even my own family thinks I ought to accept his apology for half blinding me and move on."

He was right—they needed someone older and more powerful to speak for them. But who? There were only a few people in the city who knew the truth about Eryx, and none of them could testify against the Lording without ruining themselves.

"I don't know," she said, dropping the charm-band onto the straw between them. "But we'll find something. We've got to."

Esmond shook his head in admiration. "You never give up, do you? Auradia all over again."

Coming from a boy who loved *Auradia Champion* as much as she did, that was quite the compliment. But it wasn't her love of justice that was driving Isaveth this time; it was desperation. If Papa couldn't get relief, there'd be no chance of her staying at Tarreton College; she and Annagail would have to quit school and take the first jobs they could find, just to keep their family from being thrown out on the street.

Yet she couldn't say that to Esmond. If Quiz were here she'd have poured out her fears to him, but what did this young noble, with his shining hair and spotless clothing, know about being poor? He'd likely feel sorry for Isaveth, or worse, offer her charity. And that would be unbearable.

"Maybe we can't prove that Eryx murdered Master Orien," Isaveth said, willing her voice steady. "But we could still catch him committing some other sort of crime. Bribery, or blackmail, or . . . I don't know, something. Anything."

Esmond took out a handkerchief and began cleaning his half glass, which had to be sheer habit, because he couldn't see out of it either way. "Good point. I'll keep my ears open and see what I can find out. But we can't meet here every day—it's too risky. We need a new place to leave messages."

Isaveth nodded. The loose stone by the fountain in Sage Allum's Park had served them well enough during harvest, but once the snow started falling, the walk there had become a lot less pleasant. "What about the school library?"

"Excellent idea. I recommend the agriculture section.

Find a book on crop pests or something of that sort, and nobody but us will ever look at it." He hooked his glass back on, keeping his scar averted. "I'm sorry about this. I thought . . . well, hoped . . . we'd have Eryx by now."

It's all right, Isaveth wanted to tell him, but the words stuck in her throat. Much as she didn't blame Esmond for what had happened, nothing would be right until Eryx went to prison and her family was safe.

"So did I," she said.

Chapter Four

"VETTIE!" MIMMI FLUNG her arms around Isaveth's waist—then jumped back, bristling like a wet kitten. "Ugh, you're freezing!"

"Sillyhead," said Isaveth, ruffling her sister's hair. She hung up her coat and bent to unlace her boots. "How was school?"

"Oh, never mind that! I want to hear all about the college!" She hopped onto the landing and hollered up the staircase, "Lilet! Vettie's home!"

Annagail appeared in the kitchen doorway, apron stained and wooden spoon in hand. "Don't *yell*, Mimmi," she pleaded as Lilet came tramping down from the bedroom, hugging her threadbare cardigan about her shoulders. They all looked at Isaveth expectantly.

"All right," said Isaveth. "Let me warm up, and I'll tell you all about it."

Papa was waiting at the kitchen table, big hands clasped around his mug of tea. He must have gotten home only a minute or two before she did: His cheeks were windburned, and ice pellets clung to his beard. It was hard work shoveling snow off wealthier folk's drives and walkways, and his takings were so meager they barely paid half the rent—but it wasn't her father's way to sit idle when he could be doing, any more than it was Isaveth's.

Which was why she couldn't tell him about Eryx's relief plan, no matter how much she longed to. For weeks now Papa's belief that the Lording had saved him from the gallows, and that he could count on Eryx to stand up for poor folk like himself, had kept him safely away from the illegal meetings of the Workers' Club and the other banned political groups in the city. But if Papa knew the truth, he'd be outraged. He'd try to warn his fellow dissenters, maybe even urge them to revolt . . . and that would play right into Eryx Lording's hands.

She couldn't tell her sisters, either. Annagail would only make herself sick with worrying, while Lilet would be just as furious and ready to fight as Papa. And Mimmi was far too young to hear such dark secrets, let alone keep them.

So Isaveth sat down, put on her brightest smile, and

told her family what a wonderful day she'd had at the college. "Governor Buldage came down to welcome me personally," she said. "And I start learning Sagery tomorrow."

"I want to try on your robe," Mimmi said, grabbing Isaveth's book bag and pulling it out. She draped it over her shoulders and spun around, making it ripple and swirl about her.

Lilet rolled her eyes. "It's a school robe, Mim, not a fairy dress. If you want to wear an oat sack over your clothes, I'm sure Annagail can make you one too."

"You're just jealous," Mimmi told her primly, and went on twirling.

Annagail had been listening in silence, absorbed with the potatoes she was chopping. Now she put down her knife and spoke. "I'm glad it went so well. Did you see . . . anyone we know?"

By her cautious tone she meant Meggery, but Mimmi gaped like a baby bird. "Quiz! Was he there? Did you talk to him?"

"Only a little," Isaveth said. "He's a year ahead of me, so we don't have any classes together."

"Is he coming back to see us? Did you ask if I can have his pedalcycle?"

"Enough, Mirrim," rumbled Papa, and Mimmi deflated. She folded up Isaveth's robe and put it away.

"I just miss him, that's all," she said in a small voice.

"You're too little for that cycle anyway," Lilet told her. "If he's going to give it to anyone, it ought to be me."

"Enough of that, too, Mistress Lilet," said Papa. He tamped a wad of baccy into his pipe, lit it with a deft scrape of the flint-spark, and rolled his shoulders with a sigh that was half groan—his back must be aching again. "Vettie's told us all we need to know about Esmond Lilord, and I won't have you begging for charity. We owe the lad enough as it is."

Lilet scowled, but she knew better than to argue. She shoved back her chair and went to peer into the pot Annagail was stirring, but the older girl waved her aside.

"Never mind what it is," she said with unusual tartness, "you'll be eating it anyway. Vettie, would you fetch the blessing candles?"

"I was thinking frostberry branches," said Civilla as the servants laid out the main course. "Painted white, and arranged in those big metal urns like we saw at Taia Yeng's wedding—do you remember those, Mama?"

The strained lines vanished from Lady Nessa's face. "Oh, yes, that would be lovely. Don't you think so, Eryx?"

Eryx gave his mother and sister a tolerant smile and went back to sipping his wine. He clearly cared as little about Civilla's coming-of-age ball as Esmond did, especially as they'd been hearing about nothing else since the meal began. If Lord Arvis were there he'd have cut her off long ago, but he was having one of his bad spells and hadn't come down from his room.

"It's still not perfect, though." Civilla pursed her lips as if it were the most vexing problem she'd faced all year, and Esmond had to look away. He'd been close to Civilla once, but when he'd needed her most, she'd failed him. And since then she'd grown so shallow and self-absorbed, so taken up with her gossip rags and her wardrobe and all the dinners, dances, and charity balls she'd crammed into her social calendar, that he wondered if he'd ever really known her at all.

He'd rather live with Civilla's vanity than Eryx's ruthlessness, though. Did he really think he could cut off relief to anyone who displeased him and still be seen as the champion of the poor? More importantly, was Lord Arvis going to let him do it? Esmond was wondering how to find out without making it obvious he'd talked to Isaveth, when Eryx spoke.

"I'm surprised Father couldn't join us. I'd thought he was looking quite well when we talked this morning."

The Sagelady blinked as though waking from a dream. "Oh. Yes, I thought so too. But he barely ate at luncheon, and when I went to call him for dinner, he said he wasn't hungry."

"Did you ring the healer?" Civilla asked, eyes wide. Lord Arvis missing one meal was extraordinary, but missing two was unheard of.

"Doctor Achawa says it's only to be expected for someone in his condition. He recommended hot lemon and ginger, and said to call again tomorrow if there's no change."

Civilla looked down at her plate. Then she said in a quavering voice, "Perhaps we should cancel the ball."

"Oh, no, my dear!" The Sagelady clutched her arm. "Your father would never want that! Think how people would talk. I know you're worried—we all are—but I'm sure he'll be better by the time your birthday comes."

"And even if he isn't," said Eryx, "he'll want people to believe that he is. You know what Father's like, Cilla. He'd sooner die on his feet than look feeble even for a second."

"Die!" Civilla's hand flew to her throat. "Eryx, you can't mean it. What a horrible thought."

"I was speaking figuratively," Eryx said with a touch of impatience. "Of course he's not dying, he's just got a bit of liver trouble. If he'd only quit sneaking drinks out of my liquor cabinet and cheating on his diet, he'd be fine. My point is, you've made so much noise about this party of yours that half the city's waiting for an invitation. Father wouldn't let you cancel it now if you begged him."

"Oh," said Civilla. "I suppose we'd better go on with it, then." But she sounded more relieved than otherwise, and Esmond suddenly felt sick of the whole lot of them. He dropped his fork onto his plate and stood up.

"Where are you going?" demanded Eryx.

"Anywhere but here," Esmond retorted, and walked out.

The grand staircase divided into two on the landing, a shorter flight winging off to a corridor on either side. Esmond turned right and climbed to Lord Arvis's bedchamber, then leaned against the door and knocked, listening.

No answer. Was he sleeping? Esmond eased down the latch and let himself in.

His father lay sprawled in the great bed, covers twisted around him. The spell-lamp by the bedside was dimmed, and two empty glasses stood on the table beside it: one crusted white with the dregs of his stomach medicine, and the other with a pool of golden liquor in the bottom.

"Father!" said Esmond, louder than he'd intended. "Are you all right?"

The Sagelord inhaled with a snort and raised his head blearily. "Wuh," he grunted. "Wuh d'you wan'?"

No wonder he hadn't come down to dinner. He'd boozed himself senseless, leaving Lady Nessa to make his excuses. But by his vacant look he'd passed the belligerent stage, so Esmond crossed the carpet and pulled up a chair by his side. "I came to see how you were feeling."

"Pah." Lord Arvis puffed out his lips in contempt. "That's a lie. You want something. Ever'body wants something." He slapped the bedclothes. "Out with it."

"Fine." Esmond didn't have the patience to bandy words, and in this state, his father probably wouldn't remember the conversation anyway. "Eryx wants to reform the city relief program and give workers back the right to demonstrate. Has he talked to you about it?"

"'Course. Been nagging me for days now. Wants me to bring it to council." Lord Arvis stirred restlessly. "Told him it was a stupid idea."

"You did?" Esmond was surprised. "Why?"

"Can't imagine what the boy's thinking," mumbled Lord Arvis. "Worthless rabble hate me enough as it is—practically started a riot, last planting. Had to pass the anti-dissenter law to stop 'em plotting against me, and now he thinks tossing out a few Moshite rabble-rousers'll be enough to make all the rest behave? Crazy notion."

"What about his relief plan, though?"

"Bah! Even stupider. Half those wretches have broken one law or another—am I supposed to pay a whole army of clerks to go poking about in people's houses, deciding who gets relief and who doesn't? And even the 'deserving' ones aren't going to be happy when they see their friends and relations going without." He shook his head. "Not good. 'Specially if they find out it was Eryx who came up with it."

That made sense. The past three years had seen a series of financial disasters and factory closures in Tarreton, leaving thousands of men and women jobless and bitterly angry against their Sagelord. Without Eryx's quick intervention, his repeated promises to speak up on the workers' behalf, the city would have erupted into violence months ago. How would the common folk react if they knew that their so-called champion, their shining hope, planned to cut off relief to half of them in order to increase payments to the other half?

"Upstart," his father slurred. For a moment he'd seemed almost sober; now his eyes lost focus again. "Told me he'd pass it off as my idea, and nobody the wiser. Well, I've had enough of that. Sick of being blamed for everything that goes wrong in this city, letting Eryx take the glory when anything goes right . . ." He plucked fretfully at the sheets. "Bloody gorehawks, all of 'em."

"Who?" asked Esmond, taken aback. He'd never heard his father ramble like this before.

"Hovering around me, pretending to care—hah! All they want is for me to die so *he* can take over!" Lord Arvis struggled to sit up, big shoulders pushing against the pillows. "But I'm not . . . dead . . . yet—"

Esmond reached to help, but his father swatted his hand away. "And I'm not some doddering invalid, either! You're no better than the rest of 'em."

The rebuff stung, but Esmond held his ground. "So you won't support Eryx's plan in council?" he asked. "You've decided against it?"

"It's no business of yours what I decide," growled the Sagelord. His face looked puffy in the lamplight, the whites of his eyes tinged yellow. "Quit your yapping and get out."

Esmond bowed and retreated, shutting the door behind him. Then he walked to the landing, sat on the topmost stair, and thought.

It was good to know Lord Arvis wasn't in favor of Eryx's ideas, at least not at the moment. Yet Esmond knew better than to count on the Sagelord: His father was too unstable, and his brother too cunning, for that. There was only one way to stop Eryx bringing his plan to council, and that was to utterly discredit him.

Esmond stared at the carpet, mind whirring. Yes, the confession he'd recorded on the charm-band was gone forever. But as Isaveth had pointed out, murder wasn't the only crime Eryx Lording had committed. . . .

Of course! Why hadn't Esmond thought of it before? Four months ago, he'd sneaked Isaveth into this very house to help him search for the documents that would prove her papa's innocence. Eryx had a tidy little habit of demanding written confessions from any criminals he hired, in case they became squeamish or tempted to betray him; he had to keep those letters somewhere, and his private study had seemed the obvious place.

Unfortunately, they'd been wrong, and Eryx had caught them—which was how Isaveth had ended up making the desperate bargain that had saved Urias Breck's life. At the time it had felt more like defeat than victory to Esmond: They'd had to give up all the evidence they'd gathered against Eryx and Governor Buldage, and leave a dead workman to take the blame. But when Eryx went off to fetch the man's confession and returned only minutes later, he'd unwittingly given Esmond a clue. His brother's secret documents had to be in, or very near, the house.

If Esmond could find those letters and turn them over to the Lawkeepers, not even the dullest plodder in the station would miss the implications. They'd know Eryx was guilty of blackmail to start with, and once they started arresting the people who'd written those confessions, the rest of his brother's crimes would soon come out. . . .

Esmond leaped to his feet, energy surging through him. It was the first Mendday of the month, so Eryx would soon be driving out to meet with the Tarreton Business Owners' Association, and Civilla planned to visit her friend Delicia Ghataj that evening. With Lady Nessa distracted trying to soothe her husband, the mansion would be practically empty.

He'd start hunting for the documents tonight.

Chapter Five

THE SNOW FELL STEADILY until morning, and by the time Isaveth mustered the strength to nudge Mimmi awake, squirm out of their shared cocoon of blankets, and scrape the frost off the bedroom window, the whole length of Cabbage Street was smothered in white powder. She wormed out of her nightgown and tugged on her school clothes as quickly as she could. It would be hard slogging through those drifts, and she'd have to move fast or she'd miss her tram.

Fortunately the snow proved less deep than it looked, and though Isaveth was puffing when she reached the tram stop, she'd made it with minutes to spare. Her elation faded, however, when she realized her ride wasn't coming. She was half-frozen and frantic by the time the next tram trundled toward her, crammed tight with standing passengers, and stopped to pick her up. Isaveth clutched the hand bar, toes aching as they began to thaw, and prayed that she wouldn't be the only student to turn up late to Sagery that morning.

When the tram finally stopped in front of the college, the bell for first class was ringing. Isaveth jumped off, skidding on the icy sidewalk, and pelted through the gates. The cold air seared her lungs and her feet throbbed worse than ever, but she plunged on, past the main buildings and down the narrow steps that led toward the charmery. She dashed by the Sporting Center, nearly bumping into a pair of older students wearing their slate- and sky-blue robes over their coats, and finally caught up with another first-year girl running in the same direction.

"Are you late too?" Isaveth blurted out, and a startled brown face spun toward her—only to vanish as the girl slipped, windmilled, and tumbled into a snow bank. Isaveth rushed to help, but when the other student surfaced she was laughing.

"Whoop-la!" she crowed, shaking snow in all directions. "Well, if we weren't late before, we sure will be now. Better two than one, though."

She climbed out and began brushing herself off, and Isaveth handed back her hat. "I'm awfully sorry," she said.

The girl flapped a dismissive mitten. "Don't worry about it. You're new, right?"

Isaveth nodded.

"Good! We can use fresh blood in this stuffy old place. I'm Eulalie Fairpont. You?"

"Isaveth. Pleased to meet you."

She'd left off her family name, but Eulalie didn't seem to notice. "Likewise," she said cheerfully.

They trotted down the path and the charmery rose up before them, two stories of shuttered windows and fire-blackened stone. "Why is it so far from the rest of the college?" Isaveth asked. "You'd think they *wanted* people to be late."

"Apparently it used to be closer," said Eulalie, "back when the college was first built. But that one blew up, so . . ."

"Really? How?"

"Some sillyhead trying to build a mage-bomb, I think." Her fur collar lifted as she shrugged, and Isaveth suppressed a flash of envy. It looked so soft and warm. "Anyway, charm-making's a lot safer these days, but— oh, maggots."

A square-built woman in a master's robe had stepped out of the charmery, frowning disapproval. Eulalie clutched Isaveth's arm and broke into an exaggerated limp.

"It's my fault we're late, Mistress Corto," she called. "I slipped on the path, and Isaveth stayed to help me." Which was true, but her tragic expression made the accident seem far worse than it had been.

The spellmistress stepped back, holding the door wide for the girls to enter. "You wouldn't have slipped if you hadn't been running, Miss Fairpont. As a newcomer Miss Breck has some excuse for lateness, but you do not."

"Yes, Mistress," said Eulalie meekly, then caught Isaveth's eye and winked. Hiding a smile, Isaveth followed the other girl inside.

The Sagery classroom was a barnlike space with a cement floor, exposed beams, and walls of bare red brick. A boiler squatted in one corner, exhaling a low whistle of steam. Eulalie took off her overcoat and hung it up beside Isaveth's, then hobbled to a seat in the front row. But the seats next to Eulalie were occupied, and the only empty desk was at the back of the room. Self-conscious, Isaveth edged down the aisle and took it.

"In your first term with Mistress Anandri," their teacher began, "you were introduced to the two fundamental principles that underlie all magic. Who can name them for me?"

"Affinity and Resonance," replied a boy in a lofty, nasal voice. His skin was pale as Esmond's, his brown hair slicked back, and he had the smug air of someone accustomed to being right. He was in both Isaveth's afternoon classes, but she'd never really noticed him until today.

"Mister Paskin is correct," said the spellmistress. "Now, who can give me a definition of Affinity? Miss Kehegret?"

She continued for some time in this manner, and as the students glanced at one another it was clear they were growing impatient with the review. But Isaveth was delighted, and scribbled notes as fast as her lead-point could go. She'd never learned any magical theory before; she'd only studied the recipes in her mother's Book of Common Magic and done her best to follow them. Now she was finally starting to understand why those spells worked the way they did.

At last the class ended, and their teacher dismissed them with a warning to arrive in good time tomorrow, as she would be introducing them to the basic metals, crystals, and elixirs used in charm-making.

"Which we ought to have learned today," grumbled Paskin as he got up, loud enough for everyone to hear. "If we hadn't wasted a whole class reviewing stuff most of us know already. Thanks to *her*."

Isaveth was abruptly conscious of everyone's eyes upon her. Her neck prickled and her cheeks grew warm, but she continued packing up her book bag as though she hadn't heard.

"Still, I suppose we ought to show *some* charity," the boy drawled as his mates began to snigger. "As future leaders of Tarreton, it's our duty to be kind to the poor and uneducated."

Isaveth's chest squeezed tight, and for a moment she couldn't breathe. No one had mocked her appearance yesterday, so she'd dared to hope her disguise was working. Yet in one glance Paskin had seen she was a commoner, and worse, he'd announced it to the rest of the class as well.

"The only leading you ever do is with your mouth, Tadeus Paskin," said Eulalie loudly from behind him. "And considering you barely scraped a pass in Common Magic last term, I wouldn't be so quick to call other people uneducated." Elbowing the boy aside, she marched down the aisle and hooked her arm through Isaveth's.

"Never mind him," she confided, "he's a pompous little tomfool. Shall we walk up the hill together?"

Esmond Lilord was in a beast of a mood, and he didn't care who knew it.

He'd spent the better part of last night pretending to have lost his charm-case, poking about the mansion from attic to coal cellar until the servants grew impatient with him for getting in their way. He'd even sneaked into

Eryx's bedchamber, once his older brother went out—but the lack of any wards on the door warned that nothing secret would be found there, and a thorough search confirmed it.

In short, his investigation had been fruitless. Which was hardly unexpected: After all, he'd done much the same thing hunting for the charm-band, and if he'd found no hidden panels or loose floorboards then, it was unlikely he'd discover any now. But Eryx's documents had to be nearby, so Esmond must have overlooked something obvious—and the frustration of knowing it had kept him brooding all night.

And now it was early on a dull, snowy morning, and the Sporting Center stank of wood polish and sweat, and no matter which way he turned, that idiot Hannier kept coming up on his blind side. Esmond was angry at Eryx, and even angrier at himself, because he was going to have to tell Isaveth that he'd failed *again*—

He was darting past Hannier when the other boy's elbow flew up, clipping his temple. The half glass arced away from him, charmed lens clattering against the floor. Esmond snatched up the wire frame and fumbled it back into place—then took two strides after Hannier, wrestled him around, and punched the wind out of him.

The boy wheezed and dropped to the floor. Then

came the tinny clatter of a warning bell, and a shout of "Esmond Lilord—penalty!"

The rest of his team groaned, but Esmond ignored them. Tearing off his blue team jersey, he stalked to the door, shoved it open, and plunged out into the cold.

"So tell me," Eulalie said as she and Isaveth left the charmery, "is there any reason we oughtn't to be friends? Because I could quite use one myself, and you seem a good deal nicer than any of the simpering suck-ups and puff-headed bullies I've met since I came to Tarreton."

"You mean you weren't born here?"

"Great Sages, no. We moved only a few months ago, from Listerbroke. . . . Oh no," she groaned as Isaveth's face lit up. "Don't tell me you're obsessed with that ridiculous talkie-play too."

She meant *Auradia Champion, Lady Justice of Listerbroke*, of course. Thanks to the crystal set Esmond had sent for her birthday, Isaveth hadn't missed an episode in weeks—but she'd never dare admit that now.

"It's all right," she said, trying to sound casual. "Why, what show do you like?"

"Ugh, none of them," said Eulalie. "They're all silly. I'd rather listen to Janny Mastrocelli and the Tin City Orchestra!" She spun on one foot, surprisingly nimble in her winter boots, and sashayed up the walk in the arms of an imaginary dance partner. Behind them Paskin and his friends sniggered, but Eulalie took no notice.

"Daddy says he'll take me to a concert, if they ever come this way," she continued, leaving off her three-step and dropping back beside Isaveth. "Though he only says so because he knows it'll never happen. No really good bands ever come to Tarreton." She heaved a sigh.

Isaveth did her best to look sympathetic, though she had little idea what Eulalie was talking about. Lilet was the musical one of the Breck sisters, and she had old-fashioned tastes; she'd listen to a string quartet forever, but whenever a popular song came over the crystal set she usually switched it off.

"So what brought your family—" Isaveth began, but then the door of the Sporting Center slammed open and Esmond burst out, shirt-sleeves rucked up and hair plastered to his brow with sweat. He nabbed a portly, owlish boy who'd been sneaking a smoke around the corner, plucked the puffer from his fingers, and shoved him inside.

"Tossed out for fighting, probably," one of Paskin's friends muttered, though he sounded more admiring than otherwise. "I hear that happens a lot with him."

Isaveth had seen Esmond fight, but only against bullies

and thugs. She would never have guessed he'd thump one of his schoolmates over a mere game. But here he lounged with studied insolence, contemplating the puffer in his hand as though debating whether to smoke it himself, and Isaveth's stomach gave a queasy lurch. Was this how Esmond behaved when she wasn't there?

"What is it?" asked Eulalie, noticing her sudden halt. "Did you leave something back at the charmery?"

"Probably her mop," sneered Paskin—and at the same moment, Esmond flicked away the puffer and looked up.

For a heartbeat he and Isaveth stood unmoving, staring at each other. Then with a thrust of his shoulders Esmond pushed upright and strode down the snowy path to meet her.

"Miss Breck!" he exclaimed, seizing her hand and pumping it. "Nice to see you again. How is your family? All well, I hope?"

What was Esmond thinking, making a fuss of her where everyone could see? "Y-yes, thank you," Isaveth stammered.

"Excellent." Esmond's gaze slid to Paskin and his mates. "These fellows aren't giving you trouble, are they? They seem to be hanging about where they *aren't wanted*." He adjusted his half glass pointedly, and with mumbled apologies the younger boys hurried away.

"They were being quite rude, actually," called Eulalie. "I think the masters ought to hear about it." She turned back to Esmond, adding in a normal tone, "Thanks, that was good of you. I'm Eulalie Fairpont."

"Fairpont, Fairpont . . . ah, the Deputy Justice's daughter?" Esmond rocked back on his heels, breath frosting the air, and studied Eulalie with interest. "How is your father liking his new job?"

"Well, it's an awful lot of responsibility, but it's a great honor, too. Or at least that's what Daddy says."

"I didn't know the Lord Justice had appointed a deputy," said Isaveth, recovering at last. "When did that happen?"

"A few weeks ago," Eulalie told her. "Apparently there was a bit of a ruckus about corruption inside the Lawkeepers, and the Lord Justice always seems to be out of town these days, so the Sagelord appointed Daddy to look into it."

"Which was clever of him, if you don't mind me saying so," said Esmond. "Because not only was Advocate Fairpont the one who discovered the corruption in the first place, he's an outsider—and he comes from the same town as Auradia."

Meaning that appointing him would make it look as though Lord Arvis actually cared about bringing justice to the city. "I see," said Isaveth.

"Anyway," Esmond told Eulalie, "nice to meet you. But if you'll excuse me, I'm getting chilly." He blazed a smile at Isaveth and sprinted back to the Sporting Center.

"Well!" said Eulalie, when he was gone. "You might have told me you knew Esmond Lilord. However did that happen? Everyone says he's an awful snob, even to other nobles."

"Oh?"

"Quite. He hasn't made one friend since he came here, and that's not for lack of people trying." She gave Isaveth a speculative look. "You must have made quite an impression . . . oh, look at that blush!"

Inwardly Isaveth cursed her fallowtime complexion—if her olive skin were tanned browner, her embarrassment wouldn't have been obvious. "It's not like that," she said. "We only met because he bumped into me on the street. He felt badly about knocking me over, so he's been extra nice ever since to make up for it."

Which was the truth, more or less. She was silently congratulating herself for coming up with such a good answer when Eulalie asked, "When did he meet your family, then? During the trial?"

Isaveth stopped breathing.

"I'm sorry, that was awful of me. It's just that my father *is* the Deputy Justice, so when I heard your family name was Breck, I couldn't help putting the pieces together."

Of course not. Like Paskin, she'd seen at once that Isaveth wasn't noble, or even merchant class. Only instead of mocking her, she'd chosen to pity her instead. "I should be going," Isaveth said in a strangled voice, and turned away.

"Not that it matters!" exclaimed Eulalie, grabbing her arm. "Daddy always did think your father was innocent, and I don't care a pebble about money or politics or . . . or any of those other things. I think it's marvelous you're here." She gazed up at Isaveth, brown eyes imploring. "We can still be friends, can't we? Or at least give it a try?"

Isaveth hesitated, torn between longing and doubt. Few of her old schoolmates had cared to be seen talking to a Moshite girl, let alone spend any time in her company. But here was Eulalie, whose father was one of the most powerful men in the city, practically begging to be her friend. It made no sense.

Yet hadn't she learned from Esmond that being rich never kept anyone from being lonely? Eulalie was an outsider like herself, and perhaps that was reason enough.

"Well," Isaveth said slowly, "if you're sure—"

"I am, I am!" Eulalie bounced around her. "I want to know all about you. But I've got to run or I'll be late for music. I'll see you in the dining hall, all right?"

She pelted off up the hill, boots skidding in all directions. But at the top she turned to wave, and Isaveth, dazed with surprise and dawning happiness, waved back.

Maybe she didn't have to hide who she was to fit in here, after all.

Chapter Six

GIDDY WITH THE DELIGHT of having made a new friend, Isaveth spent her history class listening to Master Eddicot drone on about the Wars of the Great Houses without really hearing a word of it. When the lunch bell rang she rushed to the dining hall, eager to see Eulalie again.

When she found her sitting at one of the long tables, however, Isaveth's excitement fizzled out. "I can't sit here," she whispered, gesturing at the gold-rimmed dishes and silver cutlery.

"Rubbish," said Eulalie. "I don't see any place cards, and there's plenty of room." She plucked a roll from the basket and began cutting it. "Come on, help yourself."

"But I brought a lunch from home. . . ." The words stuck in Isaveth's throat. Even if Eulalie already knew she was poor, it hurt to admit she couldn't afford to eat at the college.

"Don't worry. I'm sure it'll keep." Eulalie waved to one of the servers, who crossed the room to attend her. "Miss Breck will be eating lunch with me from now on. Would you add her to the Fairpont account, please?"

Isaveth started to protest, but Eulalie gave her a hurt look and she trailed off. She didn't want charity, but she didn't like to offend the other girl either. "It's very kind of you," she murmured.

"It's nothing," said Eulalie airily. "Daddy won't notice, I'm sure, and if he does he won't grumble. It's only a few cits a day, after all." She handed the roll to Isaveth and began buttering another. "Now eat up, so we can get out of here."

Isaveth sat down as the server drew up his cart and began ladling out the soup of the day—a creamy mixture of lake trout and potatoes, with a sprinkle of cheese on top. A few girls around them pushed their bowls away, but Eulalie lost no time digging into hers, and Isaveth followed her example. She wasn't sorry: The soup was the tastiest thing she'd eaten in months, and the buttery roll made it even better.

She'd nearly finished when a familiar blond head caught her eye. Esmond sat at the end of the nearest boys' table, silent amidst his jostling, laughing classmates. His spoon traced circles around his bowl, but he never raised it to his lips. Had something upset him that Isaveth didn't know about? Or was that bleak expression the one he always wore in public?

Eulalie nudged her, and Isaveth realized she'd been staring. She dropped her gaze and went back to eating her soup.

Eulalie hadn't been exaggerating when she said she wanted to know everything. They'd barely left the dining hall before she began firing off questions about Isaveth's family and how she'd come to Tarreton College. As they walked the corridors, Isaveth did her best to satisfy her new friend's curiosity—though she made little mention of Esmond, and none of Eryx Lording. She liked Eulalie and hoped she could trust her, but it might not be safe to tell her too many secrets yet.

There seemed no harm in Isaveth mentioning how she'd sold her magic-resistant paper recipe to J. J. Wregget, however, or the scholarship he'd given her in return—and when Eulalie clapped and exclaimed, "I knew you were clever!" Isaveth glowed with pleasure. She was still basking in the compliment when the other girl added, "No wonder Paskin's so cross. He made a bet with Natty Crick that there'd be no Glow-Mor scholarship this year, and he was sure he'd win because his mother knows someone who works there. Now he has to pay Natty five regals, and look like a fool besides."

Isaveth's elation burst like a soap bubble. If Paskin had an inside connection to Glow-Mor, then no wonder he'd known she was a commoner. Did he know she was Moshite as well?

"Anyway," Eulalie added, "I think Mister Wregget was right to offer you the scholarship. Nobody here likes to admit it, because Tarreton College used to be the best magical school in Upper Colonia, but in the last few years it's really fallen behind. Too stuck on old traditions, my father says."

Isaveth was beginning to like Deputy Fairpont. He sounded like a sensible man. "What traditions?"

"Oh, treating Sagery as the most important kind of magic, for one thing, when it's really too fussy for most people to use at all. It might be different if we could mass-produce charms like we do spell-tablets, but—"

"We can't? I thought it was just too expensive."

"That's only part of it. Sage-charms all have to be made by hand, and since they're attuned to the person who crafts them, there's no way to tell if they'll work for anyone else. So making charms is really just a fancy way to show you're a noble."

No wonder the other students at the college were so

keen to learn it, then. Isaveth nodded, inviting Eulalie to go on.

"Back in Listerbroke, I had a course on Common Magic in my fifth year of Primary, and we all burned our fingers and thought it great fun. Here they don't start learning it until Secondary, and everybody moans like they're being tortured."

Having seen as much yesterday, Isaveth couldn't disagree. "Yes, but what's that got to do with my scholarship?"

"Well, the point is to encourage new ideas, isn't it? That's hardly going to happen if all Glow-Mor does is hand out free tuition to the same lazy gobblewits who've been going to the college all along."

Isaveth was silent, digesting this. Maybe Wregget's eagerness to sponsor her, and even the college's decision to accept her, made more sense than she'd thought. Though she couldn't shake the feeling there was something strange going on. . . .

"You've gone all serious," said Eulalie. "What is it?"

Isaveth shook herself out of reverie and managed a smile. "Just thinking. After all, if you're right about the scholarship, that's my job."

Isaveth's first class of the afternoon was Calculation, which had seemed easy enough yesterday, but today included some unfamiliar measurements that left her baffled. What did AV stand for? Was ten AV the same as a hundred RV, or a thousand, or only one? Isaveth began leafing through her lesson book, hoping to find an explanation.

"Miss Breck," said the clear, cutting voice of Master Valstead. "This is not the time for idle page flipping. Please address yourself to the equations on the board—unless you find them too simple for you?"

His eyes were cold as a frozen lake. Hastily Isaveth flipped the book shut. "No, sir."

She was staring at the formulas, wondering if she could guess the right answer, when pain lanced into her back. She jumped, twisted around—and met the innocent blue eyes of Betinda Callender, the girl who'd accused her of showing off in Common Magic.

Yet Betinda's hands were folded demurely on her workbook, and there was no weapon in sight. Perhaps Isaveth had imagined it. Embarrassed, she lowered her eyes and turned away.

Minutes passed, and the pricking sensation had begun to fade when she felt a fresh stab, this one harder. "Stop it!" Isaveth hissed, but Betinda only smirked at her.

"Miss Breck!" Master Valstead snapped. "I do not know what behavior was tolerated at your former school—"

"Trash Heap Primary," whispered Paskin, and titters and snorts rose from his seatmates as the teacher continued.

"—but if you cannot remain quiet and face the front of the class, you will be asked to leave. Unless there is some reason you need to see Miss Callender's work in order to complete your own?"

Was he accusing her of cheating? The blood drained from Isaveth's cheeks, then flooded back again. She wanted to tell the master what Betinda had done, but the only proof she had were the two throbbing spots on her back, and she couldn't show him those without undressing.

"Well, Miss Breck?"

The whole class was looking at her. Isaveth cleared her throat. "No, sir. I'm sorry, sir."

"Good," said the master, and began chalking up another set of equations.

So now she had another teacher who despised her. And as a third savage poke made Isaveth flinch, it was clear she'd made a new enemy as well.

She tried to steel herself, gritting her teeth and sliding as far forward as the desk would allow. But the fourth jab hurt so much she couldn't help it. She gasped, and Master Valstead swiveled to glare at her. Tears stinging her eyes, Isaveth began packing up to leave.

"Excuse me, sir," said a boy. He was short and compact, with dark olive skin and a face as round as his spectacles, and there was something oddly familiar about him. "Miss Callender has been poking Miss Breck with her lead-point, sir. I saw her do it just now."

"How dare you!" exclaimed Betinda, rearing back in indignation. "What a horrible lie!"

"Miss Callender?" asked Master Valstead. "Do you require Miss Breck's attention for some reason?"

"Sir, I would never." She pressed a hand to her chest, looking wounded. "I can't think why Ghataj would accuse me of such a thing."

The master shifted his gaze to the boy, whose expression stayed resolute. At last he said, "Mister Ghataj, please exchange desks with Miss Callender. If Miss Breck's welfare is of such concern to you, you may consider yourself responsible for guarding it."

Giggles rippled through the class, and the boy winced. But he gathered his books and got up to let Betinda take his seat.

Isaveth exhaled a silent prayer of gratitude. "Thank you," she whispered to Ghataj, not daring to look back.

Around them desks creaked, papers rustled, and lead-points scratched as her classmates returned to work. Isaveth had almost given up hope of an answer when she heard his gruff, barely audible reply:

"You're welcome."

Isaveth's back was still smarting as she headed to her next class, and her head spun with questions she couldn't answer. Why would Betinda Callender be so cruel to her when they hardly knew each other? Was she jealous that Isaveth was learning Sagery when she was still struggling to bake spell-tablets? Or had she heard Paskin's snide comments about Isaveth being poor and decided to put this upstart back in her place?

She brooded over it for the rest of the afternoon, so distracted that she'd walked halfway to the gate before realizing she hadn't checked the library for a message. What if Esmond had found out something important about Eryx? Could that be why he'd made a point of greeting her and Eulalie this morning?

Squinting into the icy wind, Isaveth ran back, up the steps, and through the pillared entrance of the library. She searched the shelves for the books on agriculture, and flipped through one after another until a scrap of paper fluttered out.

Same place and time. Be careful. —Q

The *Q* was for his nickname, of course, so if anyone found the note they wouldn't guess who had written it. But the sight of the initial made Isaveth's throat ache. Quiz had been eccentric, erratic, and occasionally exasperating, but at least he'd been an equal, someone whose feelings and motives she could understand. She crumpled the note into her bag and turned away.

When she came up the stairs of the bell tower, Esmond was pacing the landing, hands clenched behind his back. "There you are," he said. "I thought you'd forgotten."

Isaveth didn't bother explaining. She crossed to the makeshift bench and sat down, waiting to hear what he had to say.

"Look, I'm sure you've been wondering about this morning. But Eryx already knows how I—I mean, he knows we're friends, so I thought it would be more suspicious to pretend I didn't know you. And acting the plummy noble was the only way I could keep from punching that noxious little weed in the face."

Well, at least he was honest about it. "What made you so angry?" she asked. "I don't mean Paskin. I mean before." And afterward in the dining hall, too. Why was he so different with Isaveth than he was around his fellow nobles? Surely they couldn't *all* be unworthy of his friendship. . . .

Esmond sighed and dropped onto the bench beside her. "I really thought I was on to something," he said. "All I had to do was hunt down Eryx's stash of blackmail letters—you know, the ones we were trying to find when we searched his study. They've got to be in the house, or so close that they might as well be. You know why, don't you?"

Isaveth nodded.

"Well, I poked through everything papery I could get my hands on—I even had a look through Father's office, just in case. But I couldn't find anything, and there's nowhere left to search." He raked his fingers up into his hair. "It's driving me mad."

Which was only half an answer, but still a relief. Isaveth had been starting to wonder if Esmond hated everyone who wasn't poor, and she didn't care for that idea at all. . . .

But then, she was beginning to have similar doubts about Eulalie. In many ways she was the kind of friend Isaveth had always dreamed of, a girl her own age who liked her just as she was. Yet the way Eulalie had insisted on buying her lunch made Isaveth feel more like an adopted pet than an equal. Did Eulalie really believe she was clever and interesting, or was it only flattery? And why had she chosen Isaveth, over all the other girls at the college?

"Isaveth?" asked Esmond, and she gazed at him blankly before remembering they'd been talking about Eryx. *Focus, Isaveth.*

"He might have moved the papers after he found us ransacking his study," she said, hoping her distraction hadn't been obvious. "Wouldn't you?"

Esmond gave a short laugh. "Eryx is far too arrogant for that. It would look like he was afraid of us."

He is, Isaveth wanted to say. *That's why he offered me two regals to stop being friends with you.* But she couldn't say so without explaining why she'd refused the money, and that would be awkward.

"Maybe he moved them for some other reason. Does Eryx have another office? At Council House, perhaps?"

Esmond shook his head. "There's a room he and Father use for meetings sometimes, but it's not private. I don't think Eryx would leave anything there."

"A secret office, then."

"Maybe," Esmond said reluctantly. "But if so, I don't know how we're going to find it. It's not like we can slip one of your tracking-tablets into Eryx's pocket and chase him around the city on my pedalcycle."

"We can't track *him*, no. But if we could put out some sort of bait for him, and attach the tablet to that . . ."

Esmond's good eye widened. "We could trace it back

to his stash! Isaveth, that's brilliant!" He flung out his arms toward her, and Isaveth's heart skipped—but then he seemed to think better of it and let them fall.

"It's got to be something juicy, though," he said, clearing his throat, "with obvious blackmail potential. And we can't just stick a tablet inside the envelope or what-have-you; he'll get suspicious."

True: She'd have to find a more subtle approach. Perhaps if she ground up the source-tablet and rubbed the paper with it? "I'll start working on it," Isaveth said. "You find something we can use for bait, and I'll give you the spell when it's ready."

She started to rise, but Esmond stopped her with a touch. "Wait—you want *me* to use your tracking spell? Are you sure it'll work for me?"

Yesterday she would have had no idea what he was talking about. But thanks to Eulalie, Isaveth understood. "It's Common Magic, not Sagery, so I can't see why it wouldn't. Besides, if the documents are at your place, you're the only one who *can* look for them. It's not like you can invite me to tea and escort me around the mansion."

"Bah." Esmond wrinkled his nose in disgust. "All this nobles-and-commoners rubbish. What I wouldn't give to be Quiz again."

So he missed those days too. It might not fix anything, but it did make her feel less lonely. "If you were a street-boy, they wouldn't let you in the house either," Isaveth pointed out. "You can't have it both ways."

"More's the pity," said Esmond. "But you're right. I'll see what I can do."

Chapter Seven

THERE WAS LITTLE HOPE of Isaveth getting any privacy for her experiments that evening; their furnace was so old and miserly that the kitchen was the only warm place in the house. But she coaxed her younger sisters into playing outside for a while, and settled Papa upstairs with a pile of blankets and a hot-water bottle to soothe his aching shoulder. So in the end, only Annagail was left to notice.

"I thought you were studying Sagery now," her sister said, lowering the sock she'd been mending. "What are you making a decoction for?"

Isaveth was brewing three at the same time, actually; each tablet needed its own bottle of potion for the tracking spell to work. She glanced into the oven to make sure her tablets were browning, and stirred each of the pots again. "It's for Esmond," she said. "He needs it for an experiment."

Annagail frowned, but she didn't protest. She knew what their family owed Esmond, even more than Papa did. "So he's not afraid to be seen with you?"

The liquid in the front pot was starting to bubble. Isaveth added a sprinkle of ground lodestone and stirred it again. "Well, he's quite busy with his classes, so we don't see each other that often. But otherwise he's been friendly."

"Oh." Annagail was quiet, looking down at her mending. At last she said, "Well, I'm happy for you. I only hope it lasts."

The back two pots were bubbling now. Isaveth sprinkled and stirred, then turned off the stove to let them cool. "What do you mean?"

"I'm sorry. I shouldn't have said anything." Annagail dropped the sock and got up, heading for the front room. Puzzled, Isaveth followed.

The window that looked out onto Cabbage Street wore a rime of frost so thick, Isaveth could barely make out Lilet and Mimmi playing in the snow. She pulled a blanket off the sofa and wrapped it around herself, shivering. "Anna, what is it?"

Her sister sighed. "I worry, that's all. Bad enough that we're poor, worse that we're Moshite, but if people find out you're Urias Breck's daughter . . ."

"Why would that matter?" It hadn't made any difference to Eulalie, and people like Betinda and Paskin hated her enough already. "The Lord Justice declared Papa innocent."

"Yes, but there are still people who think he was involved in Governor Orien's murder somehow, even if he didn't actually do it." Annagail rubbed her arms fretfully. "You saw Su Amaraq's article in the *Trumpeter*. She as good as said that the worker who confessed to the killing wasn't clever enough to have done it alone."

Which was true—but Eryx had made sure the man's confession was also his suicide note, so he couldn't tell Su or anyone else who had hired him. Still, Isaveth would have liked to give the reporter a kick in the silk-stockinged shin for stopping there, instead of digging deeper to find the truth of the story.

"Well," she said, trying to sound confident, "people might find out, but they might not. And even if they do think badly of Papa, that doesn't mean they have to think badly of—" She stopped, sniffing. "Oh no, the tablets!"

Isaveth dashed into the kitchen, scrabbling for the hotglove. Fortunately they hadn't burned, but it had been a near thing. She whisked the pan out and set it on the table. "Anyway," she continued, turning back . . .

But the front room was empty. Annagail had gone.

* * *

Once the source-tablets for her tracking spell had cooled, Isaveth started looking for ways to disguise them. She'd cut them as small as she could, but there was no way Eryx wouldn't notice a whole one. So she crushed one into powder (useless), dribbled wax over another to make it look like a seal (it didn't), mixed a third with ink (which clogged up the pen), and crumbled a fourth into a batch of homemade paper (making it far too lumpy to write on). Only when Papa tramped downstairs to chide her for not going to bed did Isaveth give up and put her spell-making ingredients away.

She woke next morning achy and sluggish, with an itch at the back of her throat. Shivering, Isaveth hurried downstairs, lit the stove, and made a pot of herb tea with honey, struggling not to cough until she'd drunk it down. Then she sat down to do the homework she'd neglected the night before.

As soon as she opened her calculation book, however, Isaveth was lost. She still didn't understand the formulas her teacher was using, and if she couldn't catch up soon she'd be in trouble. Yet judging by the cold way Master Valstead treated her, he was the last person she could expect to help.

She'd just have to look up the answers at lunchtime,

then. Resigned, Isaveth packed up and headed off to school. But when she got to the library, all the books she needed were missing.

"Hmm," said the librarian when she showed him the half-empty shelf. "Bad timing, I'm afraid. They were all taken out this morning." He snapped his ledger shut, but not before Isaveth had seen the list of borrowed books and the single name beside them: *B. Callender.*

Anger flamed in Isaveth. She'd half made up her mind to hunt down Betinda, grab her by the collar, and demand the books back, when she spotted a familiar dark head at one of the study tables.

Ghataj. Did she dare speak to him? He'd already been mocked and teased for helping Isaveth, so he might not be eager to put himself out for her sake again. Yet she had only half a bell left to get her work done, so it was Ghataj or nothing. Mustering courage, Isaveth crossed to his table.

"Hello," she said, then added quickly, "Thanks for your help yesterday. It was very kind of you."

"All right," said Ghataj, "but you've already thanked me once. What do you want?"

His bluntness didn't bother her; Lilet was the same way. Feeling bolder, Isaveth sat down and explained her problem. "Would you mind . . . ?"

Ghataj pushed his spectacles up his small, hawkish nose and regarded her levelly. "All right. Get out your notebook."

As Isaveth scribbled, he explained the terms that had puzzled her and showed how they related to one another. All were measurements used in making sage-charms, and the formulas Master Valstead was teaching were to calculate the proper balance of ingredients.

"I think I understand now," Isaveth said when he had finished. She'd always been clever with numbers, so it took her only a few minutes to finish the equations, and when she showed the page to Ghataj he gave an approving nod.

"You've got it. Well done." He leaned back, regarding her shrewdly. "Where were you last term? I'm surprised they didn't teach you this already."

"It wasn't a very good school," said Isaveth.

A frown creased Ghataj's brow, then his face cleared. "I knew you looked familiar. You came in late to the Young Politicians' Club on Mendday."

Isaveth smiled wanly at him, resisting the urge to bolt. He was the boy who'd asked Eryx about the ban on political meetings in the city. "Oh, yes. I heard everyone clapping and wondered what it was about."

"It's too bad you didn't come earlier," said Ghataj. "The

speech Eryx Lording gave was brilliant. How did you like his idea about reforming the relief system? I think it makes a lot of sense, don't you?"

It would be safest to agree, but Isaveth couldn't bring herself to do it. She liked Ghataj, and she owed him too much to lie.

"I think it would be wonderful to give more relief to families who need it," she said. "But if he can only do that by taking it away from anyone who's ever opposed the Sagelord, then I don't think that's fair at all."

"I'm sure that's not—" Ghataj began, but Isaveth pressed on.

"Even if he only means people who've broken the law, who makes those laws? You said it yourself the other day—right now it's illegal to hold political meetings or organize protests in the city. But if men and women can't get work, and their children are starving, and they can't even scrape together enough coal to keep themselves warm at night, how can they *not* protest? And is it surprising that some of them end up breaking other laws to survive as well?"

She must have spoken too loudly, because Ghataj made a shushing gesture. "Of course not," he said. "But that's the Sagelord's fault, not the Lording's. Eryx wants to fix all of that, don't you see? But he can't do it with his father in the way."

"But if—"

"I know what you're saying," Ghataj told her. "We have to make sure the law is fair before we punish people for breaking it. And it's never going to be fair as long as Lord Arvis is ruling the city. But from what I hear . . ." A smile touched his lips. "We might not have to worry about that much longer."

"What do you mean?" asked Isaveth, pulse quickening.

Ghataj opened his mouth, then shut it again. With a rueful shake of his head he swept up his books and walked out.

A few weeks ago, Esmond had told Isaveth that the rumors of the Sagelord's poor health were little more than wishful thinking, and that his father had no plans to retire. Yet Ghataj had hinted otherwise, and it troubled her. Isaveth had no love for Lord Arvis and would not be sorry to see the last of him, but the thought of Eryx ruling the city was even worse. She had to get that tracking spell working, so she could give it to Esmond.

When she got home to Cabbage Street, however, the kitchen was full. Lilet and Mimmi sat at one end of the table, quarrelling over a game of Pardon, while Annagail hunched at the other end, bracing her textbook open with her elbows and plugging her ears. Isaveth studied the three of them, weighing her options, then marched up to Lilet and Mimmi and slapped the game board shut.

"Hey!" screeched Mimmi, but Lilet folded her arms, unruffled.

"Told you you'd be sorry you cheated."

"I did not—"

"You can start a new game quietly," Isaveth said, "or you can go outside. I have work to do."

Mimmi started to protest, but Lilet quelled her with a glare. "She means *school* work, Mim. She's learning Sagery, remember? That's more important than some stupid game. Come on, let's get some blankets and start over." She scooped up the scattered game pieces, tucked the board under her arm, and headed for the front room.

"It's *cold* in there," moaned Mimmi as she trudged after Lilet. Annagail took her fingers out of her ears and gave a flickering smile, then returned to reading as Isaveth set up her next round of experiments.

Her first few attempts at dissolving a source-tablet in liquid were not encouraging: Some of the solutions had a suspicious odor, while others were too dark not to leave a stain. Water, the obvious choice, failed to dissolve the tablet properly unless she heated it, but as soon as the mixture became warm enough to bubble, the magic fizzled out. By the time she succeeded in dissolving one tablet without ruining it, Annagail was waiting behind her with apron in hand.

"I need to make supper, Vettie," she said.

It was agony to leave her experiment half-finished, but there was no way to convince her sister it was urgent without explaining why. With a sigh, Isaveth took the pot off the stove.

By the time they'd eaten and cleaned up, the sky was inky black and Isaveth had to put new light-tablets in both the kitchen lamps to see by. Lilet and Mimmi hovered on either side of her, fascinated, as Isaveth brushed a scrap of paper with the source-tablet solution and fanned it dry. Then she picked up the vial with the matching decoction, swirled it, and waited for the flecks of magewort to settle.

Please work, she prayed. *Please, please, please . . .*

Isaveth held her breath until she felt ready to explode, but at last the miracle happened: The particles swam to the side of the glass closest to her test paper, and clung there. She wanted to grab Mimmi and dance her around, but she forced herself to act casual as she laid out three more pieces of paper and brushed them with the source-tablet liquid as well. She'd do a few range tests tomorrow to make sure the spell worked, then hide the bottles in the library for Esmond.

"What does Quiz need magic paper for?" asked Mimmi, watching Isaveth pour the remaining solution into a bottle. "Are you helping him play a trick?"

Isaveth wiped her hands on her apron. "Very good, Mim," she said. "That's just what I'm doing."

"Not an unkind one, I hope," said Annagail, and Lilet scoffed.

"Don't be silly, Vettie would never. It'll be funny, that's all." She turned to Isaveth. "If it works, you have to tell us all about it. Promise?"

If the plan worked, Isaveth wouldn't need to: The news of Eryx Lording's downfall would be all over the city. But she'd still owe her family the truth about how it happened.

"Yes," said Isaveth. "I promise."

Chapter Eight

ESMOND LAID DOWN HIS PEN and sat back, regarding the finished letter with mingled apprehension and pride. It had taken all evening and a small mountain of scrap paper to get the wording right, but by the time he copied it onto the pages he'd coated with Isaveth's tracking potion, he felt certain Eryx would take the bait.

The biggest challenge had been figuring out how to tempt his brother without putting Isaveth in danger. The drawback of having hardly any friends was that there was only one person to whom he could plausibly send such a personal letter, yet somehow he had to write it without giving Eryx any information he might use to blackmail *her*.

So he'd made it sound like Isaveth was upset because he'd tried to kiss her—let Eryx wonder where and when that could have happened—and ever since she'd arrived at the college he'd been trying to get her alone to apologize, but she wouldn't let him. So he'd poured out his feelings on paper in a soppy and thoroughly degrading way, and made sure to include a few ugly slurs against his family and hints that he'd started stealing drinks from the Sagelord's private cabinet, something that would get Esmond in colossal trouble if it were true.

By the end of the letter he wondered if he'd gone too far, but why should Eryx suspect anything? He knew Esmond had been trying to write to *someone*, and if any of his spies had been lurking around the Sporting Center the other day, they'd have seen Isaveth's flustered reaction when Esmond greeted her. All the evidence fit, and since Eryx wouldn't want Isaveth to forgive Esmond, he had an excellent reason to make sure she never received the letter. But Eryx also had good reason to hold on to it, because it was exactly the kind of letter that Esmond would *not* want his parents to see.

The next trick was tempting his older brother to read the letter while appearing to want the very opposite. But the footman who handled the mail was already deep in Eryx's pocket, so it wasn't too hard. All he had to do was call Marguel aside, tell him that this was a private message and that he must make sure no one else saw it, and trust that Isaveth's name on the envelope would do the rest. With luck, Eryx would read it tonight, and add it to his files tomorrow.

And then Esmond would track it straight to his brother's hoard of documents, and expose Eryx as the lying, murdering hypocrite he was.

"I have good news for you," Mistress Corto announced the next morning as Isaveth and her classmates settled into their seats. "Today you will be making your first sage-charm."

A thrill rippled up Isaveth's spine. She sat up eagerly, waiting for instructions.

"The bad news," their teacher continued, "is that first you must complete this test." She handed a stack of papers to a student in the front corner, who took one and passed the others along. "When you have answered all the questions correctly, you may proceed to the workshop."

Groans rose from the front row, and Isaveth glanced at Eulalie, who was staring at her paper with head in hands. What she could see of the other girl's face did not look happy, and Isaveth braced herself for a challenge.

To her relief, however, the test proved simple—she had only to fill in a few blanks. She checked it over to make sure she hadn't missed anything, then brought it to Mistress Corto.

"Excellent work, Miss Breck," said the spellmistress. "You may go."

Had she really been the first to finish? Judging by the scowl Paskin was giving her, she had. Tingling with anticipation, Isaveth walked to the inner door.

It was unusually heavy, and she had to use both hands to pull it open. Once she stepped through, she saw why: Its reverse was covered in iron plates, like the hull of a warship. Bands of the same metal ran about the perimeter of the room, while thinner strips cross-hatched the ceiling. Even the windows, currently shuttered against the cold, were grilled inside to protect the glass from explosion.

As the door shut behind Isaveth, a thin young woman even paler than Esmond rose to greet her. "I'm Undermistress Kif," she said. "Come this way, and I'll help you get started."

Isaveth followed the older girl to a granite-topped table at the back of the room, where an assortment of magical ingredients was displayed. Strips of charmsilver, so light that Isaveth could have moved them with a breath; heaps of tiny crystals and semiprecious stones; vials of mysterious liquids labeled ARCANIC ACID, SAGE BROGAN'S ELIXIR, and EBONDRAUGHT.

"You'll need this to start," said Kif, pushing a stoneware

bowl toward her. "And these." She handed Isaveth a roll of leather, heavy with the tools wrapped up inside it. "What charm would you like to try first?"

There were ten different options, and all of them looked fascinating. Isaveth was leafing through the instruction cards, trying to decide, when Paskin came sauntering in.

"I'm going to make a warming-charm," he drawled, sweeping up a bowl in one hand and piling it full of ingredients with the other. He pulled up a stool at one of the workstations, lit the burner with a showy flick of the wrist, and began.

Isaveth had chosen her spell and was reading over the instructions when light flared behind her, followed by a curse as Paskin leaped back, shaking his flaming sleeve. Kif swept a siphon from beneath the table and sprayed him with it, ignoring his yelps of protest. Then, as he stood dripping and bedraggled, she began to scold him for being so careless.

The accident could have been serious, but it hadn't been, and the sight of Paskin flapping about as Kif doused him with the siphon was so funny that Isaveth had to giggle. She clapped her hand over her mouth, but a snicker escaped, and Paskin turned an ugly red. "You little—"

Kif stopped him with a warning hand. "Back to your work, Mister Paskin."

The boy obeyed, but the savage look he gave Isaveth warned her he wouldn't forget. Hastily she gathered up her ingredients and picked a workstation at the other end of the room.

The card Isaveth had chosen was a float-charm, the very spell Esmond had used to levitate himself up to her window on the night they'd confronted Eryx and saved her father. She propped it up next to the burner and unrolled her tool kit.

After a week of studying charm theory, she'd learned one heartening truth: despite Sagery's lofty reputation and the centuries of lore and scholarship that surrounded it, the actual work of crafting charms wasn't that different from Common Magic. True, it was more jewelry-making than cookery, but as long as Isaveth took her time and followed the recipe, all would be well.

Steady hand, she told herself, tweezing out a single strip of charm-silver. She passed it briefly over the flame to soften it, then dropped a flake of cloudy crystal in the middle, folded the strip in thirds, and tapped all four corners with a tiny hammer. Laying the charm into the bowl, she set it atop her burner and watched until the metal shimmered and began to turn blue. *One, two . . .* Her hands shook as she unstopped her tiny bottle of pearl vinegar. *Four, five . . .* She lifted the vial, tipping it toward the bowl. *Seven, eight—*

The drop fell, sizzling, onto the surface of the charm. Quickly Isaveth removed the bowl from the burner, then tweezed the charm out and squinted at it. It was a lop-sided square the size of her fingernail, smooth and shiny, betraying no sign of the crystal tucked inside it. She didn't know if it would work, but it *looked* all right.

Behind her the door creaked as more students filed in, lining up at the table and clamoring for Kif's assistance. Isaveth waited for the commotion to subside, hoping she could show her charm to the undermistress and get her opinion. Perhaps she'd have time to make a second one if the first wasn't good enough.

Yet the noise in the workshop only grew as Kif rushed from one impatient student to another, and there was no sign of Mistress Corto—or Eulalie, for that matter—anywhere. Isaveth was turning the charm over in her fingers, wondering what to do with it, when the girl at the workstation next to her asked, "Are you finished?"

She sounded curious, but not unfriendly. And judging by her relaxed posture and firm grip on the tweezers, she knew more about Sagery than Isaveth did.

"I think so," said Isaveth. "What should I do now?"

"Try it out, of course," said the girl, as though this were obvious. "What have you got—a floater?"

Isaveth nodded.

"It's simple, then. Toss it on the floor, make the invocation, and step on it."

"Invocation?" asked Isaveth with a flicker of alarm. She hadn't seen anything about that on the card, and Mistress Corto hadn't mentioned it in her lectures, either. "What do you mean?"

"You have to invoke the Sage who first made the charm." She turned her palm upward in an inviting gesture. "Or the magic won't work properly. Everyone knows that."

Isaveth swallowed. To call on a long-dead scholar of magic for help, as though he or she were the All-One—that might be common among Arcans and Unifying folk, but to a Moshite it was blasphemy.

"You aren't scared, are you? It's only a little floater. It won't hurt you." The girl plucked the charm out of Isaveth's hand and dropped it on the floor between them. "Go on, put your foot on it. And say 'By Sage Trofim.'"

Isaveth couldn't explain her hesitation without betraying herself and offending the other girl as well. But there seemed no reason the charm shouldn't work without the invocation. Taking a deep breath, she raised her foot and stamped as hard as she could.

Power surged into her body. Isaveth shot upward, arms flailing as she hurtled through the air. The ceiling rushed toward her, too fast—

CLANG.

Pain knifed through Isaveth as she crashed into the iron lattice. She hung suspended for a sickening instant, staring helplessly at the astonished faces below. Then the tingling in her foot cut off, and she began to fall.

"Catch her!" snapped Mistress Corto from the doorway, and the students rushed to obey. They tumbled down with Isaveth in a heap of arms, legs, and flying robes, and were still struggling to untangle themselves when the spellmistress seized Isaveth and hauled her aside. "What in the name of the Sages were you playing at?" she demanded.

Lights flashed in front of Isaveth's eyes, and the world blurred around her. She opened her mouth to apologize, and everything went black.

Chapter Nine

ISAVETH LAY HALF-CONSCIOUS on the workshop floor, her head full of lightning and thunder. Yet though she couldn't move or speak, she could hear every word her classmates were saying about her.

". . . must have been crazy! Why didn't she wait for the spellmistress?"

"Maybe she didn't know better. . . ."

"Or she was showing off. It wouldn't be the first time, I hear."

Where was Eulalie? She must have heard the crash when Isaveth hit the ceiling, just as Mistress Corto had. Why hadn't she come?

"Seffania said she didn't make the invocation," a girl piped up. "That must be why it went wrong."

There was a collective intake of breath, and then Paskin muttered, "Moshite."

"What? No! The school would never allow it."

"Even if she won the Glow-Mor scholarship?"

Another pause, as everyone digested Paskin's words. Then a flat voice spoke. "Well, that was a mistake, obviously. They must have felt sorry for her."

Anger sparked in Isaveth, filling her clammy skin with heat. She wanted to leap up and defend herself, but her body refused to obey. She was still lying helpless when the door to the workshop creaked open and Mistress Corto's firm tread crossed the floor.

"Out of the way," she commanded, and the students shuffled back. Then someone who smelled of herbs was kneeling beside Isaveth, slipping a bony arm behind her shoulders and lifting her head up. The darkness behind her eyes whirled dizzily and she began to retch, but the healer tipped something against her lips that tasted like liquid sunshine, and she swallowed instead.

It must have been a magical decoction, because the pounding in Isaveth's head receded. Her strength flooded back, and the healer eased her into a sitting position as she opened her eyes.

"You're a fortunate young woman, Miss Breck," said Mistress Corto. "You could have done far worse than knock yourself out. Can you get up?"

"I . . . think so," said Isaveth, and the healer, an

aristocratic-looking master with a wave of snowy hair and an impeccably trimmed beard, helped her to her feet. He guided Isaveth out to the classroom, and the spellmistress followed, shutting the door behind them.

"Undermistress Kif admits that she did not give you proper instructions," said Mistress Corto. "She was not expecting you to make such a powerful float-charm on your first effort, let alone behave so recklessly with it."

She *had* been reckless; Isaveth saw that now. She should have guessed that energetic charms were similar to spell-tablets: if you used sudden force to break them, they released sudden power in return. "I'm sorry, Mistress," she began miserably, but the older woman held up a hand.

"I have talked to Seffania," she said. "She admits that she encouraged you to test the charm, but she insists she told you to step gently, not stamp with your full weight. Is that so?"

She hadn't actually said "gently," but the rest was true enough. Isaveth nodded.

Mistress Corto glanced at the healer. "Master Fetheridge, does Miss Breck require any further treatment?"

"At present, no. If she avoids strenuous activity for the rest of the day and gets plenty of rest this evening, she should be fine." He patted Isaveth's shoulder. "Take care, young lady."

As the outer door closed behind him, Isaveth braced herself for a tongue-lashing. But Mistress Corto only studied her thoughtfully. "Well," she said after a moment, "I think you have learned your lesson. You will not test any charms in my class without permission again."

Isaveth's heart leaped as she realized the woman was giving her a second chance. If she'd caused a commotion like that in Master Valstead's class, he'd have marched her straight to the governor's office. "No, Mistress," she said fervently.

"Then we will say no more about it," said Mistress Corto. "Rest here until class ends, and then you may go." She strode past Isaveth, heading for the workshop.

"Mistress?" asked Isaveth, and the older woman glanced back. "What happened to Eulalie?"

"Miss Fairpont asked to be excused after the test, as she was feeling poorly. I told her she could make up the exercise tomorrow."

Strange, Eulalie had seemed well enough when class started. But perhaps she'd been putting on a brave face. Isaveth nodded and laid her head on the desk as Mistress Corto walked away.

Esmond sat through his classes that day with barely contained impatience, longing to dash home and try Isaveth's tracking spell. Surely by now Eryx had read the letter he'd written and added it to his secret file.

Mind, that was assuming he hadn't merely torn up the letter, or handed it over to their parents just for the pleasure of watching Esmond squirm—or worse yet, discovered the tracking-spell on the paper, which would tell him at once that Isaveth and Esmond were working together. . . .

No, that was unthinkable. They couldn't have failed so badly, so soon. Eryx was clever, but he also had a blind side: He was so accustomed to being the smartest person in any room he entered that he assumed other people were stupider than they actually were. He would believe the letter because it fit his view of Esmond as a boy whose impulses were stronger than his judgment, and he'd never guess Isaveth had made its pages traceable, because like most nobles, he had little understanding of what Common Magic could do.

The weekly bid committee meeting at Council House should keep Eryx occupied until half past four at least, but Esmond was taking no chances. When the last bell rang, he dashed out the gate and hailed a carriage home at once.

The butler assured him that Eryx was indeed at the meeting, and Lord Arvis had recovered enough to go with him. Civilla was at the seamstress being fitted for her ball gown, while Lady Nessa had retired to her beloved indoor garden. The house was Esmond's, so he raced to his bedroom, retrieved the bottle of tracking decoction, and set to work.

According to Isaveth, all he had to do was lift the bottle, swirl it, then wait for the floating specks inside to point the way. Mouth dry and skin tingling, Esmond did so.

Oddly, it was pointing toward Civilla's bedroom. It was hard to imagine Eryx would hide anything there, but Esmond had learned not to assume anything where his brother was concerned. He knocked, listened, and cautiously opened the door.

Inside lay a serene, rose-tinted space with mirrors on every wall, presumably so his sister could view her fashionable self from all angles. A dressing table stood in one corner, with a padded stool in front of it and a matching lounge chair stretched out beside. The only pictures were still life paintings, modern in style but utterly devoid of personality. If not for the feathery toe of a slipper peeking from under the bed, he might have taken it for a forgotten guest chamber or a display in Simkin's Category Store—anything but the bedroom of a living girl.

The last time he'd come here, he'd been eight and Civilla thirteen. Her walls had been crammed with maps and botanical sketches, her bed heaped with cloth animals, and they'd thumped each other with pillows until they could barely breathe for laughing. But then she'd started at Tarreton College and Lady Nessa began taking her out in society, and his sister had changed.

First she'd grown self-conscious, always on her dignity and determined to do everything right. She'd won academic awards for dull subjects like sociology, religious studies, and civics, and started a gardening club to help beautify the uglier parts of the city. She'd even nagged their father to stop drinking, and corrected Esmond's posture so many times that he'd started slumping just to annoy her. In short, she'd become a towering bore.

Yet even that dreary, self-righteous Civilla had been better than the sister he had now. Perhaps she'd grown tired of trying to live up to her own standards, or perhaps Eryx's gentle reminders of her inferior taste, judgment, and social skills had finally worn her down. But soon after she graduated, she'd lost interest in being respectable and set out to become popular instead. She'd cut her hair, started wearing dramatic shades of lip tint, and found a new set of friends to whisk her from one party to another. If she didn't nag Esmond or quarrel with Eryx anymore, it was only because she'd stopped caring about anyone's life but her own.

Still, he was surprised by how modest Civilla's wardrobe was. She had only one armoire, and the closet wasn't half as stuffed with dresses as he'd expected—though she did own plenty of hats and a mind-boggling assortment of shoes.

What she didn't have was a case with Eryx's documents in it. Esmond swirled the bottle again, frowning as the particles drifted back the way he had come. Had he read it wrong the first time?

Esmond spent nearly half a bell following the potion all over the house before he realized there was no point in trying further. The tracking spell kept leading him into solid walls, and changed direction every few minutes. Either it didn't work for him the same way it had for Isaveth . . .

Or Eryx had destroyed the letter, and there was nothing left for the potion to find.

After the incident in the charmery, Isaveth felt vulnerable as a newborn kit. Surely the news that she was Moshite was spreading far and wide by now. But none of her classmates troubled her, not even Paskin, and she made her way home at the end of the day in peace. Perhaps it was only the hush before the storm broke, but even so Isaveth was glad for it.

Her head still throbbed where she'd hit the ceiling, but there were no obvious bumps or cuts for her family to notice, so she did her best to smile and act as though all was well. That evening she helped Lilet wash the laundry and hang it outside to freeze dry, while the next morning she went to temple with her sisters and spent the afternoon writing a new *Auradia* story. She hadn't heard from Esmond since she gave him the potion, and she could only hope that he'd have good news for her on Mendday.

When she returned to school the next morning (not without a wistful thought of how nice it would be to have a two-day weekend), Eulalie rushed to meet her. "Did you really jump on a floater last Fastday?" she asked. "I heard Seffania telling her friends about it. Are you all right?"

"I'm fine," said Isaveth. Her head felt only a little sore now, and no one ever died of embarrassment, as Papa would say. "But what about you? Mistress Corto said—"

"Seffania actually asked me if you were Moshite, because she hadn't heard you say the invocation. Can you believe it? Anyway, I told her you must have whispered it, and she just didn't hear. After all, the spell could hardly have worked if you hadn't!" Eulalie giggled. "She didn't know what to say to that one."

Ice formed in Isaveth's stomach. She hadn't wanted to

make a show of being Moshite, but she didn't want to deny it either—especially not after what had happened with Meggery. "But what happens next time I test a sage-charm? They'll all be waiting to see if I make the invocation."

"Well, couldn't you? It's only an old superstition, you know. It doesn't really mean anything . . ." Eulalie stopped. "Why are you looking at me like that?"

She didn't understand. How could she? Isaveth hardly knew how to explain it herself. All she knew was that she couldn't do what Eulalie was suggesting. "Don't," she said hoarsely. "Please."

Eulalie blinked, then swallowed. "Oh. Sorry." She took a step back, one hand creeping to her middle. "I've—er—just remembered something. See you in class, all right?"

Despite its awkward beginning, the rest of the morning went as well as Isaveth could hope. Eulalie turned up late to Sagery, but rather than avoiding Isaveth she sought her out at once, chattering away as though nothing was wrong. And when Mistress Corto announced that first-year students were not to test any charms they made without her permission, not even Paskin complained about it. Isaveth was feeling almost cheerful until she found Esmond's note in the library:

Spell not working. Need to talk.

"Your decoction didn't seem to know where the letter was," Esmond told Isaveth when she met him in the bell tower. "I did everything you told me, but the specks kept changing direction. Are you *sure* that spell works for other people?"

"I don't know why not. All the other spells in the Book of Common Magic do."

"Then there must be some kind of interference," said Esmond glumly. "Or else I'm doing it wrong. Because I tried it when I got home on Fastday, and again after Eryx went out on Templeday, and the same thing happened both times."

Doubt stirred in Isaveth. She'd never actually checked to see if her tracking potion worked for others—before she started learning magical theory, she'd never imagined she might need to. But what if there was a reason the spell-factories of Tarreton didn't make that particular decoction? What if some Common Magic recipes were more like Sagery than she'd thought?

"There's only one way to be certain." Esmond turned to her, blue eyes gleaming with determination. "I'll have to sneak you into the house so you can try it."

Isaveth bolted upright. "What?"

"I know it's risky, but I've got a plan. My sister's coming of age this month, so she and Mother are planning a ball to celebrate. And the best part is"—he leaned toward her, dropping his voice so that Isaveth had to lean in as well—"it's going to be a *masked* ball. I suggested the idea to Civilla this morning, and she loved it. So . . ." He turned his palm up toward Isaveth, as though inviting her to dance.

A shiver of excitement ran through her. "But how could I?" she breathed. "I don't have a mask, or . . . or anything."

"Oh, I can take care of that." He winked his good eye at her. "Don't worry, I'll make sure you look the part."

She felt awkward relying on Esmond's charity, and part of Isaveth feared she'd have no more success with the tracking potion than he had. But to dress up like a noble and sneak into the fanciest ball of the season, so she could catch Eryx and bring him to justice . . . that would be an adventure worthy of Auradia Champion herself.

It wouldn't be easy, though. Not only would Isaveth have to avoid crossing paths with Eryx or anyone else who might recognize her, she'd have to find a way to search for the documents without being caught. Assuming she could convince Papa to let her go to the ball in the first place. . . .

"Well, think about it," said Esmond, misreading her

silence. "I still can't believe Civilla went for it. It's the first time she's listened to me in years." He leaned back on his elbows, gazing about as though hunting for the next topic of conversation. "So . . . you're learning Sagery now, aren't you? Is Mistress Corto a good teacher?"

"You don't know?" asked Isaveth. "Didn't you have her last year?"

Esmond looked faintly sheepish. "No, actually. Father had us all tutored at home, you see—he couldn't risk any of us embarrassing him. I'm in fourth-year Sagery right now."

Isaveth should have guessed as much, especially since she knew who Esmond's old tutor had been: Master Orien, the late governor of the college. Still, she hadn't realized he was quite so far ahead. "Can I ask you something, then?"

"Of course."

"The invocation. Is it necessary?"

Esmond frowned. "I can't see why it should be. It's mostly tradition, I think. Why?"

"Well," said Isaveth cautiously, "I made a float-charm the other day, but it didn't work quite the way I'd expected—"

"That was *you*." He scrambled upright. "I'd heard some first year nearly brained herself on the ceiling, but . . .

Were you hurt?" He reached for Isaveth, but she shied away.

"I was only unconscious for a minute. Master Fetheridge said I'd be fine."

Esmond's eyes narrowed, but he let his hand drop. "Tell me what happened, then."

Reluctantly Isaveth repeated her story. When she told him what Seffania had said to her, Esmond swore under his breath.

"She didn't tell me to step hard," she protested.

"Maybe not, but she certainly meant you to look foolish, and likely get thrown out of class as well. Why?"

It was a fair question. If Seffania had known Isaveth was Moshite, that might explain it, but she couldn't have suspected as much until Isaveth refused to make the invocation. . . .

Unless Paskin had told Seffania about her beforehand. But why would he? As far as Isaveth could tell, the two of them weren't friends, or even good acquaintances. "I don't know," she said.

Esmond blew out a frustrated breath. "Something's not right here. You don't look any poorer than some of the other girls, so why are all these people out to get you? It's almost like . . ."

"A conspiracy?" said Isaveth. "I can't see what the point

would be. It'll take a lot more than insults and pranks to scare me away from the college, and if your brother wanted to hurt me he could have done it weeks ago."

She paused, remembering the gleam in the Lording's eye as he'd spoken about his relief plan. Perhaps Eryx *did* like the idea of hurting Isaveth, but he'd hardly recruit schoolchildren to help him do it. He was far too cautious of his reputation for that.

"You're probably right," Esmond said. "But I still think there's something funny going on." He took her hand, gloved fingers warm against her own. "Be careful, Isaveth. You can't trust anyone in this place, no matter how friendly they seem."

Is that why you don't have any friends here? Isaveth wanted to ask. But she squeezed his hand in reassurance, then climbed to her feet. "I need to get home," she said. "It's my turn to make supper."

"You'll let me know, though, won't you?" Esmond called after her. "About Civilla's ball, I mean. Because if you can't get that spell working, I . . . I don't know what we'll do."

Isaveth stood still, one hand on the banister. Then she looked back and smiled.

"All right," she said. "If you find me something to wear, I'll come."

Chapter Ten

BY THE END of Isaveth's second week at the college, the whispers and murmurs of her classmates turned to excited buzzing. The invitations had gone out for Civilla Ladyship's coming-of-age ball, and all the most prominent families in the city had been invited to attend.

Isaveth received no invitation, of course, and made a point of looking wistful whenever the party was discussed in her presence. She stared at her lap when Betinda Callender boasted that she had already picked out the perfect dress for the occasion; she sighed as Paskin slipped a cream-colored envelope across the desk for his friends to see. But when she learned that Eulalie would also be at the party, it was all Isaveth could do to hide her dismay.

She agonized over the problem all weekend, and by Mendday she could bear it no longer. She caught Eulalie on their way into the dining hall and whispered, "I have to tell you a secret."

Eulalie frowned at her. Then she grabbed Isaveth's elbow and steered her down the corridor. "You look awful," she said, when they were alone. "What's the matter?"

"Esmond's invited me to his sister's party."

Eulalie's jaw dropped. "You mean it? Vettie, that's *gorgeous* news! I'd been thinking how dull it was going to be, but if you're coming too—"

"Yes, but it's not that simple." Quickly Isaveth sketched an explanation: She and Esmond had become good friends, but his family didn't want him associating with commoners, so they had to keep it a secret. She made no mention of Eryx or the search for his documents; those details were too dangerous to share. But she did admit that Esmond had coaxed his sister to make it a masked ball so she, Isaveth, could attend.

"That's why I can't spend the evening with you," Isaveth finished. "I'd love to, but I can't. If any of the other first years see us together, they'll soon guess who I am."

Eulalie raised a skeptical brow. "And the Sagelord and Lady won't suspect anything when they see you dancing with their son?"

"I—no," said Isaveth, flustered. "I don't know how, and I'm sure Esmond wouldn't ask me."

"Maybe, but you'll have to dance with *somebody* or it'll look odd," said Eulalie. "And not to be rude, but whatever are you going to wear?"

"I'm not sure," Isaveth admitted, and Eulalie rolled her eyes.

"Of course the Lilord wouldn't think of that. Boys can be so stupid sometimes! But don't worry." She bumped her shoulder against Isaveth's. "I'll sort you out."

"Oh, no, I couldn't—"

"You can, and you'd better. Besides, I wouldn't miss this if you begged me." Her face lit with a mischievous grin. "Dressing you up like the Little Queen of Uropia, and watching our classmates fall all over themselves trying to guess who you are, is going to be the best fun I've had in ages."

Eulalie insisted on starting Isaveth's dancing lessons the next day, as soon as classes were over. She met her on the steps of the Arts Building and whisked her up two flights to an empty music room, locking the door behind them.

"Now," she said, clapping her hands. "We haven't got a crystal set, so you'll have to put up with me humming, but lucky for you I've got a good ear. Let's start with the three-step, shall we?"

At first the lessons were more painful than fun—Isaveth

kept stepping on her partner's toes, and she moved so stiffly that Eulalie joked she must have dropped a poker down the back of her dress by accident. But as the week wore on, Isaveth learned to move to the music and accept Eulalie's guidance instead of resisting. By Fastday she had made enough progress to trade the old-fashioned partner dances for a livelier modern style, and soon the two girls were kicking and flapping all over the room, giddy with laughter.

"I'm hopeless at that one," gasped Isaveth. "We'd better give up." She staggered to the window and leaned against it, cooling her forehead on the frosty glass.

"Never," said Eulalie, capering to join her. "I shall make a champion hotfoot of you yet . . . say, who's that?" She pointed to the steps of Founders' Hall, where Governor Buldage was speaking to a young woman with bronze skin and a dramatic cobalt-blue hat.

"I can't tell," said Isaveth, squinting. Buldage seemed to be doing most of the talking, though from this distance it was impossible to make out his expression, let alone overhear. It wasn't until Isaveth spotted the notebook in the woman's hand that she realized who Buldage's companion must be.

"That's Su Amaraq," she said. "She's a reporter with the *Tarreton Trumpeter.*" And one of Eryx Lording's supporters, at least for now. Esmond thought Su was too clever not to see through his brother eventually, but then he'd once thought the same about Civilla. . . .

"Really?" Eulalie perked up. "There must be a scandal brewing. The *Trumpeter* always prints the juiciest stories."

"And the biggest lies," said Isaveth flatly. She'd learned that all too well after Papa was arrested—the *Trumpeter*, like the *Citizen* and all the other legal newsrags in the city, was little more than a mouthpiece for the Sagelord. "I wonder what she's after this time?"

The journalist tucked away her notebook and offered her hand to Buldage, who bowed and retreated. Then, with a smile on her lips and a confident lift of her chin, Su Amaraq strode off toward the gate.

"She's awfully glamorous, isn't she?" remarked Eulalie, gazing after her. "Like a two-reel actress. I bet she has the most exciting life."

Isaveth was silent. Not long ago she'd admired Su as well, believing the young reporter could help clear her father's name. But after reading some of the articles Su had written about Papa and his fellow dissenters, Isaveth couldn't look at the woman without feeling betrayed.

"Yes," she said, turning away from the window. "I'm sure she does."

* * *

"I found something for you," Eulalie told Isaveth the next Mendday. She glanced around the Sagery classroom to make sure the other students had gone, then pulled a package from her bag and handed it to Isaveth. "Mother bought it for me last year thinking I'd grow into it, but I stayed short and got all curvy instead." She patted her hips smugly.

Isaveth wasn't sure whether to believe her, but it would be rude to accuse Eulalie of lying, so she opened the wrappings and drew the dress out. It was a silky column with puffed shoulders, dyed a deep crane-berry red and almost Isaveth's size. When she held it up, the hem fell past her ankle, but Annagail could take it up for her—and make it fit perfectly, too.

She laid the gown back in its wrappings and gave Eulalie a hug. "Thank you," she whispered, and the other girl beamed.

"You're going to look gorgeous," she said. "I hope Betinda Callender chokes with envy. Now we just have to find you some decent shoes."

"I can look after that." She'd need a better coat as well, but she wasn't about to say so—not to Eulalie, anyway. She'd manage somehow, even if she had to swallow her pride and ask Esmond to lend her the money. "But you'd better go, or you'll be late for music."

"Eek, you're right!" Eulalie scooped up her books and dashed out.

Isaveth's next class was closer than Eulalie's, so she packed her new dress away and walked up the hill at a more leisurely pace. When she reached the Antiquities Building, however, she found the lobby crowded with students huddled around the latest edition of the *Trumpeter*. A third-year boy was reading aloud to the others:

"'. . . aware it would be a controversial decision,' Governor Buldage said. 'But Mister Wregget was most emphatic about his choice of Miss Breck, and we found no reason to refuse her. . . .'"

A cold fist closed around Isaveth's heart. The gossip Paskin had started had finally spread beyond the college—and now, thanks to Su Amaraq and the *Trumpeter*, the whole city knew her name.

All through Uropian History, Isaveth felt sick with apprehension. But she breathed slowly to ease her panic and reminded herself to stay strong. No matter what the newsrag said about the "controversial" nature of her scholarship—whether it described her as a commoner, a Moshite, Urias Breck's daughter, or all three—Isaveth had nothing to be ashamed of. So she resisted the temptation to bolt as soon as Master Eddicot dismissed them, and walked to the dining hall as usual.

It was hard to eat with so many eyes upon her—she'd seen several heads twist in her direction, even a pointing finger or two as she sat down. Eulalie prattled away on her left side, but all the other seats around Isaveth remained empty, and a group of second-year girls veered away from her as they passed. A leaden weight dropped into Isaveth's stomach. She covered her half-finished plate with her napkin and pushed it away.

Perhaps she should ask Eulalie to help her find a copy of the article, so she'd know what it said. But Isaveth barely had time to open her mouth before the other girl jumped up.

"Got to go!" she exclaimed, and dashed out of the dining hall.

That was disappointing, but Isaveth tried not to let it upset her. Eulalie might have a habit of vanishing at odd moments, but she always came back. Pretending not to notice Seffania and her friends whispering at the other end of the table, Isaveth stood up and set off to find a copy of the *Trumpeter*.

There were several newsrags in the common room, but other students were already reading them. By the time one boy finally left his copy of the *Trumpeter* unattended, the bell was ringing for afternoon classes and Isaveth had to run to Calculation instead.

Fortunately Master Valstead was late, so even after stamping her boots dry and hanging up her overcoat she made it to the classroom before he did. She hurried to her desk—and stopped short, arrested by the words scrawled in black charcoal across its surface.

NO RATS IN OUR COLLEGE

There was no use asking who had written the message. Ghataj had come in soon after she did, and the rest of her classmates were gazing blandly ahead, betraying no hint of guilt or sympathy. She was standing there helpless, a dull ache spreading through her chest, when Master Valstead strode in.

"Sit down, Miss Breck," he said curtly.

Either he hadn't noticed the writing, or—more likely, considering how big the letters were—he just didn't care. Clenching her jaw as her eyes started to prickle, Isaveth dropped into her seat and took out a handkerchief to rub the horrible words away.

Chapter Eleven

GLOW-MOR AWARD CAUSES CONTROVERSY

A four-month delay in the announcement of the coveted Glow-Mor Light and Fire Company scholarship, which offers free tuition to Tarreton College for exceptionally promising students, led many to assume that the company had found no suitable candidate this year. However, as reporter Su Amaraq confirmed in an exclusive interview with college governor Hexter Buldage (see morning edition), the scholarship has been awarded to Miss Isaveth Breck, a stonemason's daughter currently living with her father and sisters in a small rented house on Cabbage Street.

According to Governor Buldage, Miss Breck

joined the student body at the start of fallow-time term, and her work so far is satisfactory. However, her father Urias recently spent time in prison, and his dissenter views have caused some within the college to question Miss Breck's suitability as a candidate.

"I'm not saying she isn't clever," said one student who preferred not to be identified, "but I don't think it's right to teach Sagery to someone who doesn't revere the Sages. The invocation is an important part of our magical heritage, and it's disrespectful not to say it. If Moshites want the privilege of attending Tarreton College, they should learn to respect not only our laws, but our traditions."

Despite the controversy, Glow-Mor president J. J. Wregget expressed no regret. "Miss Breck has shown great promise as a student of magic," he said, "and I believe talent and hard work should be rewarded. I have every confidence that she will be a credit to Tarreton College and an asset to our city in the future."

A source close to the president, however, revealed that not all within the company share Mister Wregget's confidence, and some

are concerned that his decision may harm Glow-Mor's reputation as Tarreton's leading manufacturer of spell-tablets for home and commercial use. . . .

"Ugh!" said Lilet, slapping the newsrag shut. "What a horrible story."

She'd crumpled the pages in her anger, and Isaveth smoothed them before folding up the *Trumpeter* and setting it beside Papa's plate. An afternoon of blowing snow had left knee-deep drifts across the city, so he was still out shoveling—but this news wasn't something Isaveth could hide from him, no matter how much she wished otherwise.

Annagail's brow creased in distress. "I thought Mister Wregget promised not to say anything to the newsrags. Why would he break his word?"

The blessing candles still flickered at the center of the table. Isaveth cupped a hand around each flame as she blew them out. "I don't think he had a choice," she said. "After that interview in the *Trumpeter* this morning, it would have looked even worse if he'd refused to talk at all."

"Does this mean you have to quit school?" asked Mimmi anxiously.

"Not unless Governor Buldage says so. I just thought you should know what the newsrags are saying." People were bound to have strong opinions about the article, and it would be cruel to leave her sisters unprepared. "Now go play outside with Lilet, and I'll make you hot malty-milk when you come in."

Mimmi scampered off to fetch her coat, and silently Lilet followed. Isaveth waited until the door slammed behind them, then turned to Annagail.

"I know you were afraid of this, but at least now it's in the open. And I'm sure Mister Wregget knew it would happen eventually. The masters, too."

Annagail fetched a cloth and began wiping the table, not looking at her. "You think you can do this, then. You really think they'll let you stay."

Isaveth hesitated. She longed to pour out her troubles, from Paskin and Betinda's bullying to the message she had found on her desk, but how could she? Anna had enough on her mind already with running the household, finishing her last year of school, and studying for her healer's examinations. It would be selfish to ask her to carry any more burdens.

"Why not?" Isaveth said brightly. "I'm keeping up with my assignments, and I've done well on all the tests I've taken so far. Don't worry, Anna, it'll blow over. But . . ."

She stooped to retrieve the package from her school bag. "I need your help with something."

Annagail's hand stilled on the washcloth. "What is it?"

"Quiz invited me to his sister's coming-of-age ball, and my friend Eulalie gave me something to wear." Isaveth drew the curtains, then skinned out of her school clothes and pulled the dress over her head. It slipped down her body like cool water.

"Oh, Vettie!" Anna gasped as Isaveth turned to face her. "It's beautiful. But . . ."

Please don't ask me. Please don't.

"Have you talked to Papa about this?"

So much for that. "Not yet. I wanted to get everything I'll need for the ball first, so he'll know it won't be too expensive."

"So he'll know it's too late to refuse, you mean."

"Something like that," Isaveth admitted. "But oh, Anna, I really want to go. Wouldn't you?"

"Of course I would," said Anna with a touch of impatience. "And it was very kind of Quiz—Esmond—to invite you. But after this?" She gestured to the paper. "Vettie, you can't! When people find out who you are . . ."

"They won't. It's a masked ball, and I'll be gone before the unmasking." Besides, there'd been no picture with the articles, so most people wouldn't recognize Isaveth's face even if they saw it. "Please, Anna. Esmond asked me specially, and it's important."

"Important because he asked you? Or because you want to go?"

Annagail was usually the most sympathetic and helpful of her sisters; why was she being so stubborn? "I can't tell you any more than that," said Isaveth. "It's to do with Esmond's family, and it's private. But he really does need me, and I can't let him down."

Anna sighed and reached for her sewing basket. "All right, get up on the chair and I'll pin you. Only promise you'll tell Papa as soon as—"

The front door creaked, and a gust of cold air swept in. "Is there anything to eat in this house?" came an amiable bellow from the hallway. "I'm hollow as an old boot!"

Convincing Papa to let her go to the ball proved even more difficult than persuading Anna—especially once he'd seen the article in the *Trumpeter*, which made him scowl so darkly his brows almost hid his eyes. But Isaveth argued and pleaded with him, insisting that both Esmond and Eulalie would be looking out for her and that backing out of the party now would be letting her enemies win, until Papa groaned and waved at her to stop.

"Enough, enough," he said. "It's like trying to light a pipe in a blizzard. If your heart's set on going, Vettie, then you had better go. But be careful," he continued, half-muffled by the arms she'd flung about his neck, "and I want you home by ten bells, or Esmond Lilord will answer to me. You tell him that."

Isaveth kissed his cheek gratefully. "I will, Papa."

By the time Isaveth's tram stopped at the college the next morning, a crowd of protesters had gathered at the gate. She rubbed the frost off the inside of the window and peered out, trying to read the signs they were holding.

KEEP OUR COLLEGE NOBLE, read one. NO REWARDS FOR REBELS, said another. Then a taxi pulled up behind the tram, and with a flash of cobalt and fur-trimmed wool Su Amaraq stepped out. She'd come to report on the protest—and no doubt press Isaveth to give her an interview as well.

Isaveth squirmed lower in her seat. Bravery was all very well, but she was neither tall nor strong, and if she had to battle her way through that crowd she might never get to class at all. Besides, the last thing she needed was her picture all over the newsrags. She waited for the door to close, and rode the tram around the corner to the next stop.

Fortunately, the servants' entrance to the college was unguarded, so Isaveth made it down the hill to the charmery before the bell stopped ringing. Eulalie smiled as she came in, which was heartening—at least until Paskin stormed in, panting and red in the face, and glared at Isaveth as though she'd cheated him.

"Sneaky little rat," he muttered as he sat down. Which was when Mistress Corto turned with majestic dignity from her wall slate and asked, "Mister Paskin, where is your late card?"

Paskin looked blank. "My . . . what?"

"I see. Well, you had better go and get one." She nodded at the door. "Go on. I'm sure the governor's secretary will assist you."

Which sounded fair, except that the governor's office was all the way up the hill, on the second floor of Founders' Hall, and his secretary was one of the least friendly people Isaveth had ever met. Paskin looked stunned for a moment, then got up stiffly and walked out.

Isaveth could have hugged Mistress Corto, but that would be unwise. So she buried her face behind her workbook, hiding her smile, until her teacher finished her introduction to negation-charms and led them into the workroom.

Today's assignment was a shade-charm—not as potent as the dark-tablets in the Book of Common Magic, but a subtler, illusion-laced spell that allowed the caster to see out even as it discouraged outsiders from seeing in. Isaveth bent to the task, giving it her full attention, and a familiar contentment eased over her. She'd grown to love charm-crafting, and with Mistress Corto in charge she was safe, at least for now.

Yet despite what Su Amaraq's not-so-mysterious informer had implied, Isaveth hadn't tested a single charm, let alone refused to say the invocation over it, since the ill-fated floater. Mistress Corto had merely examined each of her finished spells with her charm-glass and dropped them into a box with Isaveth's name on it, to be kept until the end of term.

She did the same for everyone, of course, but it seemed like a waste to Isaveth. After all, her scholarship was paying for the ingredients, and it wasn't as though the charms she made were much use to anyone else. So when she noticed that Eulalie and Seffania had both spoiled their first attempts and had to start over, she discreetly pocketed her finished shade-charm and slipped back to the ingredients table to make another. The ball was fast approaching, and if anything went wrong it would be good to have a defensive spell or two that didn't immediately mark her as a commoner.

She'd just handed the duplicate charm to Kif when

the bell rang, and Eulalie bounded across the workroom to join her. "Wasn't it glorious?" she crowed as the other students filed out. "The look on Paskin's face! I hope the secretary bit his ear off."

She went on gloating all the way up the hill, describing what a nasty old fuss-cat the governor's secretary was and how she wished she could have been there to see Paskin begging her to sign his late card. But she didn't say a word about the protesters at the gate, and she bounced away before Isaveth could ask if she'd seen them.

Well, perhaps it was for the best. There hadn't been time to discuss anything serious anyway, and they'd have a better chance to talk at lunch. . . .

Only they didn't. Because when Isaveth went to the dining hall, Eulalie wasn't there.

DISSENTER GO HOME, said the mirror, in five greasy syllables of lip tint. The message hadn't been there when Isaveth entered the washroom, but it was the first thing that she saw as she emerged from the stall. She scrubbed her hands and plunged out into the corridor, looking for the girl who'd done it.

There was no sign of a culprit, however. Isaveth was watching a group of third-year boys amble into the dining hall, wondering whether to hunt for Eulalie or brave the lunch table on her own, when she felt a tap on her shoulder. Governor Buldage had come up behind her, his dark-robed figure silhouetted against the light.

"Miss Breck," he said. "I'm glad to see you're still with us."

Isaveth studied him uneasily. Was it the shadows that made his cheeks seem more sunken than she remembered, and etched those deep lines around his mouth? He looked ten years older than when they'd first met.

"I apologize for that situation at the gate this morning," Buldage continued. "I have taken steps to discourage any further blocking of school entrances, and also reminded Su Amaraq that our charter forbids her to interview students without their parents' consent."

He raised his brows, as though hoping for Isaveth's approval. Was he trying to trick her into trusting him? Did he think that if he treated her kindly, she'd forget the evil he'd done?

"I appreciate that, sir," she answered, but it came out flat, and Buldage's smile faded. He glanced over his shoulder, then stooped toward her.

"She already knew you were Moshite," he said quietly. "So I could hardly refuse to comment on the school's decision to accept you. You understand, Miss Breck, that I am in a difficult position. I have no wish to be unfair to you, but I must protect the interests and the reputation of this college."

Isaveth had never expected otherwise, but the man's pained expression baffled her. He seemed genuinely sorry for what had happened—yet how could that be? He was Eryx's henchman, and a murderer. In fact, at least one of the letters she and Esmond were searching for was certain to incriminate him.

"So I urge you to be careful," Buldage continued. "There are . . . people of influence whose children are students here, and if they wish to vent their displeasure there is little I can do to stop them. Mistress Corto did well to send Mister Paskin to my office today, but I would not count on her doing so again." He paused, his eyes hooded, then added softly, "I wish you courage, Miss Breck. You will need it."

Then he walked away.

Shaken but determined, Isaveth continued her vigil outside the dining room. Eulalie might never have known real hunger, but she loved food as much as Isaveth, and it wasn't like her to miss lunch if she was still in the college at all. . . .

"There's our little rat-girl." Paskin strolled out the door, a pair of other first-year boys trailing after him, and lounged insolently against the archway. "I knew she'd be skulking somewhere. What happened to your little friend, Mishmosh? Did she finally come to her senses and stop wasting charity on you?"

Isaveth bristled. "Don't call me that," she said, but Paskin only smirked.

"Where's your prayer scarf, Mushpot? Or are you too ashamed to show people what you really are? Not that I'd blame you. Especially with the father you've got."

Isaveth clenched her fists, blood pounding in her ears. Paskin wasn't much bigger than she was, and if she'd been Lilet, she would have thumped him until he wailed for mercy. But fighting would get her expelled for certain—even if it would be satisfying to plant her fist in that sallow, sneering face.

"My Papa is an honest man," she retorted. "Can you say the same about yours?"

Paskin's eyes turned beady. He lunged toward her—but then a pair of second-year girls strolled out of the dining room, and Isaveth seized her chance to escape. She ducked around them, pelted down the stairs, and burst outside, heading for the library.

Chapter Twelve

ISAVETH'S TEETH WERE CHATTERING as she entered the library; she'd left her coat back in the dining hall, and the air outside was cold enough to bite. But inside it was warm, quiet, and mercifully empty—except for the familiar sight of Ghataj sitting at one of the study tables, books piled all around. Cautiously Isaveth walked up to him.

"Hello," she said.

Ghataj didn't answer, or even glance at her. He turned a page and went on reading.

A sick, shivery feeling rippled over Isaveth. Now she understood: Ghataj had pitied her when he thought she was merely a commoner, but he wanted nothing to do with a Moshite . . . a dissenter . . . a *rat*. Isaveth spun away and plunged between the shelves, stumbling toward the back of the library.

Surely Esmond cared, even if no one else did. He must have read Su's article by now, or at least seen the protesters at the gate. She groped through the agriculture shelf for the volume entitled *Native Weeds of Vesperia* and flipped it open to the last page.

It was empty.

Numbly Isaveth pushed the book into place and walked to the end of the aisle, where a narrow patchwork of glass overlooked the snow-covered grounds. She braced her hands on the windowsill, breathing raggedly as she fought the urge to cry.

How stupid to think that anyone, even Esmond, would understand. She was the only one here who knew what it was like to be poor, let alone so utterly despised. . . .

"Isaveth?"

His voice was so hoarse she barely recognized it. She turned and there stood Esmond, with wind-ruffled hair and snowflakes melting all over his robe.

"I was just coming to leave you a note," he said.

Isaveth's throat knotted. She pressed her hands to her mouth as Esmond put an arm around her and drew her behind one of the shelves.

"I'm sorry," he said, low in her ear. "I could kick Su for chasing that story, especially since Eryx was probably the one who tipped her off, but there's no way to fix it now. Did you get to class all right? Those fools at the gate didn't stop you?"

He was gripping her so tightly it hurt, but if she said anything he'd let go, and Isaveth couldn't bear that either. She gave a jerky nod.

Esmond turned her toward him, peering into her face. "You look miserable. Are people being rotten?"

Isaveth tried to shrug off the question, but his sympathy undid her. Her eyes watered, and she fumbled for her handkerchief—only to find it stained black from wiping off her desk the day before. She gazed at it in dismay, and then the whole situation struck her as horribly, bleakly funny and she started to giggle.

Esmond didn't laugh. He offered his own handkerchief, pressed white linen with his family crest and initials embroidered on the corner, and waited until Isaveth had blown her nose and wiped her eyes before speaking again.

"We can't talk now—anyone might see us. And I can't meet you after school, either, because I promised Civilla I'd make all the charms for her party. But whatever they're saying about you, don't listen. You've got as much right to be here as anyone." He cleared his throat, then added in a tone so rough it sounded savage, "You're better than all of them. I hope you show them for the fools they are."

Isaveth didn't dare look at him. She kept the handkerchief to her face, breathing its soapy fragrance, as Esmond's hands tightened on her shoulders. Then something warm brushed the top of her head, and when she opened her eyes he was gone.

They'd only had a moment, yet it was enough. Isaveth felt calmer now, and able to go on. She tucked the handkerchief into her book bag, smoothed her robe, and started up the aisle toward the exit.

"Tchoo!"

The sneeze came from behind a neighboring shelf. Isaveth lunged forward, shoved the books apart—and found Ghataj on the other side, blinking at her.

"You were spying on me!" she accused, but he flung up his hands in protest.

"I didn't mean to," he said. "I didn't realize you'd said hello until you were gone, so I thought I'd wait until you came back and talk then. But then I heard you . . . I heard something, so I came to see if you were all right. I didn't expect to find you with *him*."

Isaveth's mouth went dry. Bad enough that he'd seen her with Esmond, but if he'd overheard their conversation it would be even worse. "Don't tell anyone," she blurted out. "Please."

Ghataj's brows shot up. "I am no telltale," he said

stiffly. "But I'm not a fool, either. Why were you crying? Did the Lilord threaten you?"

"Threaten me?" she echoed, bewildered. "Why would he?"

Ghataj gave her a severe look over his glasses. "Because he is a bully, like his father. Why else?"

Isaveth opened her mouth to argue, then shut it with a snap. If she defended Esmond too fiercely, he'd know the two of them were close.

"No," she said, "he didn't threaten me. He . . . he's an acquaintance, and he saw I was upset, so he stopped to lend me his handkerchief." She pulled it out of the bag, turning the crest for Gharaj to see. "He was quite decent about it, actually."

The boy regarded Esmond's handkerchief with suspicion, then came around the end of the shelf to meet her. "Acquaintance? Since when?"

"We met after my father was arrested," said Isaveth. There was no point trying to hide something that everyone knew, after all. "But his parents don't like him talking to commoners, so please don't tell. I don't want to get Esmond in trouble, and if anyone finds out . . ." She took a deep breath. "It could make trouble for me, too."

"Worse than the troubles you have already?" asked Ghataj. "That seems hard to believe."

His tone was oddly gentle, and Isaveth looked away as tears clogged her throat again. Ghataj coughed and went on, "Well, anyway. I'll keep your secret. But Miss Breck . . ."

Here it came: the part where he asked her to go away because he didn't want trouble either. It took all Isaveth's courage to look him in the eye. "Yes?"

"If you need more help with your schoolwork, just ask. I know some people think only nobles should learn Sagery, but I happen to think those people are wrong." With a polite nod, he turned to go.

"Mister Ghataj?"

He glanced back.

"Thank you," she said, sticking out her hand. "Call me Isaveth."

He shook it. "Mander. And you're welcome."

"There you are!" Eulalie trotted up as Isaveth came out of the library. "Sorry about lunch—I had to stay late after music and I only just got out. Here." She bundled Isaveth's coat into her arms, then started rummaging in her pocket. "Did you get anything to eat? I grabbed a couple of sweet buns as they were clearing the tables."

Isaveth had misjudged Mander Ghataj, thinking he didn't care. Now it seemed she'd misjudged Eulalie, too.

Grateful, Isaveth pulled on the coat and accepted the roll she offered. "What happened in music?"

"Oh, it was nothing. Just silly stuff, you know how it is. So how are you doing? Excited for the ball?"

"The ball. That's . . . all you want to talk about?"

Eulalie's face fell. "You mean you don't? You aren't backing out, are you?"

"No," said Isaveth, and then with a rush of bitterness, "but maybe I should. You read that story in the *Trumpeter*, didn't you? You saw the protesters this morning—"

"Of course I did." Eulalie put a soothing hand on her arm. "My father had to warn them he'd call in the Lawkeepers if they didn't stop blocking the gate. But it's only a few sillyheads, so don't worry. Soon they'll get tired of freezing their feet off and go away."

It was a bold speech, and Isaveth longed to believe her. It would be wonderful to think that all she had to do was ignore her enemies to defeat them. But she'd faced corrupt nobles before, and knew that the power they wielded over poor folk like herself was no illusion.

"It's not just them, though," she insisted. "It's everyone." She started to describe the insults she'd found on her desk and the washroom mirror, but Eulalie broke in before she could finish.

"Betinda Callender is not *everyone*. I know a lot of terrible things happened to Moshites in the past, but most people know better now. Betinda's been jealous of you from the start, so of course she wants you to think the whole school hates you as much as she does. I'm sure she wrote all those messages herself." Eulalie squeezed Isaveth's arm. "That's why you mustn't let her get to you, don't you see? If you give up, she wins."

She didn't understand, and Isaveth was beginning to despair that she ever would. But it was impossible to argue without sounding unreasonable. She gave a reluctant nod.

"So you'll come to the party, then? You won't let Betinda and Paskin and all those silly parents scare you away?"

As though she had any choice, with Esmond relying on her to find out what had gone wrong with the tracking spell . . . and her own future in jeopardy if they couldn't stop Eryx from carrying out his plan.

"Yes," said Isaveth. "Of course I'll come."

There was no more snow that week, only a sharp drop in temperature that froze the hairs inside Isaveth's nostrils and kept all but a few stubborn protesters away from the college gate. So when she got home from school on Trustday, she was not surprised to find Papa waiting for her.

"Something's arrived for you, Vettie," he said, beckoning her upstairs to the room he'd once shared with their mother. On the bed sat three packages, each covered in brown paper and bearing a stamp reading GARDENTOWN DELIVERY SERVICE.

Mystified, Isaveth opened the first box. Inside lay a bundle of cloth with a card tucked into one of the folds: *Miss Fairpont tells me you already have a dress, so I hope this will suit. —Q*

It was a coat, deep gray with a matching lamb's-wool collar so soft that Isaveth couldn't resist rubbing it against her cheek. Papa helped her into it, then turned her gently and studied her at arm's length.

"That's a fine thing," he said. "You look very handsome, Vettie."

But his eyes were sad, and she knew he must be wishing he could afford to buy her such fine things himself. Aching for him, Isaveth turned away and opened the second box. There lay a shiny pair of black dancing shoes with delicate T-straps and a pattern of jet beads across the toe, and in the layer beneath, a set of fur-trimmed overboots to protect them.

They fit perfectly. Either Esmond was even more observant than she'd thought, or he'd got some advice from Eulalie. She unwrapped the third box and found a feathery half mask, crested and beaked to look like a crimson berrybird. With it on, no one, not even Eryx Lording, would recognize her.

Until now the idea of attending a ball in the Sagelord's mansion had seemed like some distant fantasy. Now it felt so real that Isaveth's heart began to flutter. She shut the mask box and pushed it away.

"What is it, my Vettie?" Papa asked. "Don't you like your presents?"

"Of course I do, they're beautiful, but . . ." She brushed a finger over the label on the shoebox: EASSON'S FINE COBBLERY, TARRETON. "It feels wrong to take them. I owe Esmond—and Eulalie—so much already, and I can never pay them back."

Her father nodded soberly. "It's a hard lump to swallow, being beholden to folks who have everything." He put an arm around her. "But just because you don't have money doesn't mean you've got no worth. Your friends must think highly of you, or they wouldn't want you at this party. And who knows, you may get a chance someday to do them a favor in return."

Isaveth laid her head on Papa's shoulder, wishing she could tell him the real reason she had to go to the ball. But if Papa knew the risks she was taking, he'd never allow it.

"I hope you're right," she said quietly.

* * *

That Fastday felt like the longest of Isaveth's life. On one hand, the protests had trickled to a stop, and her enemies were too distracted by the thought of Civilla's ball to waste time tormenting her. But she hadn't talked to Esmond since Duesday, and Eulalie's gleeful anticipation of the party had become so obvious that Isaveth had to avoid her for fear she'd give the whole plan away.

At last the final bell rang, and everyone who was anyone leaped into taxis and hired spell-carriages and raced off to prepare for the grand occasion. Isaveth made her way home at a less frantic pace, but as soon as she stepped inside the cottage, her own flurry of preparations began.

Bathing, drying, dabbing her throat and wrists with rosewater; shivering in the chill of Papa's bedroom while Annagail, lips tight with concentration, made one last adjustment to the lovely dress; sitting patiently in the kitchen while her sister dampened and restyled her hair, pinning the wind-tousled locks into smooth ripples about Isaveth's face. By the time she was ready to put on the outer layers of her glamorous disguise, the sliver of sky showing through the kitchen window was dark, and even the clanging of the nearby factories had fallen silent.

"Cake," said Lilet firmly, handing Isaveth the box with her mask in it. "You have to bring us back a piece of cake at least."

"One piece *each*," piped up Mimmi, skipping after Isaveth as she walked to the back door. "And don't forget to tell Quiz I said—"

"That's enough, my Mirrim," said Papa, getting up from the game of crock-in-the-hole he and Annagail were playing and steering Mimmi away. "Your sister's got enough on her mind without all that. But you mind what I told you, Vettie. Ten bells, and no more."

"Yes, Papa." Isaveth craned around him, trying to catch Annagail's eye. "Thank you, Anna."

Annagail smiled wanly, but made no reply. No doubt she was tired after all the work she'd done, and Isaveth resolved to bring her a special treat from the party to make up for it. She hugged Papa good-bye and stepped out into the cold.

In the darkness of the coal lane, with her new coat wrapped around her and her head bowed under one of Mama's Templeday hats, Isaveth's confidence grew. She strolled up the wheel-rutted alley to Grand Street, took out the cab-hailer Esmond had given her, and cracked it in two. A blue spark arced into the air, and presently a taxi veered up beside her.

"Where to, missus?"

He thought she was a grown woman. Well, of course: What girl her age would be going out alone at this time of night? "Rollingdale Court," Isaveth said in her huskiest tone, and climbed in. Bracing herself against the bump and sway of the taxi, she unpinned her hat and slipped her crimson berrybird mask into place. Then she sat back, watching the streetlights swim over the front of the cab as it sped toward the city center.

She could do this—no, she *was* doing it. Excitement surged up in Isaveth, chasing her fears away.

"The Sagelord's house, if you please," she told the driver. "I'm going to a ball."

Chapter Thirteen

LIGHT STREAMED OUT the doors of the Sagelord's mansion, pouring down the steps like liquid honey. In the midst of the circular driveway a fountain cascaded over three tiers of gleaming marble—a shocking extravagance in this weather, especially since it would take about fifty warming-charms to keep it flowing. No wonder Esmond had been busy. Shivering with nerves and anticipation, Isaveth followed the other guests inside and gave the maid her hat and coat.

As she entered the grand ballroom, the sound of a sway band greeted her, the low plunk of a bass twining with the razz of a muted trumpet. Glow-charms hung everywhere, twinkling like tiny constellations above the crowd, and the velvety curtains were drawn, giving the room an intimate, even secret appearance. Cataracts of ice-blue silk poured down the walls, while in each corner an urn half as tall as Isaveth held ribbon-laced bundles of pine boughs and branches painted white as bone. She had never seen a room so splendid—or so full of people.

Young and old, they surrounded her on every side: men in crisply tailored suits and embroidered waistcoats; women draped in silks, furs, and cascading strands of jewels. All wore half masks like Isaveth's, but in a fantastic assortment of nature-themed styles—bristling fir needles and points of red maple, wildcats and bears and foxes, the fierce beaks of gorehawks and crows. It would be easy to pass unnoticed in a crowd like this.

Servants drifted around Isaveth, offering flutes of berry squash, trays of crisp breads layered with meats and cheeses, and platters of fancy cakes so beautifully decorated that it seemed almost wicked to eat them. Isaveth helped herself to a cheese toast and sidled across the room. Surely she'd be able to spot Esmond, no matter what mask he wore. . . .

"Psst!" came a whisper, and Isaveth turned to see Eulalie passing by on the arm of a dignified-looking man who must be her father, the Deputy Justice. She winked at Isaveth through her otter mask and vanished into the crowd.

After a few minutes of wandering, Isaveth found several

more people that she knew. First Betinda Callender, in a snowflake mask and a fluffy white gown that didn't suit her; the horned owl was Mistress Anandri, stately in earth-colored silks; and the boar in the burgundy waistcoat had to be J. J. Wregget, escorting a shy-looking sparrow who was probably his wife. Su Amaraq wore a mask of green ivy leaves, with a matching silk halter-neck and loose slacks that swirled about her ankles—Isaveth still resented the woman, but she couldn't help admiring her effortless style. And the boy coming through the door, with the frog mask made to fit around his spectacles . . .

Oh no. It was Mander Ghataj. Isaveth stiffened as his gaze swept over her, then relaxed as he turned to his companion, a dove-masked girl in gray satin who must be his sister. Funny: She looked too old to be a student at the college, yet Isaveth couldn't shake the impression that she'd met Miss Ghataj before. . . .

"Utterly mad," drawled a man on Isaveth's right, and a woman chimed in, "Absolutely. I can't see how Glow-Mor's going to walk away from this."

Isaveth's stomach jumped, but she didn't dare turn to look or her eavesdropping would be obvious. She put on a vague smile and helped herself to a pastry as the tray passed by.

"Typical J. J., though," remarked another man. "He

always was one to bet on the lame horses. And mind you, it's paid off more often than not."

"Oh, he's been lucky," said the woman with a dismissive sniff. "But he's backed the wrong horse this time. Charity's all very well, but giving a Tarreton scholarship to a Moshite? The public won't stand for it. Glow-Mor sales are sure to crash in another week or two—from what I hear, they're plummeting already."

"Crash! I don't know about that. You have to remember it's mostly commoners who buy Glow-Mor tablets, and they stick up for their own."

"Not for Moshites," cut in the drawler. "There are plenty of poor folk who think dissenters shouldn't be allowed to live in this city at all, let alone take the jobs—"

"Or the scholarships," added the woman.

"Quite right, my love—that should be theirs. J. J. Wregget may fancy himself progressive, but he's got no business sense. If you ask me, he's about to get kicked right in the profits."

"Hmm," said the second man. "That could be bad. A big chunk of Glow-Mor's sales is export, and that's mostly Wregget's doing. If his board loses confidence and kicks him out, their foreign partners may start looking elsewhere—and that's going to hurt Tarreton, not just Glow-Mor. . . ."

His words trailed off as the three of them moved away. Isaveth stood still for a few heartbeats, then moved shakily in the opposite direction.

Mister Wregget had taken a huge risk by supporting her, and now his reputation was in danger. What if the haughty couple's prediction about Glow-Mor's sales came true, and Wregget's own board turned against him? If he lost his job, Isaveth's scholarship would be the first thing to go. . . .

"Ladies and gentlemen!" boomed a voice from the dais, so loud it could only be enhanced by magic. Everyone turned to where the Sagelord stood resplendent in his Tarreton-blue suit, unmasked and gripping a sound-crystal in one beefy hand.

"It's a pleasure to have all of you here to celebrate our daughter Civilla's eighteenth birthday. My lady wife . . . Where are you, Nessa?" He half-turned, grabbed the arm of a frail-looking blond woman, and dragged her to the front of the platform. "My wife and I welcome you to this very special occasion."

If the Sagelord was unwell, as Mander had hinted, Isaveth could see no sign of it. His skin shone ruddy pink, and his eyes gleamed as he continued on. "I'm not a great man for sentimental speeches, especially not when it comes to my daughter. Every time I pay her a compliment, it seems to set her off. When she was in her last year at Tarreton College I told her to stop fretting about her marks because she was so pretty no one expected her to be bright, and she's never let me forget it—Ha! Ha! Ha!"

The crowd broke into uneasy laughter, and Isaveth winced. If Civilla Ladyship sometimes appeared distant and even icy in public, now she knew why. Who could be at ease with a great buffoon like that?

"So I'm going to step aside," the Sagelord said, still chuckling at his own joke, "and give you the real speech-maker in the family. My son and heir, Eryx Lording!"

Eryx walked out onto the dais, and the room erupted in applause. To Isaveth's left, Mander Ghataj bounced up on his toes, clapping eagerly as Eryx took the sound-crystal from Lord Arvis and stepped to the front of the stage.

"I'd like to thank you all for coming tonight," he said. "This is an important event for our family, and it's an honor to share it with our trusted friends, loyal supporters, and valued business associates. I am sure I speak for Civilla as well as the rest of us when I say that the occasion would not be complete without you. . . ."

He went on in this fashion for some time, praising various groups and individuals until the whole room glowed with self-satisfaction, and Isaveth felt a sour taste creeping up her throat. She wished Esmond were beside her, so at least she wouldn't be the only person revolted by Eryx's flattery. Where was he, anyway?

"But my chief purpose here is to honor my sister, who has indeed grown up to be an exceptional young woman. She is refined . . . perceptive . . . and as her friends well know, she takes a keen interest in other people's welfare." Eryx smiled as he spoke, as though these were the finest qualities any young woman could possess. But the thoughtful pause he left between each word implied the opposite—that Civilla was fussy, meddlesome, and controlling, and he was trying to find a gracious way to say so.

"She is also, as my father remarked—though perhaps not in the words Civilla herself might have chosen—easy to look at, which I'm sure explains the many eligible young bachelors I see before me tonight. Though for myself, I can only feel fortunate to have a sister with such . . . *excellent* taste in friends."

His voice caressed the last phrase, and his gaze lingered on someone in the crowd. All around Isaveth, necks craned as people tried to see where he was looking—but then Eryx cleared his throat and stepped back. "Honored guests, I present to you my sister, Civilla Ladyship!"

With that, he bowed and walked off the stage, taking the sound-crystal with him. So when Civilla climbed up onto the dais, she had to raise a hand and wait for the applause to die down before she could speak.

"Good evening," she said, each syllable clear and precise. Isaveth could only admire her poise—after all those back-handed compliments, she must be furious. "Thank you all for rising so magnificently to the theme of tonight's party—celebrating the flora and fauna of our beautiful country. My brother Esmond Lilord will be helping me judge the best mask of the evening, and when the unmasking takes place at midnight, our winner will receive a prize. Now enjoy the music of Syl Simms and his Royal Colonians, and let the party begin!"

The orchestra struck up a lively tune as Civilla stepped off the platform—not vanishing through a side door as her parents and Eryx had done, but walking down to take the hand of a slim young man in white who waited for her below. As he whirled her onto the dance floor, the light caught the glint of his half glass, and Isaveth realized with a start that it was Esmond.

"Er, miss?"

The voice sounded so polite, she would never have recognized it if she hadn't already known he was there. Paskin, eyes wide and hopeful behind the dark stripe of his redcoon mask, was holding out his hand to ask her to dance.

It was tempting to toss her head and turn her back on him, but while Isaveth had every reason to resent Paskin, the noble girl she was pretending to be had none. She swallowed her revulsion and let him lead her onto the floor.

"I see you're going to make me do all the talking," he teased a few moments later as they whirled through the old-fashioned dance. "The masks are just for fun, you know. You won't get a prize for being the most mysterious girl at the ball."

Isaveth smiled thinly and kept counting steps in her head, trying not to shudder at the spidery touch of Paskin's fingers against her spine. He wasn't unpleasant to look at, if a little bland and over-groomed for her taste, and no doubt another girl would have been pleased with his attentions. But nothing could erase the memory of how cruel he'd been to her, and as soon as the song ended, Isaveth dropped his hand and scuttled away.

"Was that as horrible as it looked?" muttered Eulalie as she wandered past.

"Worse," Isaveth whispered, "but thanks for the lessons." She was about to ask Eulalie where her mother was when the next set of dancers took the floor—including Eryx Lording, who came strolling up from the main entrance looking more smug than ever. He walked straight to Mander Ghataj's dove-masked sister, took her hand, and pulled her into the dance.

They made a handsome couple—though the possessive way Eryx steered Miss Ghataj about the floor, and her willingness to let him, made Isaveth feel nauseated. Especially since she'd once dreamed of dancing with Eryx like that herself. . . .

"Delicia Ghataj," breathed Eulalie. "So that's who he had his eye on."

The name jolted Isaveth: No wonder the older girl seemed familiar. A few months ago Isaveth had sneaked into a fancy garden party and overheard Delicia chatting with two other girls about politics. Her admiration for Eryx Lording had been obvious, as was her desire to see the poor folk of Tarreton treated fairly—and Isaveth had liked her for it, since at the time she'd been just as unaware of Eryx's true motives as Delicia.

She knew better now, of course, but Delicia didn't, and when Eryx drew the young woman closer and murmured in her ear, her smile was so dazzling it hurt. Isaveth shuddered and turned away.

Nine bells, Esmond had told her. That was when he'd give Isaveth the signal, and she'd slip out to hunt for the documents. But the clock had scarcely rung eight yet, so Isaveth was left to drift about the room, unable to sit in case one of her other schoolmates tried to strike up a conversation or asked her to dance. She also had to keep her distance from Eryx, who had left the dance floor and was greeting one group of guests after another, shaking hands and smiling as though he were the host of the party.

Fortunately, Civilla was doing her own socializing on the other side of the ballroom, and the crowd that had gathered around her was mostly women and a few middle-aged men—people with no reason to notice Isaveth, let alone speak to her. Edging over, she tucked herself behind a portly couple in matching beaver masks and did her best to look inconspicuous.

"So enjoyed your visit to our society meeting last week," the woman was saying effusively. "I went home and told Mister Gullinger all about it. . . ."

Civilla made some reply, but Isaveth had already lost interest in the conversation. She had drifted into a daydream where Auradia Champion marched into the ballroom with a squad of Lawkeepers and arrested Eryx, when the man in front of her spoke: "Where's Lord Arvis got to? I haven't seen him since the start of the ball."

Civilla gave a light, not quite convincing laugh. "Oh,

you know my father. He's got no patience for small talk, and he hasn't danced in years. He's probably gone off to talk business somewhere, but I'm sure my mother will coax him back eventually . . . oh!" She turned as a slick-haired boy touched her elbow, his teeth bared in a hopeful, crooked smile. "Yes, of course. Please excuse me." She followed him to the dance floor, leaving her crowd of admirers to scatter.

"Such a charming young lady," gushed Missus Gullinger as she and her husband ambled away. "She really makes quite an impression. Not like her mother, the poor darling; *she* looks like a fairweather breeze could blow her over. . . ."

Left alone, Isaveth glanced at the open door. The ballroom was growing stuffy, and she longed for fresh air. Perhaps it wouldn't hurt to step outside for a little while? She glanced at Esmond, who was still dancing, then set down her flute of berry squash and slipped out.

She knew the layout of this floor from her previous visits to the house—the library to one side of the entrance hall, a spacious lounge on the other. Both were full of noisy, puffer-smoking guests, so she passed them by, heading for the quiet of the east wing.

First came the gaming room, but when she put an ear to the door, the murmurs coming from inside told her it was already occupied by at least two people—and one of them was Lord Arvis. She couldn't make out any of the conversation, so Isaveth moved on.

She was hovering by the next door, debating whether to chance it, when a glimmer at the end of the hallway caught her eye. There stood a pair of glass doors with moonlight slanting through them, and no signs of movement within. Cautiously Isaveth sidled up, pressed down the latch. . .

And stepped forward into paradise.

The air breathed fragrance, the sweet aroma of a hundred flowers. Ferns arched from a pot beside her, while an exotic tree covered with scales of overlapping bark filtered the moonlight above. Pots dangled from the ceiling, overflowing with vines and blossoms, and beds full of dwarf shrubs and other ornamental plants lined the walls. Isaveth had never seen such a beautifully kept garden—there was scarcely a wilted leaf to be seen anywhere, and the blooming plants were spaced so expertly that there would be flowers all year around. She strolled down the aisle, gazing up at the stars through the glass ceiling, and did a little twirl for sheer happiness.

She had eased back her berrybird mask and was sniffing a cluster of heart-lilies, wondering whether the tiny yellow-capped mushrooms she could see growing nearby were edible, when the doorknob rattled. Isaveth dived behind a planter, peering wide-eyed through the foliage as the double doors opened and a woman stalked in.

Not just any woman, either. It was Civilla Ladyship, and she was furious.

"Shut the door, Eryx," she snapped. "I knew I'd regret letting you introduce me tonight, but this is unbelievable."

"What have I done that's so upsetting?" asked the Lording. "Really, Cilla, I don't see—"

"Cutting me down to make yourself look clever—that didn't surprise me. But practically proposing to Delicia in front of everyone, so they'll be talking of nothing but you and her for the rest of the night? How *dare* you."

"There's no reason to get emotional," said Eryx. "I didn't propose; I merely confessed my admiration. Surely you don't disagree? I thought you liked Delicia."

Civilla folded her arms. "I do. And that is why I never want to see you flattering her, dancing with her, or showing her any kind of special attention again."

"You can't be serious."

"I am deadly serious. Delicia Ghataj isn't just one of the brightest young noblewomen in the city, she cares deeply about making Tarreton a better place—in short, she would make an excellent Sagelady. And I will *not* stand by and watch you do to her what Father did to Mother."

"I haven't the least idea what you mean," said Eryx, but his tone was too bland, too indifferent. It was the same way Lilet talked when someone caught her misbehaving and she was trying to bluff it out.

"Very well, let me put it this way." Civilla's voice dropped lower, but its coldness was no less intense. "If I catch you slithering around Delicia or any of my friends again, I will *ruin* you."

"Oh, come now, you can't mean—"

"Don't test me, Eryx. You need me on your side."

Isaveth gripped the edge of the planter, trying desperately to ignore the cramp in her leg. If she moved even a little, they'd spot her.

"Very well," said the Lording at last. "But jealousy doesn't become you, Cilla. Just because Delicia doesn't despise me doesn't make her any less your friend."

He really was a snake, thought Isaveth. How could she ever have admired him? Anyone who could twist words like that . . .

"No, it doesn't," retorted Civilla. "But neither does it make me any less hers. Charm-swear it, Eryx. I won't let you off until you do."

Eryx gave a long-suffering sigh. He drew a silver case from his pocket, opened it with a practiced flick of the thumb, and tweezed out a charm, holding it up before his lips as he spoke.

"I, Eryx Lording, pledge to show no more attention to Delicia Ghataj after this night than I did before, until and unless my sister, Civilla Ladyship, approves. I also vow not to court any other friends of my sister, Civilla Ladyship, without her consent." He arched one dark brow at her. "Does that suffice?"

Isaveth wanted to shout a warning—there had to be a loophole in that promise, a cunning trick that would enable Eryx to get his way. But even if she'd dared to reveal herself, it was too late. Civilla nodded, and the charm flared green as Eryx murmured the invocation and snapped it in two.

"For your keeping," he said, handing Civilla one of the broken halves. "Now, if we're quite done here, it's time we were getting back to the ball."

Heart thumping, Isaveth forced herself to stay hidden until the door closed and the sound of their footsteps had faded. Then she rose stiffly and crept toward the exit.

Chapter Fourteen

WHEN ISAVETH RETURNED to the ballroom, she found more couples dancing than ever. Eulalie was skipping about with Mander Ghataj, whose reluctant manner made Isaveth suspect that she'd asked him to dance instead of the other way around. J. J. Wregget guided the Sagelady about the floor, holding her so lightly she might have been a soap bubble, while Eryx seemed to be waging a silent battle with Su Amaraq over which one of them should lead. And judging by the way Betinda Callender kept tossing her curls and giggling, Paskin had found a willing partner at last. . . .

"There you are," said Esmond in her ear, and Isaveth jumped. "Good. Now turn around and try to look surprised. I'm going to ask you to dance."

She didn't need to try: Her startled reaction was genuine. "What?"

Esmond made her a half bow and held out his hand. "We need to talk," he muttered, "so will you please cooperate before people start staring?"

He had a point. If she refused to dance with the Sagelord's son, everyone would wonder. So as the musicians struck up a slower tune, Isaveth put her hand into Esmond's and let him walk her out onto the floor.

"Try to relax," said Esmond as they turned to face each other. "I know this is awkward, but it was the only way I could think of to get a proper conversation. Is everything all right? I saw you go out a few minutes ago."

"It's fine. I only wanted some fresh air." She was silent a moment, wondering how to tell him about Eryx and Civilla's conversation, then asked, "Esmond . . . what's charm-swearing?"

He made a face. "It's a way of holding someone to a promise they don't really want to make. Like when my father made me charm-swear to always wear my half glass in public, and never dress like a street-boy again." His fingers tightened on Isaveth's waist, swinging her away from the other dancers. "If you break your word, both halves of the charm start flashing and blaring the words you said when you made the promise. So everybody knows you're a liar."

His gaze slid to Eryx, who stood listening gravely

to a woman in a wolf mask and her matching escort, both of whom seemed upset for some reason. Betinda Callender hovered behind them, simpering and batting her eyelashes—hoping Eryx would dance with her, no doubt.

"My brother loves charm-swearing," said Esmond distractedly, "because it makes people think they can trust him. What nobody seems to realize is that Eryx never vows to do anything he didn't mean to do in the first place . . . but anyway." He drew Isaveth closer, lowering his tone. "I left the bottle of tracking potion behind the mantle clock in the dining room—go out the side door and you'll find it. Just try not to bump into any of the servants."

"I'll be careful," Isaveth said breathlessly. His face was very near, and she felt a shy impulse to lean away. "Anything else?"

"Father's holding court in the gaming room, and people keep going in to talk to him. So you'd better stay clear of all that, too." He glanced to his right, where Civilla was dancing with a fish-faced man who kept squinting as though he'd lost his spectacles. "Poor Cilla. Every time she gets a chance at the spotlight, Eryx finds a way to steal it."

Isaveth couldn't argue with that. Yet she couldn't help thinking that the Civilla she'd seen in the conservatory seemed sharp enough to take care of herself.

"Esmond," she said, and he looked at her quizzically. "What would happen if your sister turned against Eryx? Does she know something that could hurt his reputation, or spoil his plans in some way?"

"I wish," said Esmond. "But she's too busy fussing over Mother and gadding about with her society friends to pay attention to politics these days. I don't think she cares what Eryx gets up to as long as he leaves her out of it." He steered her aside as another couple danced too close. "Anyway, what could she do? He's Father's heir, and the whole city adores him. Even if she knew something, she'd never dare say it without proof."

Isaveth nodded, her gaze wandering over the crowd. Lady Nessa had finished her dance with Wregget and was talking quietly to his wife, who kept patting the Sagelady's hand as though to soothe her. But she didn't look upset so much as weary, as though the effort of hosting such a grand party had drained her of what little strength she had.

I won't stand by and watch you do to her what Father did to Mother, Civilla had told Eryx in the garden. Surely she couldn't mean that the Sagelady had once been as bright and full of life as Delicia?

"Isaveth," said Esmond, and she blinked to attention. "Are you sure you're all right?"

He probably thought she'd lost her nerve. But after the things she'd seen and heard tonight, Isaveth felt more determined to stop Eryx than ever.

"I'm fine," she told him. "Just give me the signal, and I'll go."

"You danced a lot better with him than you did with Paskin," whispered Eulalie as she passed by, and Isaveth nearly spilled her punch. Was it that obvious she was so familiar with the way Esmond moved, and so sure he wouldn't mislead her, that she hadn't needed to think about where her feet were going at all?

If so, she could only hope nobody else had noticed. Isaveth hurried to the opposite side of the ballroom, putting as much distance between herself and the dance floor as possible, and attached herself to Su Amaraq's circle of admirers instead.

". . . can't imagine it'll pass in council," one man was saying. "Too heavy-handed. Sounds more like something Lord Arvis would do than Eryx, if you ask me."

"Of course it sounds like Lord Arvis," replied Su with a dismissive tilt of her glass. "My guess is that he refused to even discuss it until Eryx came up with an idea he liked better."

"Well, either way it's radical. I know cutting relief to

Moshites makes more sense than riling up half the commoners in the city, but even so . . ."

Isaveth froze.

"He didn't say *all* Moshites," objected a deer-masked girl. "Only the ones who refuse to pledge allegiance to the Sagelord and take an oath of nonviolence. After all, if they won't do that they're clearly up to no good, aren't they?"

Nausea rushed over Isaveth, and the room darkened around her. She clutched at an urn to steady herself.

"Except, my dear, that Sage Moshiel forbade his followers to swear oaths or pledge loyalty to anyone but the All-One," remarked a familiar voice from behind his boar mask. "So we're not just asking them to be good citizens, we're asking them to convert."

"Why, Mister Wregget," exclaimed the girl. "I had no idea you were such a sympathizer."

"Not taking sides here, young lady, just stating a fact. . . ."

Isaveth couldn't bear to listen any longer. She plunged through the crowd, heading blindly for the stage and the half-open door beside it. Now she knew what Eryx meant to do to her people—not just the ones who'd been arrested or caught protesting anymore, but every Moshite in the city—there wasn't a moment to waste.

The dining room stood empty, with only a few glasses and abandoned plates to show that anyone had passed this way. Instrument cases lay all around the fireplace, and Isaveth stepped carefully past them, reaching up behind the clock to retrieve her tracking potion. Fingers trembling, she raised the vial—

The door across the room banged open, and a young man in servants' livery burst through. "Don't you lecture me!" he shouted over his shoulder. "I know my duties as well as—oh, sorry, miss." He bobbed her a bow. "May I help you?"

"Oh," gasped Isaveth. She'd thrust the vial behind her back just in time, but her mind was blank with panic. "No. Thank you. I was only . . ."

The waiter raised his brows.

". . . looking for the toilet," she finished lamely.

"Ah. This way." He crossed the tiled corridor, opened another door, and gestured to the brass-fixtured washroom inside.

"Thank you," said Isaveth, with a smile she hoped looked less ghastly than it felt. She backed in and shut the door, then whipped out her tracking potion.

At first glance, it appeared to be working perfectly. The sparkling flecks of magewort pointed in a roughly northwest direction—away from the ballroom, toward the back of the house. She swirled it a second time to be certain, then opened the washroom door and peeked out.

The hallway stood empty, and Isaveth was about to make a dash for it when a side door swung open and a maid with a tray of drinks backed through. That must be the entrance to the kitchen—how could she get past without anyone seeing her? Isaveth dug into the pocket Annagail had sewn inside her skirt, fingering her small assortment of charms and tablets, but none seemed to offer any solution.

She'd have to be bold, then, and trust her berrybird mask to protect her. Isaveth took a deep breath, pelted to the end of the hall, and flung herself through the door, slamming it behind her.

Cold air stung her face, and it was so dark that Isaveth thought she'd blundered into the meat larder. But no, this was the underground tunnel she'd come through on her first visit, the weather-passage between the mansion and the carriage house. Isaveth fumbled for a light-tablet and crushed it between her fingers, then pushed her mask to the back of her head and shook the bottle again. Was she on the right track? Or would the potion mislead her like it had Esmond?

The answer came in a flash, as all the floating grains raced to the opposite side of the bottle. One hand glowing and the other clutching the vial, Isaveth ran for the end of the passage.

The door moved easily, opening into further darkness. Isaveth climbed the stairs to the floor of the carriage house and paused, frowning at the Sagelord's black sedan and the sleek gray sportster beside it. Had she reached the end of the trail already? Esmond had searched this place weeks ago, so it hardly made sense. . . .

The grains pressed against the left side of the bottle, urging her onward. Shoes crunching on the salt-stained concrete, Isaveth followed it between the carriages—then stopped, bewildered, as the particles dropped to the bottom of the vial. Could Eryx's documents be *under* the carriage house? It was hard to imagine: The floor looked solid, with no sign of a trapdoor anywhere. But perhaps he'd used an illusion-charm, or . . .

Reflected in the carriage window, Isaveth's eyes opened wide. Of course. What a fool she'd been! She thrust the vial into her pocket, reached for the door handle—

And a deafening blare shattered the night.

Isaveth leaped back, clapping both hands to her ears. Then with renewed horror she realized she'd still been holding the pieces of her light-tablet. Frantically she swatted at her hair and stamped the glowing crumbs to powder, then rushed around the dark carriage house, desperate to escape.

But how? If she went back down the tunnel, she'd run straight into Eryx, or whoever else was coming to investigate. If she fled outside, she'd freeze—not to mention leave a clear trail of footprints in the snow.

There was no way out. What was she going to do?

Chapter Fifteen

EEEEAAAAHHHH . . . EEEEAAAAHHHH . . .

Like the bray of some maddened donkey, the magical alarm droned on. Isaveth crouched atop the rafter with a float-charm in one hand and a shade-charm in the other, stomach cramping with fear. She was safe for the moment, but if the manservant circling Eryx's sportster looked up . . .

"Who's been fooling about in here?"

Isaveth's insides knotted tighter. The new arrival was Eryx Lording himself.

"They must have bolted when the alarm went off, sir." The footman gestured to the side door of the carriage house, which Isaveth had suggestively left open. "I came as soon as I heard it, but—" He raised his voice to be heard above the din. "There was nobody here."

Eryx's mouth flattened. He tapped the sportster's door

handle and the alarm cut off, leaving Isaveth's ears ringing. "Then look for them, man. They'll have left footprints, surely, unless . . ." He rubbed a finger across his chin. "Unless they used magic to hide their trail."

"One of the guests, then, milord?" The servant craned outside, sweeping the night with his spell-torch. "No prints."

The Lording pivoted slowly, scanning the carriage house. Isaveth held her breath. *Merciful All-One, don't let him look up!* True, all he'd see was shadow at first, but if that torch swung toward her . . .

"Probably one of Esmond's idiot schoolmates," said Eryx at last. "Lock up and we'll deal with it tomorrow."

"Yes, milord." Ice rasped as the footman pulled the side door shut. He glanced about one last time, then snapped off the lights and followed his master out. The lower door slammed, and Isaveth was alone.

Isaveth let out her breath, tension draining from her body. But she was freezing, filthy—and even more worrisome, stuck. She'd used the floater to get up to the rafter, but how to get down?

She didn't dare touch Eryx's spell-carriage a second time, and its soft top likely wouldn't hold her anyway. The Sagelord's sedan looked more sturdy, but what if she set off another alarm? Isaveth shinned forward, peering at the darkened floor. Could she roll off the beam, dangle by her hands a bit, then drop?

Maybe, but she'd also stand an excellent chance of breaking an ankle. Besides, the rafter was too wide to give her a proper grip. Isaveth sighed and backed up to where she'd started.

Little by little the darkness lightened as her shade-charm lost its power. Her body grew heavy, and the rafter dug into her thighs. She was shivering uncontrollably, and she couldn't hold on much longer. . . .

"Isaveth?"

Her muscles melted into butter. "Esmond!" she gasped as he climbed out of the stairwell, a light-charm glowing in his hand.

One glance was all it took for him to grasp her predicament. Esmond dropped the charm into his pocket, scrambled onto the roof of his father's sedan, and stretched out both hands to help Isaveth down. For an awful second the metal groaned beneath their combined weight—then he swung her off the far side of the carriage and hopped to the floor beside her.

"You're freezing!" he exclaimed, rubbing her cold-pebbled arms. "Here, take my jacket." He draped it around her, and gratefully Isaveth wriggled into the sleeves.

"H-how did you f-find me?" she asked, her teeth still chattering.

"Well, the alarm was a bit of a giveaway. Not that most people heard it over the orchestra, but when Eryx rushed out, I knew something was up. I followed him far enough to guess what must have happened, but I didn't dare come after you until the tunnel was clear. And he'd locked the door, so I had to hunt for a key. . . ." He looked her up and down. "What were you doing?"

"Eryx's car." She clutched at him, grimy fingers digging into his sleeve. "The tracing potion said to look inside, but when I touched the handle—"

Esmond stared at her. Then he pulled away and covered his eyes with his hand. "Stupid," he groaned. "So stupid."

"Well, I like that! How was I supposed to know?"

"Oh, great Sages, I didn't mean *you*. I meant me." He seized her cold hands and began chafing them. "No wonder I couldn't get the tracking spell to work, because I kept waiting to try it until Eryx was out. Driving around the city. *In his carriage*."

Isaveth mouthed a silent *oh*.

"I should have guessed ages ago. He's always so fussy about letting anyone touch his car. . . . But you, Isaveth!" He twirled her around in a triumphant dance. "You're not stupid, you're brilliant. I could—"

He stopped, gazing into her uplifted face. "Yes?" asked Isaveth faintly.

Esmond stepped back, releasing her. "I couldn't be more lucky to have a friend like you," he said. "But there's no way you can go back to the ball like that."

He wasn't wrong. Esmond's light-charm cast only a faint glow around them, but even so the dirt that streaked Isaveth's dress was plain to see. Her palms were black from clinging to the rafter, her mask gray with cobwebs and dust, and she didn't need a mirror to know that her hair was a mess as well. Embarrassed, she ducked her head—but a gentle touch on her chin brought it up again.

"You're still the prettiest girl I know," said Esmond. "Wait here. I'll fetch your coat."

When he returned to the house, Esmond expected to find the back corridor as busy as he'd left it. But the hallway stood empty, and the whole house was eerily still. Even the music had stopped.

". . . some bad news." That was Eryx's voice, echoing from the ballroom beyond. "My father the Sagelord has taken ill, and my mother and sister have gone to attend him."

Esmond's heart lurched. *No,* he thought. *Not now.*

"I'm sorry to end the party so soon, but I know I can count on all of you to understand. . . ."

Isaveth. He had to get her out of the house. Esmond sprinted across the lobby, plunged into the coatroom, and rummaged madly until he found a coat and overboots he recognized. He was less certain about the hat, but its slight dowdiness reassured him; no noble girl he knew would wear something that was more than two seasons old. . . .

"There you are!" Eulalie Fairpont popped up in the doorway. "I've been looking all over. Where's Isaveth?"

There was no time to hesitate. He thrust Isaveth's gear at Eulalie and dragged her out the door. A maidservant squeaked as they barged past, but Esmond kept moving, steering the sputtering Eulalie around the staircase to the kitchen passage.

"Door at the end," he said. "Get her out of here, quick."

To her credit, Eulalie didn't argue. She clutched the bundle to her chest and ran.

He'd left his jacket with Isaveth, but there was no help for that. Hurriedly Esmond rolled his sleeves up to his elbows, loosened his top button, and raked his fingers through his hair. Let everyone think he'd sneaked off for a puffer, or a stolen kiss in the coatroom, and had no idea what had happened in his absence.

"Oh, my dear boy," gasped Lady Marcham as the first wave of guests surged into the lobby. "I am so very—"

She recoiled, blinking at his disheveled appearance. "Esmond, where *have* you been?"

Out the corner of his eye he saw Eulalie dart past, with a hatted and coat-muffled Isaveth behind her. He could only hope they'd made it out of the tunnel without being seen. "What?" asked Esmond, doing his best to look innocent. "What's going on?"

"Your father's taken ill. They've sent for a healer—"

That was all the excuse he needed. "Pardon me," said Esmond, and bolted up the staircase.

Civilla was pacing the corridor outside their father's room, hands clasped tight together. The shoulder of her ice-blue gown was stained red on one side, and beneath the rouge her cheeks were ashen.

"I just heard," Esmond said. "What happened?"

"Mother found him unconscious in the gaming room. He'd been sick—" She swallowed and shook her head.

It must have been bad, then. Civilla wasn't usually squeamish. Bracing himself, Esmond opened the door and went in.

Two footmen bustled about the Sagelord, wiping his sweat-beaded face and tucking the bedclothes around him. A cloying stench hung heavy in the air. Lady Nessa hovered by the far side of the bed, dabbing her eyes with a handkerchief—but when she saw Esmond her face crumpled, and she flung herself into his arms.

He held her a moment, then guided her to an armchair. She wilted into it as the door opened and Eryx strode in.

"All of you, out," he commanded, and the servants hurried to obey. "You too, Esmond."

His mother's trembling fingers touched his wrist, and Esmond stood straighter. "I'm staying."

Eryx gave him a hard look, then bent over the bed and thumbed their father's lids open. "His eyes are yellow. Was he drinking?"

The Sagelady looked at her lap. She did not speak, but Esmond could guess the answer.

Silence fell over the bedroom, broken only by the rasp of Lord Arvis's breathing and the muffled noises of the guests departing below. Esmond took his mother's hand, feeling the frailness of her bones. He couldn't remember the last time she'd touched him.

"Where's that healer?" muttered Eryx, and stalked out again.

Esmond sat down heavily on the arm of the chair. Occasional bouts of liver trouble were one thing, but this sudden collapse was another: There could be little doubt that Lord Arvis was gravely ill. Yet he'd eaten a hearty supper, and not long ago he'd been well enough to stand in front of two hundred guests and give a speech. . . .

A groan rose from the bed, and Esmond jumped up. "Father?"

"Boy." He turned his head feebly toward Esmond, then grabbed the front of his waistcoat. "Don't let . . ."

The stench of alcohol on his breath made Esmond's gorge rise, but he swallowed it. "Don't let who? Do what?"

The cracked lips moved, shaping soundless syllables. "Need to . . . Eryx."

"He's just left. Did you want to talk to him?"

"All . . . against me. Even my own . . ." His hand thumped Esmond's chest. "Poisoned . . . *ahh!*" He clutched his stomach, convulsing.

A chill raced through Esmond. "Father," he said quietly. "What do you mean, poisoned?"

But Lord Arvis was lost in delirium now, his head thrashing on the pillow. "Guilty . . . have to . . . no!" He jerked upright, voice rising to a howl. "Not you, not . . . *Get out!*"

Esmond whirled. Civilla was standing in the doorway, looking more ashen than ever. "The healer's arrived," she said as the Sagelord sagged again, unconscious.

Lady Nessa moaned, and Civilla rushed to her side. "I'm here, Mama, don't—" She stopped as though something had surprised her. "What's this in your hand?"

"It's nothing," sobbed the Sagelady, "just some rubbish I found in the chair. No, please, I have to stay. . . ."

Civilla slipped a hand under her elbow. "It's all right, Mother," she said, shaky but resolute. "We'll go somewhere quiet and talk about it, and everything will be all right."

They'd barely left the room when Eryx returned with Doctor Achawa, a lean, bronze-skinned man who strode to the bedside and dropped his healer's bag onto the carpet with a thump. He stooped over Lord Arvis and began listening to his chest as Eryx moved discreetly to watch.

Esmond backed toward the door, watching his brother. There was no hint of triumph on the Lording's face; he looked concerned, even anxious, as a good son ought to be.

Or as a poisoner would pretend to be, if he didn't want anyone to suspect him.

Chapter Sixteen

"UGH! THIS STINKS! Vettie, what have you got in here?"

It was the morning after the ball, and already the events of last night seemed like a dream to Isaveth. She looked up as Lilet marched into the kitchen, holding her school bag at arm's length.

"Only my schoolbooks," Isaveth replied, puzzled—and then the stench hit her, acrid and sickly-sweet at once. Gagging, she pinched her nose, then grabbed the bag from Lilet and dumped it out onto the table.

At a glance, nothing seemed unusual. Workbooks, textbooks, the crumpled first draft of a history assignment, the box that held her lead-point and the bottle pen Papa had given her. . . . Isaveth turned the bag upside down, looking for stains on the bottom.

Lilet backed away, fanning herself in revulsion. "It

smells like something *died*," she said as Isaveth unbuckled a side pocket and the limp body of a woodrat fell out.

It hit the floor with a sickening soft thump, and Isaveth stared at it in horror. Then she lunged for the dustpan, scooped up the dead rodent, and hurled it out the back door into the garden.

Still the odor lingered, clinging to her books and especially the satchel itself. She'd have to scrub the bag inside and out before she went back to school on Mendday.

"How did it crawl in there?" asked Lilet, opening a jar of pine oil and waving it in all directions. "Was it trying to get at your lunch?"

"It must have been sick already," said Isaveth, struggling for calm. "It was probably looking for a quiet place to die."

Lilet wrinkled her nose skeptically and set the jar down. "Well, I hope you know a spell to get rid of rat stink. Because I don't think soap's going to be enough."

Isaveth cast a despairing look at her belongings, then shoved them back in the bag and set it out on the step. It was time to leave for temple, and she could only hope the smell in the kitchen would clear before Papa got up.

Outside the sun shone brightly over Gardentown, but its beaming face was deceptive. It offered no warmth, only a dazzling brilliance that glinted off the snow and made Isaveth's head ache. It was a long walk to Wisdom Hall, and by the time the Breck sisters climbed the steps of the Moshite temple Isaveth's feet felt like two chunks of ice inside her boots.

Inside, however, it was warm—so cozy, in fact, that Isaveth and her sisters glanced at each other in surprise. Usually they had to keep their coats on during fallow-time, since Wisdom Hall was one of the poorer Moshite congregations and its building was too old and drafty to heat well. Yet when she and Annagail put on their prayer scarves and walked into the sanctum, Lilet and Mimmi trailing in their wake, they found a brazier full of fire-tablets on either side of the room.

"What does it mean?" Isaveth whispered to Anna. If it was a special occasion, there was nothing in the temple calendar to say so. But her sister only shook her head, equally baffled.

Isaveth was still puzzling over it when the first chant began, the women's lilting voices alternating with the sonorous tones of the men as they sang praise to the All-One and gave thanks for the wisdom of Moshiel. Hastily she joined in—but as the service went on her thoughts began to wander, first to the dead rat in her school bag and then to the shocking discoveries she had made the night before.

Did the Sagelord support Eryx's new plan to cut relief to Moshites? Would the protests against Isaveth's scholarship hurt Glow-Mor as badly as that couple at the ball seemed to think? Now that she'd found Eryx's secret documents, how were she and Esmond going to get to them? And why had the party been breaking up when Eulalie whisked her out of the mansion last night?

Anna nudged her, and Isaveth realized she was still sitting while everyone else had risen. Embarrassed, she rose and lifted her hands to join her fellow Moshites in prayer.

At last the meeting ended, and Isaveth was folding up her scarf when Mister Yeltavan, one of the older men, came by. "Your father's doing good work, I hear," he said, with a meaningful look at Annagail. "Now we just need to get him back to temple, eh?"

Anna gave him a half smile and a little nod in return. She didn't seem surprised by the comment, but Isaveth was: No one at temple had said anything when Papa was doing good work as a stonemason, so why praise him now that he was shoveling snow?

"And congratulations to you, Miss Isaveth. In fact . . ." He stepped into the aisle, coughing loudly and waving a hand for attention. The murmur of conversation subsided, and all the members looked around as Mister Yeltavan raised his voice to speak.

"As I'm sure you have noticed, we are enjoying a generous donation of fire-tablets today, thanks to the Moshite Women's Charitable Council. They were purchased from the Glow-Mor company in support of our first member to attend Tarreton College, Miss Isaveth Breck!"

Applause broke out, and Isaveth's cheeks turned hot as Mister Yeltavan went on.

"Our overseers have met with the Long Street and Willowdell congregations, and agreed to buy as many Glow-Mor light- and fire-tablets in the coming weeks as we are able. We must not give our enemies the victory by failing to support our friends! So please, remember to give your business to Glow-Mor, and pray for the All-One's protection for Mister Wregget and his company. And, of course, for our own dear Isaveth."

The hush in the sanctum turned to an excited babble as everyone lined up to congratulate her. Some offered words of comfort and reassurance, while others encouraged Isaveth to stand up and show the world what a Moshite girl could do. One woman even apologized for not being more kind to Isaveth and her sisters when their father was in prison, and vowed to urge all her friends to buy Glow-Mor tablets to make up for it.

There were twenty thousand Moshites in Tarreton: a

small minority compared to the hundreds of thousands that made up the Arcan and Unifying churches, and most of them poor. But there were also wealthy folk with Moshite connections, openly or in secret. If they worked together to support Glow-Mor until the public outcry had passed over, then perhaps Isaveth wouldn't lose her scholarship after all.

"Be brave, little one," whispered old Missus Dzato, brushing a dry, papery kiss against Isaveth's cheek. "Your mother would be proud of you. We all are."

Isaveth's eyes welled. "Thank you," she said hoarsely. "I'll try not to let you down."

"All right," said Eulalie on the way to Sagery the next morning, tucking her arm possessively into Isaveth's. "What's going on with you and Esmond?"

Isaveth stiffened, but resisted the impulse to pull away. "What do you mean?"

"What the two of you were up to." Eulalie lowered her voice as a pair of fourth-year boys strode by. "I'm not silly, you know. I *notice* things. What were you doing in that tunnel? And don't tell me you were smooching, because I won't believe you."

Isaveth spluttered. "Eulalie!"

"Of course you weren't. You're far too proper." Eulalie

elbowed her teasingly. "Out with it. Was it something to do with the Lording?"

"Why would you think . . ."

"You were avoiding him the whole night, and Esmond went after you practically the minute Eryx came back from chasing that alarm. Oh, don't worry," she added as Isaveth gazed at her in dismay, "I don't think anyone else heard it. I only did because I was in the washroom."

Which was off the same corridor that led to the tunnel. Isaveth's heart sank. "I really shouldn't say," she began, but Eulalie cut in.

"He's up to something shady, isn't he? I *knew* he was too good to be true!"

Isaveth bit her lip. Eulalie was so close to the truth, there seemed no sense in deceiving her. But did she dare to give away a secret that was Esmond's as much as hers?

"I'm not going to take his side, silly," Eulalie said impatiently. "I'm from Listerbroke, remember? The Lording's just another politician to me, and I don't even think he's good-looking. There's something creepy about the way he smiles. . . ." She gave a theatrical shudder.

That decided Isaveth. Eulalie had done as much as anyone could to prove her loyalty, and she had to take a chance sometime. "You're right," she said. "Eryx isn't what he seems at all."

Keeping her voice low, she told Eulalie everything she knew about the Lording, from his role in Governor Orien's murder to his scheme to offer more relief to the Arcan and Uniting commoners who supported him by denying it to Moshite families like her own. Then she explained about the documents. "Esmond knew they were somewhere in the house, but he couldn't find them. That's why he had to smuggle me into the ball, so I could use a spell I know to track them down."

Eulalie's brown eyes lit up. "A Common Magic spell, you mean? How clever! Eryx would never suspect something like that." She squeezed Isaveth's arm. "This is so exciting! So did you find them, or . . . No, wait. They were in his spell-carriage, weren't they? That's how you set off the alarm."

Isaveth nodded. "So now we have to find a way to get into Eryx's sportster without him knowing it." Which could be even harder than finding the documents in the first place. But Eulalie's remark about Common Magic had sparked a thought in her mind. . . .

She was just about to tell Eulalie her idea, when the bell rang. They dashed for the charmery, and there was no more time for talking.

"They say it was the fish he ate for supper, and he's fired the whole kitchen staff."

"That's not what I heard. Daddy says he was off in the gaming room all evening getting roaring drunk, and—" Betinda broke off, glaring at Isaveth. "Do you mind? This is a *private* conversation."

Isaveth had no desire to cross Betinda, so she quickly walked on. But she'd heard enough to know what her classmates were talking about, and it chilled her. Could Mander Ghataj have been right about Lord Arvis? Was Eryx closer to becoming Sagelord than she'd thought?

When the bell rang for lunchtime, Isaveth went straight to the library, looking for a message. Sure enough, Esmond wanted to meet—not after school, but right away. Somehow he'd got a key to the room where the old college records were kept, and he was already waiting for her.

Glancing about to make sure she was alone, Isaveth ran up the staircase to the top level of the library and knocked—*tap tatta-tap-tatta-tap-tap-tap*, the familiar beats from the opening theme of *Auradia*. The door opened at once, and she slipped in.

The storage room was cramped and windowless, lined with shelves and cabinets on every side. The lone spell-lamp cast a pool of amber-tinted light—and in it stood Esmond, his thin face lined with strain.

She knew that look: She'd seen it every day in the

mirror when her mother was ill. Stricken, Isaveth touched his arm. "Oh, Esmond. Is it that bad?"

"Bad enough." His voice sounded husky, as though it were the first time he'd used it all day. "The healer says his liver's failed. They're trying to make him comfortable, but—" He looked away, the gleam of his half glass vanishing in shadow. "My father's dying."

Isaveth drew a shaky breath. "How long?"

"A week or two, maybe. The healer wasn't sure."

So it made no difference anymore whether Eryx had his father's support or not. As soon as Lord Arvis died, Esmond's brother would become the next ruler of Tarreton, free to bring his new relief plan to city council whenever he pleased. Worse, since it was Eryx, the council would probably agree with him.

Yet Isaveth knew what it was like to lose a parent, and this wasn't the time to talk about her worries, no matter how pressing they might seem. "I'm sorry, Esmond."

He gave a bitter laugh. "Then you're the only one. I think half the city is already celebrating, including Eryx. *Especially* Eryx."

"Because now he can do whatever he wants?"

"Because he's the one who poisoned him."

"What?"

"Why are you shocked? Remember what he said to

me before he did this?" He flicked a finger toward his scarred eye. "If Eryx was ready to poison Father then, why wouldn't he do it now?"

Isaveth could think of at least one reason: that by killing Master Orien to spare his father the trouble, Eryx had won the Lord Arvis's confidence and the two of them had been working together ever since. Yet wicked as the Sagelord might be, part of Esmond plainly longed to believe in him, so revealing the truth about Orien's murder now would only be cruel. After all, Lord Arvis would soon face the All-One's justice, even if he'd managed to escape everyone else's. . . .

"Doesn't it seem a bit obvious for Eryx, though?" she asked. "Why would he poison him in the middle of Civilla's party? Why not do it gradually, and make it look natural?"

"Maybe he was trying to," said Esmond grimly. "I don't know what happened yet. Father keeps babbling about being poisoned, but he doesn't seem to know who did it—so far he's accused the healer, the butler, half the guests at the ball, and everyone in the family by turns, including Civilla and my mother."

Which was no help at all, and also raised a serious problem. If they could prove Eryx had poisoned the Sagelord, he'd be arrested for certain—but what if he hadn't?

"Well," Isaveth said slowly, "your father's got no shortage of enemies. And there were a lot of people going in and out of the ballroom that night—"

"I know that!" Esmond snapped, then winced and passed a hand over his eyes. "Sorry. You're right. But even if Eryx wasn't the one who actually gave Father the poison, it still comes back to him in the end. He's the motive even if he isn't the means, if you know what I'm saying."

Isaveth's thoughts flashed back to Mander Ghataj clapping as the Lording took the stage, and his sister's rapt expression when Eryx whirled her into the dance. "Did the healer *say* it was poison?"

Esmond sat down on an empty book cart, which creaked beneath his weight. "I told him what Father said, but he dismissed it as raving. Father's been having liver troubles for a couple of months now, and he'd had at least two drinks that night, so Doctor Achawa says there's no mystery about it."

"Do you think Eryx bribed him?" After all, it wouldn't be the first time the Lording had paid someone off to hide the evidence.

"Not Doctor Achawa. He's not the sort to line his pockets at a patient's expense. I did think he might have overlooked something, though, so I searched the gaming room and took samples before the servants could clean up."

She'd heard all the same episodes of *Auradia Champion* he had: She knew what that meant. "And?"

"I don't have the results yet, I only brought them to Master Robard this morning. But he said he'd get back to me by the end of the week." Esmond stood up and started to pace. "I know he probably won't find anything. But I had to try."

Isaveth nodded.

"Father doesn't seem to remember who came to visit him in the gaming room, or whether they offered him anything. So I'm going to talk to some of the servants and find out what they know." He turned back to her. "You're awfully quiet. What's wrong?"

"It's just . . ." She lowered her eyes, smoothing her robe self-consciously. "I keep thinking about those documents. I'd love to help prove that Eryx poisoned your father, but what if we can't? That's why I think we still need to find out what charms he's using to protect his sportster. So we can find a way to counter them before he . . . does anything worse."

Esmond looked crestfallen. "Of course. I'm an idiot. I'll look into it tonight."

Isaveth breathed out in relief. He'd seemed so obsessed

with his new plan to stop Eryx, she'd feared he might be annoyed with her for even bringing up the old one.

"But counter-charms are tricky stuff, Isaveth." Esmond stepped closer, regarding her seriously. "Even if we can find the right formula, we'd need a fully trained Sage to help us make one. I'm not sure even Mistress Corto—"

"If there's a sage-charm to cancel out Eryx's defenses, he probably knows about it already." And taken all the precautions needed to guard against it. "What if we use Common Magic instead?"

Esmond's brows shot up. "You think you can?"

"I don't know, but I'm sure going to try. Only I'll need sample copies of whatever charms he's using, so I can experiment."

A slow smile spread from one corner of Esmond's mouth to the other. "You really are marvelous," he said. "All right, meet me in the bell tower tomorrow. I know what to do."

Chapter Seventeen

"WHAT'S THIS I HEAR about you questioning the servants?"

Quickly Esmond shut the book on protection-charms he'd been reading, turning it face down so Civilla couldn't read the title. "Sorry?" he asked, doing his best to sound innocent.

"You heard me, Esmond." Civilla shut the library door and sat down across from him, her eyes—the same uncertain blue-gray as their mother's—holding his. "Olina tells me she heard two of the footmen gossiping about it, and I want to know why."

Olina was the grimly efficient lady's maid who dressed both Civilla and his mother, and she had no use whatsoever for anyone else in the family. Esmond had avoided the older woman for that reason, but he should have guessed he couldn't keep her unaware.

"Why do you think?" he said defensively. "Doesn't it seem a little odd to you that Father collapsed on the night of your ball, even though he'd been perfectly fine at dinner?"

"He *said* he was fine," retorted Civilla. "That doesn't mean anything. You know what Father's like, especially when it comes to the public—I wouldn't put it past him to dose himself with Pep-a-Tonic or even use an illusion charm to make sure nobody knew he was unwell. If he was healthy, don't you think he'd have made at least *some* effort to mingle at the party, instead of hiding in the gaming room all night?"

Esmond squirmed deeper into the armchair. Frivolous or not, Civilla still had an uncomfortable knack for picking out the flaws in his logic. "Maybe, but he still talked to plenty of people. Including your friend Delicia—"

"Delicia!" Civilla sat up, startled. "Why?"

"Apparently he sent for her. After Eryx practically drooled over her from the platform, I can see why he might have been curious. Anyway, he also had a visit from an older fellow done up like a beaver—"

"Mister Gullinger," said Civilla.

"And a couple in wolf masks. Do you know who they were?"

Civilla sighed. "No. I didn't talk to them."

"They talked to Eryx, though. That could mean something—"

"Esmond!" Civilla leaned forward, fists clenched as though resisting the urge to throttle him. "Enough blather. What is all this about?"

Did he dare tell her? At this point, it was more a question of whether he could afford not to. Civilla's curiosity could be dangerous if she didn't know what the stakes were, and Esmond couldn't risk her getting in the way.

"I think Father was poisoned."

Civilla stiffened. She stared at him, her eyes ringed white with horror.

"If I can find out who went to see him that night and what they talked about, I might—"

"No." Civilla's voice was shaky but fierce. "Esmond, this has to stop right now. You're alarming the servants, you're accusing our friends, and you're going to upset Mother terribly. I know Father keeps talking about poison, but he's delirious—there's nothing in it. You're not Auradia Champion; you're not even a Lawkeeper. You're just a boy who fancies himself a detective, and you have *no right*."

He should have known she wouldn't understand. All she cared about was keeping up appearances and making everything pleasant for her and Mother and their silly society friends.

"I'm not a fool, Cilla," he snapped. "I know what I am. But I also know when something fishy is going on in my own house, and it's *my* father who's dying."

He hadn't planned for his voice to crack on that last phrase, but it had an extraordinary effect on Civilla. Her face softened and she reached out to touch his hand.

"Oh, Esmond," she said. "It's awful, feeling helpless. I know. But calling it poison, and finding someone to blame for it, isn't going to stop what's happening to Father. All you can do is accept it."

"Like my eye, I suppose?" said Esmond. "As I recall, you thought that just *happened* too." He flung himself to his feet, careful to keep the book he held turned inward, and stalked toward the door.

"Esmond, stop." Civilla drew herself up. "You need to promise you won't pursue this any further."

"Or what?"

"Or I'll tell Eryx."

His fingers clenched around the door handle. "You wouldn't."

"I will if I have to. You may hate him, Esmond, but he's going to be Sagelord soon, and he doesn't want a scandal any more than Mother and I do. If you won't listen to me . . ."

So that was how things stood. He'd thought there was

nothing between Civilla and Eryx but indifference, but now it was clear whose side she was really on.

"Fine," he said flatly. "No more questions."

"She might as well have threatened me," Esmond told Isaveth the next afternoon. "No, what am I saying? She *did* threaten me."

They were standing just inside the bell tower, chill seeping through the stones around them. Isaveth cast a longing glance at the landing, but Esmond, still warm in his woolen greatcoat and striped Tarreton-blue-and-white scarf, didn't notice. He thumped the banister irritably as he went on. "As if it wasn't enough for Eryx to own half the servants already, now he's got my sister protecting him as well."

"Do you think she knows you're still investigating?"

"Well, if she does, she can't prove it. I haven't questioned anyone in the house since . . . but then, I didn't need to." He pulled a list from his pocket and handed it to her. "These are all the people the servants saw going in or out of the gaming room that night."

The list was longer than Isaveth had expected, but that wasn't all that surprised her. "J. J. Wregget?"

"Wregget's wife is a friend of my mother's, so they stopped by to greet him. They left the door open, and the maid heard everything they said—nothing suspicious there."

That was a relief. It would be horrible to think that Wregget might only have offered Isaveth a scholarship because he was secretly working for Eryx. "Eagle mask," she read. "Wasn't that Eulalie's father?"

"Ah. I thought it might be." Esmond pulled a stub of lead-point from his pocket and scribbled the name out. "Never mind."

Isaveth didn't have to ask why. Deputy Fairpont was still an outsider and a relative newcomer, with a strong reputation for integrity. He might have come to report to Lord Arvis, but surely not to murder him. "Wolf couple?" she asked.

"One of the maids saw a man and a woman going to visit him halfway through the evening. She couldn't describe their faces because of the masks, but the man was slim and dark-haired and the woman was fair."

Perhaps theirs were the voices Isaveth had heard on her way to the garden. And if it was the same couple she'd seen with Eryx later, they hadn't been too pleased with how the conversation turned out. Yet they hadn't been the only ones to visit Lord Arvis before his attack. . . .

"Delicia Ghataj? What was she doing there?"

"I don't know, but according to the maid Father sent

to fetch her, she didn't stay long." His expression turned pensive. "I wonder what he said to her. I danced with her after she got back, and I could tell she wasn't happy."

Isaveth could have slapped herself. She'd forgotten to tell him. "I have an idea," she said, and went on to relate the argument she'd overheard between Civilla and Eryx in the conservatory.

"So that's why you asked me about charm-swearing," remarked Esmond. "Well, it's nice to know Cilla can stand up to Eryx when she wants to." He made a face. "She just won't do it for me, apparently."

Isaveth had no answer for that. It seemed impossible that two people raised in the same house could be such strangers to one another, but perhaps that was what happened when you lived in a mansion instead of a cottage.

"Do you think it's important, though?" she asked. "After all that fuss Eryx made over Delicia, it seems odd he'd give her up so easily. Unless he already knew your father didn't approve."

"Or she'd already served her purpose. You don't see Eryx's name anywhere on that list, do you? Of course not: He'd want to keep his distance from the actual murder to avoid suspicion. Just like he did with Master Orien."

The thought of Eryx wooing Delicia to poison the

Sagelord for him, only to abandon her as soon as the deed was done, made Isaveth feel queasy. She wrapped her arms around her stomach and gave a reluctant nod.

"It's all guesswork at the moment, though," Esmond said. "I'm still waiting for those test results. In the meantime—" He clapped his gloved hands together. "We have some charms to make."

Isaveth cast a dubious glance around the tower, and Esmond laughed—the first real laugh she had heard from him in a long time. "Not here! I mean in the charmery. I'll go and get everything ready, you wait a bit and follow. I'm sure the way's clear by now."

True, they'd stood here long enough that most of the other students had left the grounds, and many of the masters would be on their way home as well. But if anyone spotted the two of them, separately or together . . .

Esmond backed toward the door, tossing his scarf over his shoulder. "Come on. It'll be an adventure."

There was a feral gleam in his eye; all at once he looked more like Quiz the street-boy than the Sagelord's youngest son. Isaveth relaxed, and smiled.

"All right," she said.

Isaveth waited in the bell tower, rubbing her arms and pacing, until she felt sure Esmond had reached the charmery. Then she pulled her scarf up over her nose and slipped out after him.

Crossing the main drive and running down the steps to the valley made her feel horribly exposed, especially when she passed the Sporting Center and heard the thumps and squeaks of a ring-ball game echoing inside. But the doors stayed shut, so Isaveth pressed on.

When she reached the charmery, she found the front door locked. A quick scout around the building led her to a smaller entrance on the workshop side, where Esmond was waiting for her.

"I suppose you stole the key to this place too?" she asked, squeezing by as he held the door open. The doorway was narrow, and his breath stirred her hair as she passed. "Or did you pick the lock this time?"

"Neither. Master Orien gave me a key, back when he . . . when I was helping him."

His voice wavered at the end of the sentence, and Isaveth was abruptly reminded what a dear friend Orien had been to Esmond. No wonder he found it so easy to believe that Eryx had poisoned their father, when he'd spent a lifetime watching his brother destroy everything he loved.

"Anyway," Esmond went on, "I took a look at Eryx's sportster last night. He's got a warding-charm and a sealing-charm on it, and probably another one of each on the case itself." His mouth quirked ruefully. "It's under the passenger seat, by the way. The night Eryx drove you home, you were sitting on it."

The irony of that, after he'd caught her and Esmond in his study searching for those very documents, must have kept Eryx amused for weeks. Isaveth entertained a brief fantasy of her younger self pulling the case out from under the seat and bashing the Lording over the head with it as she took off her hat and coat.

"A warding-charm and a sealing-charm," she repeated. "So I need to find a spell that will counter both."

"That's right. And if we make three or four of each kind of charm, you'll have plenty to practice on." Esmond led her to the table where he'd laid out their ingredients, along with an assortment of tools and a heavy leather-bound book titled *A Master's Compendium of Sagery, Vol. III.*

"Right, then," Esmond continued, rolling up his shirtsleeves. "We'll start with Sage Armus's Ward, then, since that's the one you set off when you touched the carriage." He flicked the burner alight and handed Isaveth a pair of gloves to put on. "First you lay two strips of charm-silver crosswise, and twist the ends like this . . ."

Isaveth tweezed the strips into the earthenware bowl

and nudged them into position as Esmond propped the book up for her so she could read the instructions. One by one he passed her the ingredients she needed, explaining what the unfamiliar liquids were and how to dispense them, and showing her how to use a few tools she had never seen before.

"This is a tricky bit." He stepped behind her, so close she could feel his warmth against her spine. "Do you mind if I help? Because if the timing isn't perfect we'll have to start over." He reached around Isaveth and pinched a fleck of red jasper in the tweezers with one hand, then folded his other around the dropper she held in her right. "Steady . . . the stone goes first . . . wait for the flash . . . now!"

Heart galloping, Isaveth squeezed the bulb of the dropper. A hiss went up as the liquid touched the stone, and a thin, rising wail rang out before dying away. Giving her a quick squeeze of triumph, Esmond stepped aside as Isaveth tipped the charm out onto the anvil and folded the ends shut to make the spell complete.

"Brilliant," Esmond pronounced, when he'd inspected it with his charm-glass. "Couldn't have done it better."

Little tingles were still running up Isaveth's back. She had to flex her hands to stop them from trembling. "That wasn't too hard."

"Not if you've got the knack for it," said Esmond, leaning both elbows on the table and grinning up at her. "Good thing you do."

Isaveth drew a slow breath, willing her pulse to calm. "What next?"

"I'll let you make another one," said Esmond, pulling a second burner toward him, "while I whip up a couple of sealing-charms." He flicked three strips of charm-silver into his bowl and bent to work.

Now that she'd gotten over her initial nervousness, Isaveth found she liked making magic with Esmond. Even though they were both concentrating too hard to talk, there was something companionable about it. Isaveth tweaked and twisted, layering the charm-silver with the other ingredients until she was ready to perform the maneuver Esmond had shown her. Stone first, flash, then the drop of liquid—yes!

Absorbed in their spell-crafting, neither of them heard the door to the workroom open. Not until a foot tapped pointedly behind them did Isaveth realize that they were not alone. Heart plummeting, she spun around to find Spellmistress Anandri standing behind her.

"So," she said. Her cool gaze flicked to Esmond, then back to Isaveth. "This is unfortunate. Miss Breck, come with me."

Chapter Eighteen

DRY-MOUTHED WITH APPREHENSION, Isaveth followed Mistress Anandri into the adjoining classroom. The spellmistress shut the door, then asked, "Did Mistress Corto give you permission to come here?"

There was no use lying: It would be all too easy for the woman to check her story. "No, Mistress," said Isaveth miserably.

"Does she know that Esmond Lilord has been tutoring you in Sagery?"

Isaveth shook her head.

Mistress Anandri's face hardened. "Then why would you do such a foolish, reckless thing? Do you realize that working in the charmery after school without a master present is grounds for expulsion?"

Isaveth's stomach felt like it was being squeezed through a wringer. She fumbled for a chair and sank into it.

"Esmond may be safe from the consequences of his actions, but you are not. However eager you may be to learn Sagery, Miss Breck, and no matter how willing he might be to help you, there is no excuse for doing what you have done. Do you understand me?"

So it was over. She had risked everything, and what did she have to show for it? Nothing but the four meager test charms she'd scraped into her pocket and the brief warmth of Esmond's touch on her hand—a reassurance that meant nothing, now. Had he really believed she could walk away from this just because he could? She should have known better than to trust her safety to a noble, however charming or well-intentioned; she should have realized she couldn't be friends with Esmond without paying a bitter price for it.

"Yes, Mistress," she whispered.

"Good," said Mistress Anandri. "Then you will not do it again." She pulled out the chair behind Mistress Corto's desk and sat down, adding in a milder tone, "Thank the All-One that I was the first master Meggery found when she came to report you. If it had been anyone else, you would be explaining yourself to the governor right now."

Isaveth's heart skipped a beat. "Mistress?" she said uncertainly.

"Meggery saw you coming out of the bell tower." The

woman's dark eyes met hers, grave but no longer angry. "Still, that is a minor offense compared to being caught in the charmery, and no reason to expel you. I told Meggery I would make sure you received a proper punishment, and I will. Do not be so careless again."

Faint with relief, Isaveth slumped in her seat. "I thought you hated me," she said—and then it hit her. "You just thanked . . . you're *Moshite*?"

"Privately, yes," said Mistress Anandri. "I have been for several years." Her dark brows crooked together. "What made you think I hated you?"

"Because you were so cold to me when I was in your class. I thought—" Isaveth rubbed a hand across her face. "I thought I must have done something to offend you."

"Ah, yes." The spellmistress sounded pensive. "I can see how that must have appeared. But it was not you I was angry with that day. You should have been in Mistress Corto's class from the start, but your schedule was altered. Someone hoped to stop you from learning Sagery."

"They can't have hoped very hard, though. They must have known you'd spot the mistake."

"And that," said Mistress Anandri, "was the other reason I had to be cautious. I had already explained to the other masters that a mutual acquaintance had spoken highly of your skill at Common Magic, and that I had seen enough proof to think you worth mentioning to Mister Wregget. But that was as much partiality as I could give you."

She did not explain further, but Isaveth understood. If she showed too much warmth to Isaveth in front of the other students, it could be dangerous for both of them. Especially once it came out that Isaveth was Moshite.

"By rights, I ought to report this to Governor Buldage," the older woman mused. "Especially since it was Meggery who spotted you coming here. If I say nothing, I put my own position in jeopardy."

Isaveth's breath caught.

"But Lady Nessa was one of my first and brightest students, and I have known Esmond since he was born. I have no desire to see him humiliated, you expelled, and J. J. Wregget suffer yet another injury to his reputation. So if anyone should ask . . ."

The spellmistress leaned back, brown fingers tapping her arm as she thought. "You were on your way out of the college when you noticed that the door to the bell tower had been left open. Being curious, you entered, and climbed to the top to see the view. You spotted a strange object on the pathway near the charmery, so you left the tower and went to find out what it could be."

"What was it?" asked Isaveth, caught up in the story.

"A hat," said Mistress Anandri. "Which you showed me when I came to find you. I put it in the Found Box, of course, but I also reprimanded you for going into the bell tower. Your punishment is to clean the ovens in the spell-kitchen, which you will do tomorrow after school."

Hard work, but infinitely better than expulsion. "Thank you, Mistress," breathed Isaveth.

"By now Esmond will have tidied up the workshop," the spellmistress said, lifting her hood over her close-cropped hair, "and found a discreet way out of the college. I will accompany you up the hill and tell Meggery what came of our meeting." Her mouth tightened. "And let us both pray that will be the end of it."

Still dizzy from her narrow escape, Isaveth caught the tram home, raced through her chores, and spent the evening searching the Book of Common Magic for a spell that might cancel sage-charms. But all the recipes in the book were of a homely sort—tablets to light a room or darken it, decoctions to numb toothaches or help find a missing child. She'd have to look elsewhere.

Perhaps her neevil-paper—what Wregget called Resisto-Paper—would work, if she covered the charms with it? If it could keep magic from leaking out of a cracked spell-tablet, it might stop Sagery too. Isaveth hunted through the satchel she kept her spells in, took out a scrap of the paper, and laid it over the warding-charm she'd made that afternoon. Then, cautiously, she touched it.

No sound—not even a peep. Excitement surged up in Isaveth—then drained away as she studied the ward through her charm-glass and found its magic still glowing. So why hadn't it made that blaring noise? Puzzled, Isaveth prodded and poked the charm until she realized her mistake. Of course the ward wouldn't react to her, because she was the one who'd crafted it in the first place!

She turned to Annagail, sitting quietly with her sewing in the corner. "Anna, would you do something for me?"

Her older sister did not look up. "Lilet," she said, "go and help Vettie, please."

Lilet put down her book and struggled out of the armchair, a blanket clutched about her shoulders. "All right. What is it?"

Isaveth was surprised: Lilet wasn't normally so obliging, especially not with a book in hand. Then she realized the shirt Annagail was mending was the same red-flowered blouse that Lilet had worn to school that morning. It had looked perfect then, but now one sleeve was ripped half out of the seam.

"How did that happen?" asked Isaveth.

Lilet shrugged. "I caught it on a hook at school. What do you need me to do?"

"Touch this," said Isaveth, sliding the paper-covered charm toward her. "Not hard, just—"

EEEEAAAAHHHH, came the familiar wail. Isaveth grabbed the charm to silence it, then looked up to find all three of her sisters gaping at her.

"It's an experiment," she said. "For Sagery. Sorry, I should have warned you."

"That was scary." Mimmi hugged her doll, lips trembling. "Don't do it again."

No, thought Isaveth with sinking heart as Lilet stomped back to the armchair. She wouldn't.

The next morning Isaveth walked on snail shells, fearing she'd be called to the governor's office at any moment. But Meggery must have been satisfied with Mistress Anandri's report, because no one asked Isaveth why she'd been in the bell tower, much less the charmery, at all.

That wasn't her only worry, however. All last night she'd brooded over what the spellmistress had said about J. J. Wregget and his reputation. How badly had Glow-Mor's sales been affected by Su's article about Isaveth? Would her fellow Moshites make up the difference, or was Wregget already regretting his choice to support her?

"You're awfully quiet today," said Eulalie as they sat together at the lunch table. "And you haven't eaten much, either. What's wrong?"

Isaveth explained her worries, but Eulalie dismissed them with a shake of her head. "I'm sure it's not as bad as you think," she said. "Maybe a few people switched to Power-Up or Fuller's Firelights because of you, but they'll soon switch back again."

"How do you know?"

"Because nobody likes wasting money. Glow-Mor tablets aren't just cheaper than everyone else's, they work better—and that's *your* doing, remember. So it would be silly for Mister Wregget to quit supporting you now."

Isaveth had almost forgotten about telling Eulalie she'd invented Resisto-Paper, but the other girl had a point. It was her recipe that had enabled Glow-Mor to lower its prices and increase the quality of its wares, while other spell-factories still had to use dampening wax, which protected the tablets but also made them weaker. Perhaps she didn't need to worry about Wregget having second thoughts after all.

With that heartening thought, Isaveth's appetite returned. She had almost finished eating when she spotted Mander Ghataj on his way out. Quickly Isaveth excused herself and caught up with him. "Can I ask you something? In private?"

Mander gave a neutral shrug and followed her into the corridor. Once away from the dining room, Isaveth lowered her voice and said, "A while ago you told me Lord Arvis might not be Sagelord much longer. Had you heard something that made you think he was going to die?"

The boy's placid expression vanished. "I should never have said that. It was only—a guess." But his eyes darted away as he spoke, and she knew he was lying.

"Who told you he was sick?" Isaveth persisted. "Was it Delicia?"

"No! Not like that. She would never—" He stopped, frowning. "Wait. How do you know my sister?"

"I don't, not really," Isaveth said. "But she's good friends with Civilla Ladyship, isn't she? And from what I hear . . ." She spoke carefully, watching Mander all the while. "She's *quite* close to Eryx, as well."

Mander's shoulders drooped. "I wasn't trying to eavesdrop," he muttered. "The door wasn't shut properly, and I thought they were talking about politics, not anything . . . personal."

So Eryx had told Delicia about his father's liver trouble. But had he done so as part of a plot to poison his father, as Esmond thought? Or had he been at the Ghataj house for some other reason? Isaveth was about to ask what else Mander had heard, but the boy shook his head and backed away.

"I'm not telling you any more," he warned. "If Esmond Lilord wants to know what's going on, he can talk to Delicia himself."

Helplessly Isaveth watched him go, then walked back to the dining hall. She was not surprised to find Eulalie still there—except that now Betinda Callender was standing next to her, and the two of them appeared to be having a heated conversation.

"What was that about?" she asked the other girl once Betinda had gone. But Eulalie shook her head miserably, then got up and left without another word.

Chapter Nineteen

WHEN CLASSES ENDED Isaveth looked for Eulalie again, hoping to find out what had happened between her and Betinda. Yet the other girl did not appear, so at last Isaveth gave up and headed for the spell-kitchen.

The main room stood empty, with only a few battered tools and a half-empty box of scouring powder to greet her—Meggery's way of making her task as unpleasant as possible, no doubt. Sighing, Isaveth filled a bucket, tied on an apron and kerchief, and set to work.

She'd thought to clean the dirtiest oven first, but they were both so crusted with black grime that there was little to choose between them. Isaveth had her head and shoulders well inside and was scraping away when someone spoke her name, and she startled so violently she cracked her head on the roof of the oven. "Ow!"

"Sorry!" Esmond helped her out and pulled up a chair

for her. "Didn't mean to startle you. Are you all right?"

He looked so contrite that Isaveth nearly forgave him at once. But then she remembered yesterday and hardened. "No, I'm not," she said. "You almost got me expelled. What are you doing here?"

Esmond leaned back against the worktop, crossing his long legs at the ankle. "I left you a note at lunchtime, but you didn't come to the bell tower. I had to ask Mistress Anandri where you were."

"And she told you to stay away from me, no doubt," said Isaveth. She knelt by the oven again, digging at a stubborn lump of char with the metal scraper. The box of scouring powder bore the slogan, "Works like Magic!" but so far it wasn't doing much at all. She'd be here all night at this rate.

"Actually," said Esmond, "she asked me to give you these."

He tossed a pair of wrapped disks in front of Isaveth, each the size and thickness of her palm. She'd never used one before, but she knew what they were—industrial-grade cleaning tablets, magically enhanced and more effective than any powder. She frowned up at him, uncomprehending.

"And I made you a few more charms to practice on, if that helps any," Esmond continued, digging a handful out of his pocket and dropping them onto the counter. "We might even have time for an experiment or two, unless you'd rather clean ovens. Do you know how those soap things work?"

A few minutes later, a tablet was foaming away behind each oven door, and Isaveth was telling Esmond about the trouble she'd been having with Eryx's sage-charms. "I couldn't find anything useful in the Book of Common Magic," she said as she sat beside him on the countertop, waiting for the grime inside the ovens to soften. "And the school library was no help either. Do you think Mistress Anandri might have some more Common Magic recipes I could try?"

"I don't know," said Esmond, hopping off the counter. "Let's look around and find out."

A search through the kitchen cupboards yielded nothing of interest—only mixing bowls, canisters of flour, and other basic spell-baking supplies little different from what Isaveth had at home. The only books she found were a few battered editions of *Spell-Baking for Beginners*, and those were no use at all.

"Nothing here," she said glumly as she shut the pantry door—then glanced about in surprise as she realized Esmond was no longer there. She was about to call his name when he leaned out the door of the adjoining room, beckoning her to join him.

Had he gone mad? That was the sunroom, glass-roofed and lined with windows on three sides. Isaveth shook her head and backed away.

"It's all right," said Esmond. "The glass is privacy-charmed, so people outside can't see us. Well, unless they come right up to the window, but I don't think that's likely with all this snow."

Reassured, Isaveth followed him into the sunroom. There, inside the cabinet, stood a full shelf of books on Common Magic. With Esmond's help she carried a pile back to the kitchen and sat down at the table to examine them.

The first few volumes were pure theory, comparing Common Magic and Sagery in language so abstruse she could barely understand a word of it. Others chronicled the history of Common Magic over the centuries, but Isaveth had more urgent concerns in mind. She kept on, leafing through each book and pushing it aside, until at last she came to a small, handwritten volume bound in cracked leather. It was a journal, its first entry dated nearly a hundred years ago.

Once she'd puzzled through the first few pages of crabbed writing, Isaveth realized she'd found a treasure: the diary of a Moshite country-mage, a woman who had spent her life seeking out herbs, roots, and fungi with magical properties and cooking them into spells. Some of the recipes were similar to those in the Book of Common Magic, but others surprised her. Had this woman really invented a decoction that could cure warts overnight?

She was still reading when Esmond cleared his throat. "Not to rush you," he said, "but it's getting late, don't you think?"

Sure enough, the light from above was fading. It must be past five bells, and she still had to wipe out the ovens. Isaveth jumped up and ran to do so, while Esmond grabbed a pile of rags to help.

"Do you think Mistress Anandri would be angry if she knew what we were doing?" Isaveth asked when they were finished, dropping the last black-stained rag into the laundry hamper and tossing her apron on top. The cleaning tablets had made the job easy if not exactly pleasant, but she'd made sure to dirty all the tools and sprinkle a bit of scouring powder about so that if Meggery came by it would look like she'd cleaned the ovens the hard way.

Esmond lifted her overcoat off the hook and held it for her. "She's not particularly fond of Eryx, if that's what you're wondering. His first year at the college, he tried to bribe her into giving him the top mark in Common

Magic, and she's kept a wary eye on him ever since."

Perhaps, thought Isaveth as the coat settled on her shoulders, but being suspicious of Eryx wasn't the same as believing him a criminal mastermind. She'd have to be careful not to test Mistress Anandri's generosity too far. She stacked up the books on the kitchen table and carried them back to the sunroom—all except the journal, which she tucked into her school bag for further study. Surely the spellmistress wouldn't mind if she borrowed it for a day or two.

Isaveth fingered the handful of charms in her pocket, then buttoned up her coat and turned to Esmond. "I think I've got all I need for now," she said. "Thanks."

Esmond didn't reply, only gazed at her. His teeth grazed his lower lip, and his good eye took on a wistful, questioning look.

"What is it?" asked Isaveth, but Esmond huffed a laugh and turned away.

"Nothing important."

That night Isaveth stayed up as late as her father would allow her, searching the old journal for ideas on how to undo Eryx's charms. By bedtime she'd found a couple of recipes that looked promising—including one that claimed to dissolve metal. But it called for ingredients she didn't have, so Isaveth put the book away and resolved to talk to Esmond about it tomorrow.

The next morning Isaveth looked for Eulalie, but there was no sign of her. Even when the bell rang and all the other students were seated, her friend's desk remained empty.

"Faking sick again, probably," said Seffania.

The girl next to her rolled her eyes, and Paskin snickered. But a defensive spark lit inside Isaveth. "What do you mean, faking?"

"Well, she doesn't *look* sick, does she? She's got all the energy in the world when she wants it, but the minute things get unpleasant, off she goes. You can't count on her for anything."

"That's not true," said Isaveth. "You don't know her."

Seffania gave a short laugh. "Oh, don't I? You're not the first one she's latched onto, you know. Wait and see."

Just then Mistress Corto tapped her pointer and called the class to attention. Dutifully Isaveth opened her notebook, but her thoughts churned with unhappiness and a small, nagging whisper of doubt. Eulalie had been kind to her, and she owed the other girl a great deal. Yet it *was* odd that she didn't seem to have any other friends at the college besides Isaveth. . . .

She had almost decided to ignore Seffania and put the

matter out of her mind when Miss Kehegret, Seffania's seatmate, leaned across the aisle and slipped a note onto Isaveth's desk.

Ask E what she told DW about S at the Harvest Dance. Nobody likes a girl who can't keep secrets.

Isaveth had hoped to borrow some money from Esmond for the ingredients she needed, so she could buy them on her way home and try out the metal-dissolving spell that night. But the message she left him went unanswered, and there was no sign of him at lunchtime. What if he'd been called home suddenly, because his father was about to die?

Dread clutched at Isaveth. *Please, not yet,* she begged silently. *I need more time.*

She turned on the crystal set as soon as she got home, but there was no news about the Sagelord's health. Then Aunt Sal turned up at the door, insisting she had to go out and needed someone to come and look after her two children at once. Annagail was busy scrubbing the kitchen floor with soap ends, so Isaveth had no choice but to go—and by the time she got back, it was too late for experiments. All she could do was read the last few pages of the country-mage's journal and pray for better luck tomorrow.

When she checked the library the following morning,

there was still no news from Esmond. Eulalie turned up to Sagery class, but all she would say about her conversation with Betinda was, "It makes me cross when people say horrible things," and she dismissed her absence with a vague, "I just wasn't feeling right."

She showed no sign of having been ill, however, and the doubt inside Isaveth sank its roots a little deeper. Eulalie might have a reputation for giving away other people's secrets, but she clearly had no trouble keeping her own. So Isaveth was too distracted to pay much attention when she passed a cluster of girls outside the dining hall and heard Betinda Callender announcing loudly, "I got it for my birthday. Daddy had it sent all the way from Uropia—he says it's just like the one the Little Queen wears."

Betinda boasting was hardly unusual, so Isaveth rolled her eyes and walked on. By the time Calculation class started, she'd forgotten all about it.

"Open your notebooks to the third chapter," said Master Valstead. "Today we will begin Lesson Seven, which . . ."

"Oh!" Betinda exclaimed, clapping a hand to her throat. She dived under her desk, then popped up again, scanning the floor in all directions.

"Miss Callender!" their teacher commanded. "Sit down at once."

"But sir," she gasped. "I've lost my diamond pendant. It must have fallen off—I can't find it anywhere!"

Privately Isaveth thought it served Betinda right, but the girl wept so noisily into her handkerchief that Master Valstead gave in. "Very well, all of you get up and look for Miss Callender's necklace."

Everyone did so, with much milling about and creaking of desks and chairs. But there was no sign of the pendant.

"It had the prettiest golden chain," Betinda wailed. "And the diamond was shaped like a teardrop, with little sapphires all around it. . . ."

"If it was so valuable, Miss Callender, you should not have worn it to school," said Master Valstead severely. "When did you last have it?"

"At the bottom of the stairs, before I came up to class. Oh, please let me go look!" She half-rose, but their teacher raised a forbidding hand.

"Enough. I will deal with this."

He strode out the door and returned a few minutes later, announcing that the housekeeper and her staff were on the way to search the building. Then he walked back to his note stand and continued the lesson.

The bell rang for the end of class, but the door remained shut. Master Valstead sat down, and all the students began whispering to one another.

"If they haven't found it by now . . ."

"Someone must have pocketed it."

"Did anyone come late? Maybe they saw . . ."

A knock rattled the door, and Master Valstead rose to answer it. He stepped outside for a brief, muttered conversation, then returned looking even more stony than usual.

"Your necklace is found, Miss Callender."

"Oh, thank the Sages," breathed Betinda, scrambling to her feet. "Where was it?"

"You may reclaim your property from the governor's office after school," their teacher continued, ignoring the question. "For now, proceed to your next class."

Isaveth picked up her school bag and started after the others, but Master Valstead blocked her path. "Miss Breck. Remain here, please."

"But, sir—" she began, then faltered silent as the last of her classmates vanished out the door and Meggery marched in. A nervous-looking maid trailed after her, carrying a bundle of black cloth.

"That's her," said the housekeeper, nodding at Isaveth. "She's the one."

Chapter Twenty

FOR ONE WILD MOMENT Isaveth could not make sense of what was happening. Her first thought was that it must have something to do with the bell tower—but if Meggery wasn't satisfied with Isaveth's punishment, why would she bring it up here, and now?

"You are certain?" Master Valstead asked. "You have witnesses?"

Meggery nudged the maid, who stepped forward. "I found the necklace, sir. Harlin was searching the coatroom with me, he saw it too."

"And where did you find it?"

"In the pocket of this, sir." She shook out the overcoat she'd been carrying, and Isaveth's knees wobbled. That slightly shabby collar, the mismatched button on the lapel—it was hers.

"But that's impossible," she whispered.

Master Valstead regarded her coldly. "This is a serious charge, Miss Breck. What do you have to say for yourself?"

Her mouth felt parched, her tongue thick with disbelief. But she had to speak before this madness went any further. "I didn't do it, sir—I couldn't have. I was in the classroom before Betinda lost her necklace."

Meggery huffed. "So she claims, master, but I'll warrant her classmates tell a different story. No doubt Governor Buldage will find the truth of it."

"Indeed." Master Valstead straightened up grimly. "Miss Breck, come with me."

Heart hammering, Isaveth followed Master Valstead out of the building, with Meggery and the maid at her heels. They crossed the snowy cobbles to Founders' Hall and climbed the stairs inside.

Even as they approached the governor's office, Isaveth was too distracted to recognize the greater danger. Not until she found herself face-to-face with his secretary did the full horror of the situation crash in, and by then the woman had already seen her.

"What is *she* doing here?" the secretary demanded, pointing an accusing finger at Isaveth.

"Excuse me?" asked Valstead, frowning. "Do you know this young lady?"

"She turned up the week Master Orien passed,

claiming to be a cleaning maid. Asked me all manner of impertinent questions about his death." She surveyed Isaveth with displeasure. "Morra, wasn't it?"

Isaveth shook her head, though the sick feeling inside her warned that the truth would be no help now. "I'm Isaveth Breck."

The secretary's face closed up like a slamming door. "Well," she said. "How *interesting*."

"We need to speak to the governor," said Master Valstead. "Is he available?"

The woman picked up her earpiece, listening. Then she pressed a button on her desk and the inner door swung open.

Governor Buldage rose as they entered, pale and haggard as a prisoner called to his execution. "Good day," he said hoarsely. "How can I help you?"

"Miss Breck is accused of theft," announced Master Valstead, and Buldage blinked, his color returning. Whatever he'd expected when Isaveth arrived in his office, it hadn't been this.

"How so?" he asked.

Valstead gave him a brief summary of what had happened in the classroom, then gestured to Meggery to step forward and tell how she and the servants had discovered the necklace in Isaveth's pocket.

"'Twas my idea to search the coatroom," she concluded smugly, "as I thought some greedy girl might have seen it fall and snatched it up for herself. And I was right."

"Yet Miss Breck insists she was in the classroom before Miss Callender arrived, and therefore could not have taken it," said Valstead. "I was not present at the time, so I cannot say. We will have to question the other students."

Governor Buldage sat back, running a finger across his lips as he studied the pendant. "I will speak to Miss Breck in private," he said at last. "You may go."

Master Valstead bowed out at once, but Meggery lingered. "Sir, if I might say a word—"

"Thank you, Missus Jespers. That will be all."

Isaveth had never heard the housekeeper called by her family name before, and even Meggery seemed taken aback. She scurried away, taking the maid with her.

"Sit down, Miss Breck." Governor Buldage gestured her to a chair. "Tell me what happened."

He spoke so gently that Isaveth's eyes began to burn. She had to shut them as she repeated her story. "I didn't take Betinda's necklace. I didn't even look at it. I would never—"

"No," said Buldage, "of course not. That would be foolish and greedy, and from what I have seen, you are neither."

Hope leaped up in Isaveth. "Then you believe me?"

"I do. However . . ." He sighed. "I doubt it will make any difference."

"But you're—"

"The governor? Indeed. But Miss Callender's parents are powerful nobles and patrons of this college. They will not be satisfied until someone is punished, and they have every reason to want that person to be you."

"But someone must have planted the necklace in my pocket. If we could—"

"Find out who might wish to see you expelled from the college? There is no shortage of suspects. Including, it appears, my own secretary."

So he had heard. He knew now, if he hadn't before, that she had come to this very office four months ago looking for clues to Master Orien's murder. Buldage rose, his tall figure looming over her, and Isaveth shrank back—but he only walked to the window, lacing his hands behind him as he gazed out over the grounds.

"I hoped," he murmured, "that I could make amends. But to do that, I would have to be free." He turned back to her, looking more weary than ever. "I am sorry, Miss Breck, but I must protect the interests and the reputation of this college. Until we have fully investigated this matter, I have no choice but to suspend you."

* * *

Isaveth stumbled through the front door of her cottage, the school bag slipping off her shoulder to fall with a thump to the floor. The house was empty and icy cold, but that was nothing compared to how she felt inside.

Suspended, not expelled. That was some comfort. There was still a chance that whoever had put the necklace in Isaveth's pocket would be caught . . . or that at least some of her classmates would agree she couldn't have taken it.

But an investigation would unearth other details that could ruin Isaveth just as surely. The governor's secretary could tell how she'd disguised herself and pried into college business; and Meggery would be quick to report how she'd seen her sneaking out of the bell tower. After hearing all the trouble Isaveth had gotten into, the board of masters might well decide that thief or not, the school would be better off without her.

"Why did you let me come here if you knew this could happen?" she'd asked Governor Buldage at the end, too anguished to hold back any longer. "Was it Eryx Lording's idea to humiliate me? Or did you really think being kind to me could make up for helping murder Master Orien and letting my father take the blame?"

Her words had struck home: Buldage's nostrils flared on an indrawn breath, and his face turned more sallow than ever. "I will pretend that I did not hear that," he said tightly. "You may go, Miss Breck."

There'd been no time to leave a message for Esmond or talk to Eulalie. As soon as she came out of the governor's office his secretary had called for the porter, who'd escorted Isaveth off the school grounds.

After nearly a week without protests, threats, or nasty messages, Isaveth had dared to hope that her enemies had lost interest in her. Now it was bitterly clear that they had only been biding their time.

Yet one thing hadn't changed. No matter how crushed she felt, no matter what Betinda's parents might say or the masters decide, Isaveth wasn't giving up. She was fighting for her family and her people, even if they didn't know it, and she had work to do.

She unlaced her boots, hung up her coat, and went to light the stove for her next round of experiments.

"You're home early!" exclaimed Mimmi. Her cheeks were still rosy with cold, her hair fuzzed where she'd carelessly dragged off her hat. "What are you making? It smells good. Is it for supper?"

Isaveth glanced at her little sister distractedly, balancing the journal in one hand as she stirred her latest decoction with the other. This one claimed to be an antidote to curses, which nobody really believed in anymore. But a curse was a kind of spell, at least in theory . . . and until she could get the ingredients for the metal-dissolving potion, it was the best she could do.

"No," she said. "It's magic."

"Oh," said Mimmi, lip jutting in disappointment. Then she brightened and began to chatter about the soap carving she'd made at school. Isaveth let her little sister's words wash over her, nodding at intervals. At least someone was happy.

"Where's Lilet?" she asked, when Mimmi paused for breath.

"She had to stay behind. I think she was fighting again."

Isaveth nearly dropped her spoon. "*Again?* How many fights has she been in?"

"A few. She usually wins, though."

The liquid in the pot was simmering, tiny bubbles rising toward the surface. Isaveth added a pinch of null-pepper and began to stir in the opposite direction. She'd had no idea Lilet was getting into trouble at school—she'd been too consumed with her own troubles to notice. How much else had she missed these past few weeks?

"Does Papa know?" she asked, but she already knew the answer. Lilet would never admit to causing trouble, or even being in it, until she was caught.

"No, and she said she'd thump me if I told him. She

didn't tell me not to tell you, though," Mimmi added, proud of finding the loophole.

Isaveth rubbed a hand across her brow. She had one piece of bad news to share already; now Mimmi had handed her another one. It was going to be an unhappy evening in the Breck household. . . .

Unless, of course, she said nothing. Not just about Lilet fighting, but about her suspension as well.

Guilt pricked Isaveth at the thought of keeping more secrets from Papa, but it made sense. As far as her family knew, she was under Esmond's protection, had a loyal friend in Eulalie, and even the scandal of Su's article had soon been forgotten in the buzz of fresh gossip after the ball. Would it really hurt to let them go on believing all was well, at least until she knew for certain that it wasn't?

Isaveth lifted the spoon and let the liquid ooze back into the pot, testing its thickness. Then she dribbled it over the warding-charm and the sealing-charm Esmond had made for her. Holding her breath, she took out her charm-glass to inspect them. . . .

They still glowed just as brightly. The decoction had made no difference at all.

The dull pain in Isaveth's chest pushed up into her throat, and her eyes blurred. But she told herself it was too soon to despair. Since she couldn't go to school on Mendday, there'd be plenty of time to try the remaining spell; all she had to do was sell the beautiful new coat Esmond had given her and buy the ingredients she needed.

Yes, things looked hopeless right now. But Lord Arvis hadn't died yet, and Eryx couldn't bring his plan to council without the Sagelord's permission, so there was still time.

Her next experiment would work. It had to.

The next day was Templeday, so none of the shops were open. The snow lay thick over the sidewalks, and Isaveth and her sisters had to wade through several drifts to get to Wisdom Hall. But the sanctum was warm again, and Mister Yeltavan's announcement that sales of Glow-Mor tablets had risen across the city cheered her a little. It would be a bad blow for Mister Wregget if she was expelled from the college, but at least there was still hope of keeping her scholarship if she wasn't.

Mendday morning was the usual flurry of activity as Isaveth and her sisters scrambled to get ready and Papa shoveled the front step, clearing away the snow that had blown over it last night. Mimmi and Lilet were first out the door, hats pulled low and scarves high to keep out the bitter wind, while Isaveth filled a flask with tea and packed up her book bag as though she meant to use it.

"Have a nice day at school," she said to Annagail as the two of them put on their coats.

Anna flicked a glance at her. "And you," she said colorlessly.

Something was troubling her, and as a good sister Isaveth ought to ask about it. But if she'd been going to school as usual, she wouldn't have time. She gave Anna an apologetic smile, tugged on her mittens and went out.

Last night she'd wrapped up her new coat, not without a pang of regret, and hidden it under the back step. Isaveth waited until Papa left the house—without his shovel, oddly enough, so he must have some special business to attend to—then slipped back to fetch it. She caught a westbound tram into the heart of the city, and by the time the town clock tolled noon she had sold the coat at the Relief Shop, used the money to buy the ingredients she needed, and returned home to start her next experiment.

She'd ground the bitternuts to a paste and was chopping the dried scorch-pepper when a firm rap sounded at the door. A visitor at this time of day? Isaveth put the knife down and sidled up the front hallway, craning her neck to see who it could be.

"I can see you, Miss Breck." An amused female voice floated through the mail slot, and gloved fingers waggled at her from beneath the flap. "It's Su Amaraq from the *Trumpeter*, and I'd like to ask you a few questions."

Chapter Twenty-One

AS ALWAYS, SU AMARAQ sounded like the perfect reporter: friendly, competent, and interested only in the truth. But after the last couple of articles she'd written, Isaveth had no faith that the woman would treat her fairly.

"I have nothing to say to you," she replied, one hand pressed to her thumping heart. "Please go."

Silence followed, then a sigh and a crunch of footsteps, growing fainter until they faded away. Cautiously Isaveth crept to the door and raised herself on tiptoe to look out.

Su's face popped up in the window, and Isaveth jumped back with a shriek. "You look familiar," the woman said, her voice muffled by the glass. "Have we met before?"

They had, once, when Isaveth was looking for information on her father's case. But she'd pretended she only wanted to become a journalist, and they'd parted without Su even asking her name. Isaveth swallowed, fingers curling into her sweaty palms. "Does it matter?"

"Maybe," said Su. "Look, I understand why you don't trust me. I wouldn't either. But I'm not the villain here, I just want to know what's going on."

"So you can print it in your newsrag and turn the whole city against me? No thank you."

"The story's going to break eventually, whether I write it or not. I got a tip that you'd been suspended. Somebody's out for blood, Miss Breck, and it appears to be yours. I'm starting to wonder why."

"Isn't it obvious?" She knew she sounded bitter, but there was no point in hiding it. "They hate me because I'm—"

"Moshite. That explains some of it, no doubt. But I get the feeling my ever-so-helpful informant is playing a bigger game." Su pressed a gloved hand to the window, imploring. "Come on, Miss Breck, help me out. I'll even keep your name out of it, if that's what you want. I'll quote you as an unnamed source at the college."

It wasn't that generous an offer. But if she could get Su to investigate a little further, instead of writing up her article at once . . . Isaveth wiped her hands on her skirt, sent up a silent prayer for courage, and opened the door.

Su stepped inside, unbuttoning her fur-collared coat—then paused, sharp eyes focusing on Isaveth. "Oho," she said softly. "It's my little journalist."

It was no use pretending otherwise. Isaveth nodded and led her through to the kitchen.

"Right, then," said Su, sitting down and taking off her gloves with practiced elegance. Her gaze swept the room, lingering briefly on the hallow cabinet in the corner, then returned to Isaveth as she flipped her notebook open. "Let's start at the beginning, shall we? How did you first learn about the Glow-Mor scholarship, and what made you decide to apply?"

"I didn't," said Isaveth. "Mister Wregget liked my . . . work, so he offered it to me."

"Your work? Ah, yes. Your homemade fire- and light-tablets. A family recipe?"

Isaveth smiled faintly, relieved that Su had jumped to such a safe conclusion. "My mother's."

"Your family must have been quite proud when you got the scholarship. Especially after your father's, ah, recent difficulties. How did you feel, coming to Tarreton College? Excited? Nervous? Anxious to do well?"

"All of those things." Su looked up, black brows arched against her coppery skin, and Isaveth felt compelled to say more. "I knew people wouldn't want me there, and I hoped I could . . . convince them . . ." She looked away, unable to finish the sentence.

"So you were aware that you were being watched, and that it was important to keep up a good reputation. Did you enjoy learning Sagery? Were you good at it?"

"I think so." Actually she knew so, but she didn't want to sound arrogant. "I liked it very much."

"You don't think there's anything disrespectful about a Moshite making sage-charms?"

Heat flooded into Isaveth's face, but she kept her anger in check. "Some of the greatest sages were Moshite," she replied. Or at least they had been until the Concord of Abirene, the centuries-old treaty that had stripped Moshites of their lands, destroyed their books of magical lore, and forbidden them to practice Sagery. "I don't have to worship the sages to respect them, or learn what they taught."

Su tapped the end of her lead-point against her lips. "How did you feel when the story appeared naming you as the winner of the Glow-Mor scholarship?"

"It was horrible," said Isaveth flatly. "And don't you mean *your* story?"

"My name was on the article, yes. But it was edited before it went to print." Her lips pursed with displeasure. "One might even say butchered—and *not* in your favor."

"You mean someone at the *Trumpeter* was bribed into changing the story?" asked Isaveth, pulse quickening. "Why would anyone care what the newsrags say about me?"

Su sat back, appraising her. "Good question, Miss Breck. Have you made any powerful enemies lately?"

If she thought she could trust this woman, Isaveth would have told her everything. But she'd seen Su at the ball only a week ago, flirting with Eryx and defending him to Civilla's friends. Still, if she could get her to doubt the Lording even a little . . .

"I've never met Lord Arvis," she replied cautiously, "so I don't know what he would have against me. And if he didn't want me at Tarreton College, all he had to do was say so. But I heard that Eryx Lording wants to deny relief to Moshites, so . . . maybe he feels differently."

Su went still—but then she smiled, and Isaveth's hope died out. "Oh, I can't imagine that. I'm sure you misunderstood. But let's get back to the point. Why don't you tell me, in your own words, what happened the other day?"

Su did not ask many questions after that, and stayed only long enough to hear the briefest version of Isaveth's story. She jotted a few cursory notes, then rose from her seat with a neutral "Thank you, Miss Breck," before pulling on her gloves and heading for the door.

"Miss Amaraq!" Isaveth hurried after her. "When will you—I mean, if there's going to be a—"

"Governor Buldage expects the investigation will be done by tomorrow," said Su. "So you can look for my article on Worksday morning." She strolled out to her waiting taxi, and was gone.

Isaveth shut the door and went back to chopping ingredients, wondering if she'd made the right decision by talking to Su or whether she'd soon regret it. After all, if the reporter had been telling the truth, anything favorable or even fair to Isaveth wouldn't make it into the *Trumpeter* anyway. Eryx Lording would make sure of that.

Yet if Eryx was behind all of this, it seemed like a strange way to punish her. Why allow her to go to Tarreton College and even study Sagery for half a term, before . . .

What, exactly? Coaxing Betinda Callender to lose her expensive necklace, and Meggery to plant it in Isaveth's pocket? How could Eryx do that without risking his reputation, and more importantly, why would he? He had no reason to believe Isaveth posed a threat to him, and his new plan to cut off relief to Moshites would ruin her just as surely.

Unless he needed to make Isaveth look like a criminal in order to convince the council that Moshites didn't deserve charity? Could it be that simple?

The question still nagged at her as she read over the instructions in the country-mage's journal one last time, making sure she hadn't missed anything. This spell could be dangerous if she didn't follow the steps exactly. She unstopped the glass jar she'd washed for the purpose, then began measuring and pouring in the ingredients.

Once she'd prepared the base mixture, Isaveth set the jar in a pot of water and put it on the stove to simmer. The journal warned that this step could take two bells or more, so she walked to the front room and turned on the crystal set.

There would be no new episode of *Auradia* until tomorrow, but she could always listen to one of the daytime talkie-plays, or a comic show like *Silly Sailor*. She fiddled with the dials, tuning the crystal from one station to another.

"—not just the flavor, it's the savor! Try Perram's Puffers for long-lasting—"

"That was Janny Mastrocelli and the Tin City Orchestra with 'That Darling Girl o' Mine'—"

"—Sages have mercy, Master Lyle! Can't you see the poor child is dying?"

Not in the mood for gloomy stories, Isaveth settled on a station that was playing music and began to wipe up the mess she'd made of the kitchen counter. The bright, brassy tunes proved cheering, and she was scrubbing along to the beat when the melody abruptly cut out.

"We pause this program to bring you a special report. Shortly after eleven bells this morning, Sagelord Arvis was pronounced dead by the Healer-General. . . ."

The cloth crumpled between Isaveth's nerveless fingers. She stared blindly at the wall, cold spreading beneath her ribs.

". . . sources report the cause of death as liver failure, though the Healer-General has declined to issue a statement until a full investigation has been made. Lady Nessa, now Dowager Sagelady, accompanied the body to Sage Johram's Hospital along with the new Sagelord Eryx and the other members of the family. . . ."

The ice inside Isaveth cracked, and a pang of grief burst through. "Oh," she whispered. "Oh, Esmond."

Right up to the end, Esmond had hoped for a miracle. Not that his father would get well: He knew it was too late for that. Whether it was poison or merely drink that had done it, Lord Arvis's liver was too damaged for medicine or even magic to repair.

Yet two nights ago he'd dreamed that the Sagelord had woken from his delirious sleep and sent for him. He'd called Esmond to his bedside and told him he was sorry for not being a better father, but he loved him and was proud of him . . . all that stupid, sentimental nonsense that dying men said to their sons in the talkie-plays.

It was only a dream, of course. Before he died, the last person his father had spoken to—really spoken, in a wheezing murmur too low for anyone else to hear—was Eryx.

All at once Esmond's neck-cloth felt like it was strangling him. He clawed the knot loose and dropped his head into his hands, breathing hard.

He'd sat there for some unknowable time, when someone touched his shoulder. He dragged his sleeve across his face, furious at the interruption—to see Civilla standing beside him, looking as wrung out as he felt.

"You should eat," she said.

Esmond shook his head, anger fading. He'd thought it was Eryx come to gloat, but he should have known better. Eryx would be in his study by now, pouring himself a drink and making plans for his glorious reign as Sagelord, and likely hadn't spared a thought for anyone else at all.

Part of him envied his brother for that. If only the

footman hadn't rushed out to stop Esmond getting into the carriage this morning, he could be at Tarreton College right now, too distracted by facts and formulas to think of his father dying.

No, not dying anymore. Dead.

"Esmond, please," Civilla urged. She'd lost the remote, haughty expression she'd been cultivating for the last year or so; there were blue shadows beneath her eyes, and her lips were trembling. "We need to talk. I can't do this alone."

"Do what?" Esmond said, but it came out harsh. "If you want help with something, ask Eryx. You know, the one who poisoned our father, and *you* let him get away with it?"

Civilla stiffened, and Esmond braced himself for a slap. But instead she whirled and stalked from the library, slamming the door behind her.

It didn't matter, Esmond thought dully as the click of her footsteps faded. He had nothing to say to her anyway. The only person he wanted to talk to was surely at the college right now, dark head bent over her workbook, nibbling the end of her lead-point as she thought.

Isaveth had worked hard these past few weeks. He hoped she'd do well on her midterms and be happy for a while. She'd hear the news about his father's death eventually, but they could talk about it when Esmond got back to school.

After all, Eryx was Sagelord now, and all their plans to stop him had failed. There was no hurry anymore.

It wasn't too late, Isaveth told herself, though dread clawed her stomach and she felt weak in every limb. Even as ruler of the city, Eryx needed the council's support to carry out his reform plan, and they wouldn't meet until after Lord Arvis's memorial. If the potion she'd just made could dissolve charm-silver, there was still a chance to get hold of Eryx's documents and show them to someone with the courage, integrity, and power to do something about it. Like Eulalie's father, the Deputy Justice . . .

She'd removed the jar of potion from its hot-water bath a few minutes ago, and strained its contents through a piece of gauze-cloth until only a thin pinkish liquid remained. Licking her lips nervously, Isaveth tweezed up one of her test charms from the table and dropped it in.

It slid to the bottom, tiny bubbles escaping from all four corners, and landed with a clink. Isaveth was squinting through the glass when the front door creaked and she heard boots stamping on the mat.

Too light for Papa. "Anna?" called Isaveth, resisting the impulse to hide. School was almost over anyway, and she could always claim that her last class had been cancelled. "Is that you?"

There was no answer. Reluctantly she tore her eyes from the still-bubbling charm—and there was Annagail in the hallway, taking off her coat.

Perhaps Isaveth had been wrong not to confide in her, the one person who'd always listened when she needed to talk. If she could share her worries, it would take a huge weight off her mind . . . and maybe then Anna would feel free to do the same.

Yet it had been weeks since they'd had a proper conversation, and Isaveth hardly knew where to start. "So . . . how was your day?"

Anna straightened up slowly, staring at the wall. Then she whirled on Isaveth. "Stop it," she snapped. "Just stop."

Isaveth's chest fluttered. "What do you mean?"

"I mean, stop pretending to care about anything but your precious college and your noble friends. You've changed so much since you got that scholarship, I hardly know you anymore." Annagail snatched off her scarf and threw it onto the hook. "Don't you care that Lilet's been getting into fights at school because of you?"

"Me?" Isaveth was aghast. "Why?"

"Because she can't bear to hear anyone speak ill of you, and the other children know it. If she keeps on like this she's going to get expelled." Anna tugged up her stockings and stepped into their mother's old house slippers. "But you're so taken up with your Sagery and your fancy balls and everyone making a fuss over you at temple, you can't spare a thought for anyone else."

"Anna, that's not—"

"For two days I've been in agony, not knowing what to say to Papa." Swiping a knuckle over her wet cheeks, Annagail started up the stairs. "Especially after Mimmi told me she'd talked to you about Lilet first. So you knew. You've known longer than I have. And you just went on fussing over your sage-charms and said nothing at all."

With every accusing word, the knot of pain in Isaveth's chest grew tighter. She wanted to tell Annagail she had it all wrong, and yet how could she? She *had* ignored Mimmi's report, telling herself it was none of her business and that Lilet could handle herself. And after she'd worked so hard to convince her family she was happy, how could she blame Anna for believing it?

"I—I'm sorry," she stammered. "But Anna, it's not like you think. If you'd only listen—"

Annagail, three-quarters of the way up the staircase, gave no sign of having heard. "I've tried so hard . . ." She faltered, then started over in a more determined tone,

"I've tried to be patient. To imagine what I might feel like in your place. But you've made that very difficult, Isaveth."

She'd never liked being called Vettie, or so she'd thought. Yet hearing her sister speak her full name was like a cold knife in Isaveth's heart. Her mouth opened, pleading, but by the time she found her voice Annagail was gone.

Isaveth was sitting at the kitchen table, gazing listlessly at her still-undissolved charm, when Lilet tramped in the door with one mitten missing and her hat askew.

"I heard the Sagelord died today," she said, kicking off her boots. "Is it true?"

Isaveth nodded.

"Finally," said Lilet with relish. "Also, Mimmi said to tell you she's at Aunt Sal's, playing with Pem." She came into the kitchen, took a cup from the shelf, and began pumping herself a drink of water. "What's the matter with you? I thought you'd be happy. Sagelord Eryx and all that."

Isaveth couldn't bear it any longer. She pushed the glass jar away and buried her face in her hands.

"Vettie?" Lilet dropped the cup into the sink and came over. "What's wrong? Is it Papa?"

Isaveth had never wanted to burden her sisters with

the knowledge she carried, or the fear that had driven her since she first heard Eryx Lording talk about his plan. She'd told herself that Anna was too guileless and Lilet and Mimmi too young to keep such dangerous secrets anyway. But she had to talk to someone or her heart would burst. . . .

And Lilet had fought for her. That meant she cared.

"No, not Papa," she said, struggling to speak past the sobs heaving her chest. "Lilet, if—if I tell you something, will you promise to listen and not tell anyone?"

Lilet sat down next to her, spine straight and chin raised in determination. "You can tell me anything," she said. "I won't say a word."

So Isaveth spilled out her story, broken words tumbling over one another as her younger sister sat quietly, absorbing it all. She told Lilet nothing about her suspension—it wasn't important now. But she explained how Eryx Lording had murdered Master Orien and framed Papa, his plan to deny relief to the Moshites of Tarreton, and all that she and Esmond had done to try to keep him from becoming Sagelord.

"This decoction was supposed to dissolve metal," she finished miserably, gesturing at the jar. "Only it doesn't seem to work on charm-silver. And now I don't know what else to do."

Lilet huffed out a breath as though listening so long had exhausted her. Then she lunged forward and grabbed Isaveth in a fierce, bony hug.

"I knew it!" she exclaimed. "I knew you weren't just working on some silly prank with Esmond. You were far too serious about it." She sat back, adding more soberly, "I think you should tell Papa about Eryx, though."

"How can I? It was dangerous enough to cross Eryx before, but now he's Sagelord it's ten times worse. You know what Papa would do if he—"

"Where are my girls?" The front door burst open and their father lumbered in, shedding snow in all directions. "Did you hear the news? A new Sagelord at last!"

"Papa?" Annagail rushed downstairs, losing a slipper in her haste. "You mean . . ."

"Yes!" He tore off his coat and flung it over the banister, then swept Anna into a hug that lifted her off the floor. "Now we'll really see some changes in this city!"

Isaveth shot an agonized look at Lilet, but Papa was too busy dancing Annagail about like a tipsy bear to notice. "Brom and I are calling the first official meeting of our new Moshite Workers' Union tonight," he announced. "As soon as the memorial for Lord Arvis is over, we're going to see Eryx and sort out this relief business, and then we can all sleep sound again." His black beard split in a grin. "I've never been gladder to work so hard for so little!"

Annagail leaned her head against his shoulder, looking happier than she had in weeks. "Oh, Papa, I'm glad too. I was so worried about you."

Isaveth got up and began filling the teakettle, struggling to digest what she'd just heard. She'd never given much thought to what her father did when it wasn't snowing, but now she understood—he'd been making the rounds of the local factories and taverns with her uncle Brom, Aunt Sal's husband, and rallying other Moshites to stand up against Eryx's relief plan.

Except, of course, that he didn't know the idea had come from Eryx. Like Su and most other people in the city, Papa thought any political decision that seemed cruel or unjust must be Lord Arvis's fault.

She should have known Papa would hear about the plan, whether she told him or not. She should have known he wouldn't sit by and wait for others to fight when he could fight for himself. And now that her father had made up his mind, not even the truth about Eryx would turn him from it. If he'd been ready to start a rebellion against the old Sagelord, he'd be just as quick to defy the new one.

Yet when Eryx found out about the newly formed,

illegal Moshite Workers' Union, he'd have all the proof he needed to show the city council that Moshites were lawless radicals who didn't deserve their support. . . .

It might be a hopeless cause, but she had to try. Isaveth set the kettle on the stove with a clang and turned to face her father.

"Papa," she said, "there's something I have to tell you."

Chapter Twenty-Two

ISAVETH DID ALL SHE COULD to warn Papa about Eryx, short of revealing the plans she and Esmond had made to stop him. She told him the Lording—now Sagelord—was as wicked as his father had ever been, and that all his grand speeches about equality and justice were a lie. She'd even blurted out that Eryx had plotted Master Orien's murder, and possibly Lord Arvis's as well. But her words were so garbled with panic that Papa finally waved at her to stop.

"I think you've been listening to too many talkie-plays, Vettie," he said. "I can't make sense of such a tangle, and I don't know how you can either. If Lord Eryx is as wicked as you say, time and testing will prove it. But I'm not seeing any proof just now."

The worst of it was, Papa was right. The proof was still locked up in Eryx's spell-carriage, so all she had was suspicion and hearsay to go on. How could she expect to convince anyone, even Papa, with that?

Isaveth barely slept that night, and by morning she felt as though she hadn't gone to bed at all. Yet she dressed mechanically, ate her breakfast, and went through the motions of heading off to school. She walked to Sage Allum's Park and left a note for Esmond in their old letter drop, praying he'd look there when he couldn't find her at the college. When she felt sure the house was empty, she sneaked home by the coal lane.

She'd take a nap, she told herself as she came in the back door, just a short one, and read over the journal again. Even if all the spells she'd tried so far had failed, there had to be *something* she could do. But when she went to hang up her coat she found a note lying under the mail slot, announcing that J. J. Wregget wanted to see her.

Somehow, he must have heard about her suspension. And now she'd have to account for what had happened. Wearily Isaveth tucked the note into her pocket and went out to catch a tram to the Glow-Mor office.

The route to the industrial core of the city was less direct than the one to the college, and with all the stops, starts, and transfers it was nearly eleven bells before Isaveth arrived at her destination. She walked the slushy pavement to the Glow-Mor factory, the sounds of machinery pounding like a nervous heartbeat in her ears.

"I'm here to see Mister Wregget," she said to the woman at the front desk.

The receptionist's gaze narrowed, studying Isaveth. Then she tapped a button on her call box. "Good morning, Tambor, it's Vernice. *She's* here."

The hint that everyone in the office had been expecting her made Isaveth more uneasy than ever. The last time she'd been here the receptionist had simply waved her through, but now she rose and took Isaveth by the elbow, marching her down the corridor to the president's suite.

J. J. Wregget was waiting for her, no longer the robustly cheerful figure she'd met a few weeks ago but a subdued and even shrunken man. "Thank you, Tambor," he murmured as his private secretary took her coat. Then, with a nod to the receptionist, he ushered Isaveth into his office.

"I didn't do it, sir," she blurted out as the heavy door swung shut. "After all you've done for me, I would never—"

Wregget waved a hand to stop her. "Of course not, my dear. I had all the details from Mistress Anandri yesterday, and she is convinced that you are as innocent as I am." He sighed. "For all the good it does either of us."

"Sir?" asked Isaveth, taken aback. If he hadn't called her here to ask for an explanation, what did he want?

The president paced behind his wooden desk, picking up a paperweight and setting it down again. "We are in similar straits, Miss Breck. Last night my board of directors voted to replace me."

Isaveth's lips parted in dismay. "Because I got suspended?"

"By no means!" exclaimed Wregget with a spark of his old spirit. "I would be a poor excuse for a businessman if I laid all my troubles on the shoulders of one young lady. No, I fear they have been growing restless for some time. I can only blame myself for not seeing it sooner."

He motioned for Isaveth to sit, then rolled back his own chair and did likewise. "My directors claim that my poor judgment in selecting you as a candidate drove them to action. They say I've exposed the company to scandal, and that firing me is the only way to save Glow-Mor's reputation and ensure its continued success. But that's all fiddle-faddle—our sales these past weeks have been better than ever."

He drummed his fingers against the desk. "What they really want is to sell the company to my biggest rival, who's made them such a handsome offer they can't see beyond their own pockets. But I built this company up from nothing, and I won't let it go without a fight!"

Isaveth sat forward. "Your biggest rival? That would be Power-Up, wouldn't it?"

"That's right. Ever since we started using Resisto-Paper to wrap our spell-tablets, we've leaped ahead of them in the market. Especially when it comes to exports—and Power-Up's owners are shipping folk, so they don't like that at all."

A suspicion was taking shape in Isaveth's mind, but it was still hazy. She needed to know more. "So how can you fight them? If your own board wants to get rid of you—"

"Ah, but I have one advantage they can't afford to lose." He puffed up proudly. "The secret ingredient for Resisto-Paper, which only you and I know."

Neevils. Little black bugs that infested grain and flour, neevils were usually sifted out and discarded early in the process of making spell-tablets. But since Isaveth had sold her recipe to Wregget, he'd been putting them to good use instead.

"How can that be?" Isaveth asked. "The workers who make the paper know, surely?" And though Wregget seemed to have forgotten it for the moment, Esmond and Mistress Anandri knew as well.

"They know the recipe includes a black powder which comes to them ready-ground," said Wregget. "But I'm too clever a hen to keep all my chicks in one coop, Miss Breck." He waggled a finger at her. "The secret ingredient comes from an off-site supplier, through a long-time associate whose loyalty is to me and not Glow-Mor. The supplier delivers the powder to him, and he delivers it to the company that makes the wrappers, so nobody knows where it comes from. You see?"

Isaveth did, though she wasn't sure what any of it had to do with her. "So the board can't fire you without losing the recipe, which is the reason Power-Up wants to buy your company in the first place. Do they know that?"

"They do now," Wregget said, with a dangerous gleam in his eye. "I gave them my ultimatum this morning. They have until Trustday to decide whose side they're on . . . and then, my dear, we shall see."

Already he seemed happier, more like his old confident self. Yet Isaveth feared his troubles were only beginning. "But sir, I'm still suspended from the college. And I don't think they'll let me come back."

She was about to add that when Su's story broke it would hurt Glow-Mor's reputation even more than the news that their scholarship student was a Moshite, but Wregget interrupted her. "Bullying and slander won't stop me, Miss Breck, so don't let them stop you either. One way or another, we'll get you back in that school where you belong. Even if I have to go begging to Er— excuse me, to Sagelord Eryx himself."

A lot of good *that* would do. "Thank you, sir," Isaveth replied, trying not to show her disappointment. "I appreciate it. Was that why you sent for me?"

"I beg your pardon?"

"I mean, why you sent the note asking me to come here," explained Isaveth, and when the president looked blank she added, "This morning."

J. J. Wregget's brow furrowed. "I didn't send for you. I thought you'd come on your own. Do you still have the note? May I see it?"

"It's in my coat," said Isaveth, starting to rise, but Wregget waved her down again.

"Tambor!" he bellowed, and after a brief pause the secretary opened the door. "Bring the young lady her overcoat."

"Yes, sir," said the man promptly, and returned a moment later to help Isaveth put it on. She reached into her pockets, but both were empty.

"I don't understand," she murmured. "I had it when I left the house." Could it have fallen out on her way from the tram?

"Hmm. Quite the little mystery." Wregget heaved himself from his chair, extending one big hand in farewell.

"Well, whatever your reasons, I'm glad you came. We'll get through this, Miss Breck. Don't lose heart."

Isaveth walked slowly away from the Glow-Mor factory, collar turned up and head bowed beneath the brim of her bell-shaped hat. Her head spun with all that J. J. Wregget had told her, and she kept mulling over the details, trying to make them fit.

So Wregget's board had turned greedy and wanted to sell out to Power-Up. Could that be why they hadn't tried to stop him offering Isaveth the scholarship? They'd known his decision would be controversial, so all they had to do was leak Isaveth's story to the newsrags and hope the backlash would give them the excuse they needed to get rid of him.

Except it hadn't worked. Isaveth's fellow Moshites had rallied around her and shored up Glow-Mor's sales until the kettle-storm of controversy died out. So Wregget's enemies were forced to try again. . . .

But who were those enemies, exactly? Could they include the couple she'd overheard predicting Wregget's ruin at the ball? Perhaps they were the same wolf-masked pair who'd visited Lord Arvis in the gaming room, and he'd made the fatal mistake of telling them something they didn't want to hear?

Lost in thought, Isaveth wandered straight past the tram stop and had crossed two more streets before she realized that none of the factories and warehouses about her looked familiar. By then it made no sense to turn back, so she continued on.

"Give us a smile, pretty!" crowed a voice across the street, to the tune of whistles and rough laughter. Isaveth's face flamed and she hurried to the next stop, hoping the tram would come soon.

Delivery wagons clopped in and out of the factories, and passing spell-carriages sprayed slush over Isaveth's feet. She was craning to see into the distance, wondering if the tram had met with an accident, when a taxi pulled up next to her. "Where to, miss?"

"Oh," said Isaveth, backing away. "I'm sorry, I didn't call for you."

"Are you Miss Breck? A Mister Wregget called, and he's paid your fare home."

Isaveth hesitated.

"Come on then, miss, I can't sit here all day!"

Part of her felt foolish for not getting into the cab at once. Yet something didn't feel right to her, so Isaveth shook her head. "No, thank you."

Shrugging, the man rolled up his window and drove away. Isaveth walked back to the curb, restless with nerves and impatience. There! A tram at last. She climbed on and dropped gratefully into a seat.

As the spell-powered trolley picked up speed, Isaveth calmed herself and tried to focus. What—or who—was the connection between her troubles and J. J. Wregget's? The loss of Betinda's necklace was too cunningly timed to be coincidence, so it seemed likely that the Callenders were involved. Perhaps they worked for Glow-Mor or held some stake in the success of its rival?

The quickest way to find out would be to pay a visit to Power-Up. But Isaveth was too young to be out of school at this time of day, and any questions she asked would raise suspicion. The safer option was to look up the company in the city records office, which could give her the names of Power-Up's owners at the very least, and perhaps a listing of its directors and other employees as well.

Isaveth rode the tram to the city center, pulled the bell cord, and stepped off. The sloppy crust of snow that covered the sidewalks elsewhere was all but melted here, and grit crunched beneath her boots as she dodged past wandering shoppers, beggars, and street-boys, heading for the records office.

"I'm looking for information on Tarreton's factories," she told the clerk in her most grown-up voice, chin lowered so he could see little more than the brim of her hat. "Do you have a directory?"

"Right here," said the man, leading her to a back shelf and taking it down for her. "Anything else you need?"

"Not at present," said Isaveth with dignity, lowering herself into a chair. She was afraid to take off her gloves in case her hands looked too childish without them, so she opened the book and began clumsily turning pages.

She found the entry for Glow-Mor first, with J. J. Wregget listed as president and founder, and below it a brief history of the company since its beginnings some twenty years ago. It had grown quickly thanks to early investments from a noble named Lord Segravius and, to Isaveth's surprise, Mistress Anandri.

She ran a finger down the list of current board members, scanning one name after another. Hodgston, Bowerill, Jinh . . . none of them seemed familiar, so she leafed ahead to the entry for Power-Up and began to read.

"There you are!" A man's voice rang out across the office, and Isaveth started in alarm. She clapped the book shut and pushed back her chair, but too late: The stranger seized her elbow and yanked her to her feet.

"Sneaked out of school again, the little minx," he told the clerk confidentially as Isaveth struggled in his grip. She tried to cry out, but a charm pressed against her wrist and her whole body went numb. She could barely move, let alone speak.

"I hope my daughter hasn't been a nuisance," the stranger continued, sweeping Isaveth toward the exit. "I do apologize. Good day."

Isaveth tripped over the doorstep, but the man did not break pace. He dragged her to a waiting spell-carriage, shoved her into the back, and climbed in after her.

"Go," he told the scarf-muffled driver, and the carriage veered out from the curb. Isaveth rubbed her wrist where the sage-charm had bruised it, feeling her strength return—but she was locked in, and they were speeding too fast for her to jump anyway.

"Stop," she pleaded, tugging at the door handle. "Let me out."

"Oh, don't worry," drawled her captor. "You'll be going for a nice little walk soon."

She'd heard that voice before, Isaveth felt certain. And when the driver added in crisp but feminine tones, "Probably sooner than you'd like," her stomach lurched—they were the couple she'd overheard on the night of the ball.

But the smirk on the man's lips seemed familiar, too . . . and after what she'd just read about Power-Up, she knew why.

She'd been kidnapped by Paskin's parents.

Chapter Twenty-Three

GOVERNOR BULDAGE HAD given Esmond the week off to mourn his father, saying he needn't worry about midterms or anything else at present. But after just one day of Lady Nessa's tears, Civilla's silence, and Eryx's sober-faced hypocrisy, Esmond couldn't stand it any longer. He'd ordered an early breakfast and dashed off to school.

Yet he couldn't find Isaveth. He checked the message drop in the library and scanned the tables for her at lunch, but all he found was Eulalie Fairpont, poking glumly at her food as though hoping it would eat itself. When she got up, Esmond crossed the room to intercept her. "Where's Isaveth?"

"You haven't heard?" the girl exclaimed, then winced. "Of course you haven't. Sorry."

Everyone who talked to him was sorry, these past two

days. He'd heard the word so many times it had lost all meaning. "Heard what?" he demanded, resisting the urge to seize Eulalie by the shoulders and rattle her.

"She's been suspended. She hasn't come to school since Fastday."

"What? Why?"

"Governor Buldage won't say, and the masters aren't talking either. But Betinda's been telling everyone Isaveth stole her necklace—"

"Betinda Callender?" Esmond spun in place, scanning the tables. He'd danced with the girl at Civilla's party—her mother chaired the city arts committee, or some such—but she'd been wearing a snowflake mask and he could remember little else about her.

Not like Isaveth, with her straight thick brows and curling wedge of hair, her olive-brown skin that turned rosy when she blushed, the bow mouth that might have been coy if not for the firm, even stubborn angle of her jaw. If he'd been an artist, Esmond could have painted her without looking.

And now she was gone.

"Yes, Callender," said Eulalie. "She's such a spiteful little polecat, I wouldn't be surprised if she got Isaveth in trouble deliberately. She's been picking on her all term."

Isaveth had never said anything about that. Apart from

the day he'd caught her weeping in the library, she'd never complained about any of her fellow students at all. How much else had she left unsaid, all those times in the bell tower?

"Tell me." Esmond took Eulalie's arm, steering her out of the dining room. "From the beginning. Everything you know."

They'd taken Isaveth to a warehouse a few blocks from the harbor, stacked high with crates of Power-Up tablets ready to be shipped across the lake to the neighboring country of Federatia, or out the eastern seaway to the provinces beyond. None of the toiling laborers paused or even glanced up as the Paskins strode past, dragging the charm-numbed Isaveth between them, and shoved her into a narrow, windowless room with a wooden table, a few chairs, and a single spell-lamp dangling overhead. They tied her hands and feet to one of the chairs and stepped back to appraise her.

"So," said Missus Paskin, "you're the girl who invented Resisto-Paper. Who would have guessed? But it certainly explains why J. J. was so keen on you." She whisked off her mannish hat, absently fluffing her blond curls into shape. "I'm sorry for the ropes, but after all the trouble we had finding you, we can't risk you getting away."

Isaveth pressed her lips together. She didn't need to ask why the Paskins had kidnapped her; the real question was what they meant to do if she didn't talk.

"Look here, Miss Breck," said Mister Paskin, drawing up a chair next to her. "This doesn't have to be unpleasant. Just give us the recipe and you can go."

And then Wregget would lose his company, which would be a poor way to repay him for all the kindness he'd shown her. Glow-Mor would vanish into Power-Up and there'd be no more scholarships for commoners, let alone Moshites. "I don't know what you're talking about," said Isaveth.

The woman sighed. "Very loyal of you, I'm sure. But there's no point in lying. Someone *very* close to you already told us what we need to know."

Until that moment, Isaveth had supposed that someone at Glow-Mor must be working for the Paskins and had eavesdropped on her conversation with Wregget that morning. Yet he'd shut the door—a padded privacy door thick enough to block all sound—as soon as they entered. And apart from Esmond and her own family, there was only one person close to Isaveth who knew she'd invented Resisto-Paper. . . .

"So," continued Mister Paskin, taking a puffer from his breast pocket and tapping it on the table, "let's discuss terms. What did J. J. pay you? I'm sure we can match it, and add a little extra for your trouble."

There was no telling what these people might do to get what they wanted. But it would take more than bribery, or even threats, to make Isaveth betray a friend. She closed her stinging eyes and said nothing.

Missus Paskin made a little clucking noise of pity. "You have no idea how money works, do you? No wonder Wregget bought you so easily. Do you realize that if you'd filed a patent on that recipe instead of selling him the rights, you'd be rich by now? And there'd be no need for all this unpleasantness." Her voice dropped confidentially as she moved closer, slinging a hip over the corner of the table. "He's not worth your loyalty, my dear. Even with that scholarship, he got you cheap."

Isaveth swallowed. She'd been so thrilled to learn that Wregget wanted to buy her recipe, and so dazzled by the five imperials he'd offered, she'd never stopped to wonder if there might be a better way. She couldn't blame Papa for not thinking of it, but why hadn't Esmond?

"Of course it's too late to fix that now," the woman continued, "but there's no reason you should have to suffer. So how about this? Give us the recipe, we'll pay you double what J. J. did—*and* we'll clear up that unpleasant business at the college for you."

Blood pounded through Isaveth's temples. She felt as though the earth had shifted beneath her and there was nothing left for her to cling to, nowhere safe that she could go. "How?" she asked hoarsely.

"Oh, I'm sure we can find someone who saw the housekeeper slip that necklace into your pocket. From what I hear, she's made no secret of disliking you, so she had good reason to do it." Her red lips curved in a smile. "Help us, and you'll be back at school by the end of the week."

So Meggery wasn't part of their conspiracy—not knowingly, at any rate. That made sense: much as the housekeeper resented Isaveth, she wouldn't risk her job by planting false evidence against a student, any more than Isaveth would have risked her scholarship by stealing. That was the way of spoiled, wealthy folk like Betinda and the Paskins, who could afford to be dishonest because they had nothing to lose.

"I don't know," Isaveth mumbled. "After everything . . . I'm not sure I want to go back."

"Don't be absurd," said the man, with a languid wave of his puffer. "A girl like you going to Tarreton College? You'd be a fool to throw away a chance like that."

It was true, of course—yet she wasn't just feigning reluctance. Isaveth was tired of being the only student in her classes who knew what it felt like to go hungry, to spend nights shivering under the blankets because there wasn't enough coal, to have to keep wearing old shoes long after they were outgrown. Tired, too, of hiding her friendship with Esmond and living in fear of his brother's spies. And if Eulalie had betrayed her, she would never trust any of her schoolmates again.

"Maybe," Isaveth said thickly. "But I won't go back if it means costing an innocent woman her job. Especially since it was *your* son who put Betinda's necklace in my pocket."

A muscle jumped in Mister Paskin's cheek, and his wife sat up sharply. If they'd counted on Isaveth not guessing their identities, they knew better now.

"I see," said Missus Paskin. "Aren't we clever. Well, let me put it this way." She leaned closer, her painted face close to Isaveth's. "We are one of the most powerful families in this city. You are an insignificant little chit of no breeding whatsoever, and your father is a known radical who was recently accused of murder. Do you really think you're in a position to bargain? Give us that recipe or we'll ruin you. *That* is our final offer."

The intensity in her black-rimmed stare was terrifying: She clearly meant every word. Isaveth pressed back, squirming against the ropes that bound her—but even if she could free herself, what difference would it make? The Paskins would catch her before she'd taken a step.

What do I do? Merciful All-One, help me!

But no insight burst upon her, and no peace flooded in to wash her fears away. Isaveth gulped and burst into hiccupping sobs.

Mister Paskin shifted uneasily, tapping puffer-ash onto the floor. "Darling, why don't we step out for a moment? Let her calm down a bit, and I'm sure she'll see reason."

"We can't wait all day," snapped the woman, but he gave her a beseeching look and she sighed. "Oh, all right." She strode out and her husband followed, closing the door after them.

Isaveth rubbed her wet cheek against her shoulder, struggling for calm. She wasn't strong enough to break her bonds or flexible enough to slip out of them; there was nothing here she could use to cut herself free. Her only hope was rescue—but at this time of day, who would notice her missing, or know where to look for her even if they did?

She was slumped in the chair, eyes swollen and nose stuffed up from crying, when the door eased open and Mister Paskin slipped in. He cast a furtive glance behind him, then took out his handkerchief and began awkwardly wiping Isaveth's face.

"My wife is, er, a passionate woman. I'm sorry she frightened you. When she gets over her temper, I'm sure she'll be sorry too."

Isaveth turned her nose into the handkerchief and blew as hard as she could. The man's face spasmed in disgust, but he composed himself and folded the sodden cloth away.

"In any case," he went on reasonably, "there's no need to use threats on a bright young lady like yourself. Now you've had some time to think it over, I'm sure you recognize how short-sighted it is to risk your whole future over some silly recipe. Why, you wouldn't even be in this situation if old Wregget wasn't so greedy about keeping your invention to himself."

Or if you weren't so greedy about wanting it, thought Isaveth.

"Resisto-Paper is a great invention, and it was clever of you to discover it. But right now your recipe's only putting more money into J. J.'s already silk-lined pockets. Wouldn't it be better to share, and help all of Tarreton's spell-factories at once? Think of the new workers we could hire, once we cut our production costs. Your father, for instance."

Isaveth's head jerked up at that, and Mister Paskin gave an encouraging nod. "That's right," he said. "It's not just about Glow-Mor or Power-Up, it's what's best for everyone. If Wregget's board could see that, surely you can too. Don't let that old fox flatter you into protecting him—as my wife says, he doesn't deserve it. And you can't save him anyway."

Isaveth tensed. "What do you mean?"

Mister Paskin sat down on the table, relaxed and confident. "I mean he's going to lose his company one way or another. Lord Arvis might have been happy to let Wregget do as he pleased, but there's a new Sagelord in charge now, and he knows who his real friends are."

"So you're working for Eryx?" asked Isaveth. "Or is he working for you?"

The man smiled, as though her ignorance charmed him. "Never mind that," he said. "Let's keep it simple. Tell me the recipe, and you can go home right now. I'll even call you a taxi."

So much for doubling Wregget's offer, or restoring her to the school's good graces. The more these people bargained with her, the less she had to win. "What if I don't?"

Paskin's father shrugged. "Then we send J. J. a note telling him you've been kidnapped—and that if he doesn't give up the recipe we'll kill you."

Chapter Twenty-Four

"MANDER GHATAJ, ISN'T IT?"

The boy glanced up and turned a shade paler. "Milord," he said, starting to rise.

"No need to be formal." Esmond circled the table, pulling out a chair for Eulalie and another for himself. The librarian made a shushing gesture, but Esmond ignored him. "We're practically family, if the way Eryx looks at your sister is any indication."

He'd meant it as dry humor, but Mander froze like a hunted deer. "What?" asked Esmond, and then it struck him. What had Isaveth said about the oath Eryx had sworn to Civilla? Something about not paying any more attention to Delicia after the ball than before. . . .

"They're engaged, aren't they?" Eulalie breathed. "They were just waiting for Lord Arvis's blessing to announce it."

"Except," Esmond finished slowly, "he said no. Or at least, not yet. That's why your sister was unhappy."

Jaw clenched, Mander began stuffing books into his bag, but Esmond stopped him. "Even if it's true, it doesn't matter right now. I'm here to find out what happened to Isaveth."

The boy's shoulders drooped, and he let the bag go. "I tried to tell the masters she couldn't have taken the necklace. But Betinda and her friends said I was lying."

No surprise there. "Eulalie says you've stood up for Isaveth before. When did Betinda start bullying her?"

Mander said nothing.

"Look," Esmond said with growing impatience, "I'm trying to find out how Isaveth got suspended from the college and if there's any way to get her back. Do you want to help, or do you only care about toadying up to my brother?"

"If I did," Mander shot back, "I'd have told *your brother* when I saw you talking to Isaveth in the library. But she asked me not to, so I didn't."

So he did have a spine after all. "Good for you," said Esmond. "Tell me about Betinda."

Mander glanced at Eulalie, who gave him an encouraging nod. Then he adjusted his spectacles, cleared his throat, and explained how he had ended up sitting behind Isaveth in Calculation. His voice was level, but

Esmond saw the spark of anger in the boy's eyes and felt his own fury rising to match it.

"I'm a fool," Esmond said bitterly, when Mander had finished. "I knew it wasn't easy for her after Su wrote that article, but I didn't realize they'd turned on her so soon." He slid his fingers under his half glass, pressing away a twinge of headache. "Why would they single Isaveth out even before they knew she was Moshite? And why would anyone hate her enough to do *this*?"

A gloomy silence descended over the table, until Eulalie spoke. "Paskin danced three times with Betinda at your sister's ball," she pointed out. "And they've been seeing a lot of each other since."

Tadeus Paskin. The boy who, according to Eulalie, resented Isaveth for winning the Glow-Mor scholarship and spoiling his five-regal bet. There was more to it, though; there had to be. "Paskin," muttered Esmond. "Why is that name familiar? Who are his parents?"

"His mother's a shipping heiress, I think," said Eulalie. "And they own some sort of spell-factory. . . ."

"Power-Up!" Esmond's fist thumped the table. The librarian popped up, ready to scold him, but he was already halfway to the door.

"Where are you going?" Eulalie asked, running after him. "Can we come?"

Mander had followed as well. Esmond looked from the boy's sober face to the girl's eager one and shook his head.

"Not yet," he said. He needed to think about what he'd just learned, collect some more pieces of the puzzle . . . and one of those pieces, he suspected, would be waiting under a loose brick in Sage Allum's Park. "When I need you, I'll let you know."

Isaveth gaped at Mister Paskin, too appalled to speak. She'd known these people were greedy and ruthless, but she'd never thought they'd go as far as murder. . . .

Except there was a chance they already had. What if they'd poisoned Lord Arvis because they knew he planned to stop them taking over Glow-Mor?

"But you can't," Isaveth spluttered. "When Mister Wregget gets the note, he'll know who it came from. He'll go to the Lawkeepers—"

"Who will dutifully investigate, yes," said Mister Paskin. "But they won't find enough evidence to trouble us. I have that on the very highest authority." He gave her a wolfish smile. "Think how upset old J. J. will be when he realizes he's put a sweet young girl in danger. I don't think he'd let you die just to keep his recipe secret, do you?"

Isaveth closed her eyes in despair. If she couldn't

escape, couldn't bargain, and couldn't be sure her captors wouldn't hurt her, there was only one thing to do. "All right. I'll tell you."

The man leaped up. "Laraine!"

Missus Paskin strolled into the room and sat down, taking a notebook out of her purse. "Go on," she said. "I'm ready."

Isaveth's shoulders drooped. She hung her head and whispered, "Null-pepper."

The woman leaned closer, lead-point hovering over the page. "What did you say?"

"Six parts null-pepper," Isaveth repeated huskily, "to one part magewort. That's what you need to make Resisto-Paper."

Missus Paskin raised a sculpted brow at her husband, who answered with a shrug. "Thank you, Miss Breck," he told her. "We'll have our people test your recipe, and get back to you if it turns out."

Panic fluttered in Isaveth's chest. She'd thought to buy her freedom, or least a more comfortable prison. "You're leaving me here?"

"Of course," said Missus Paskin. "We're not fools, you know, and we have business matters to attend to. But don't worry," she added slyly as she turned off the spell-lamp, "you're quite safe here. For now."

Then she shut the door and left Isaveth alone in the dark.

Isaveth's note was waiting in the old letter drop, just as Esmond had hoped—and feared. She'd been suspended for three days, and he'd been too busy mourning a man who'd never cared two cits for him to realize his best friend was in trouble. Esmond sat on the edge of the fountain, its stony chill seeping through his overcoat, and read the message over again. Then he jogged back to the main road and hailed a taxi.

Overnight the temperature had soared above freezing, an unseasonable thaw that made the roads filthy as well as slick. A shroud of gray mist hung over the rooftops as the cab splashed into the factory-dotted neighborhood known as Gardentown—named not for its flowers, but for the pathetic little vegetable plots its residents cultivated to survive. At last they turned down Cabbage Street, bumping over the ruts and potholes, and halted in front of Isaveth's tiny cottage. "Wait here," Esmond told the driver, and ran to knock on her front door.

No answer. He peered through the window, cupping both hands around his eye for a better view, but inside all was dark.

Where would Isaveth go, in this weather? Frowning,

Esmond returned to the taxi and directed it to the shops on Grand Street. Yet even after searching the dry grocer's, the butcher's, and several more local businesses, he found no trace of her. Frustrated, Esmond was about to climb back into the cab when he caught sight of a skinny girl stomping up the far side of the street, fists clenched as though daring the whole world to fight her.

"Lilet!" he shouted, and her head snapped up. She splashed across the road to meet him.

"Splendid boxer's eye you've got there," Esmond said, taking her by the chin to admire it. "Is that why they sent you home?"

Lilet pushed his hand away. "Maybe. Why aren't *you* in school?"

"I'm looking for Isaveth, but she isn't home. Do you know where she might have gone?"

The eye that wasn't swollen shut narrowed in suspicion. "Of course Vettie isn't home. She's supposed to be at the college."

So her family didn't know she'd been suspended. "Ah, yes," he said quickly. "I must have missed her somehow." He turned toward the taxi, but Lilet grabbed his arm.

"Something's wrong, isn't it? You're worried. Is Isaveth in trouble?"

It was tempting to put her off with some light-hearted

answer, but Lilet was too sharp to be fooled easily. If he lied to her, he might well regret it.

"I don't know," Esmond admitted. "But I'm starting to think she might be."

Lilet chewed her lip. "You'd better come home with me, then. Maybe she left a note."

"Help me! Please, someone, help!"

Isaveth had shouted herself hoarse, but no one answered, and she felt miserably sure that they never would. If none of the workers had reacted when they saw the Paskins dragging her through the warehouse, why would they take pity on her now?

"Help," she whispered. The rope around her wrists chafed, her ankles throbbed, and her bladder felt as full as her stomach was empty. But the Paskins wouldn't care about that.

Isaveth drew a long breath and screamed until her air ran out. Then she sagged, panting, and prayed for an answer. But all she heard were clomping boots and muffled voices, the distant creak of a pulley, a clatter of hooves and cart wheels as a new load arrived on the warehouse floor.

Desperately she cast her mind back over the last fifty-six episodes of *Auradia Champion*, remembering all the ways the intrepid Lady Justice had escaped captivity. But most involved her having a secret charm or weapon hidden in her clothing, and the rest required some brave ally like Wil Avenham or Peacemaker Otsik finding her at the last moment. Isaveth had no such advantages . . . and, it seemed, even fewer friends than she'd supposed.

Nobody likes a girl who can't keep secrets.

Isaveth yanked her wrists against the rope, focusing on the pain to keep back fresh tears. Had Eulalie truly betrayed her? Had she been spying for Isaveth's enemies, willingly or unwillingly, all along? Isaveth didn't want to believe it. Yet her mind kept returning to the memory of Betinda talking to Eulalie in the dining hall, and how evasive her friend had been afterward. What if she'd been less upset with what Betinda had said to her than ashamed of what she'd said herself?

Misery squeezed Isaveth's throat, but she swallowed it down and tried to think of a new plan. Now that her eyes had adjusted, the room wasn't completely dark; she could make out the shadows of the furniture and the dim outline of the door. If she could get close enough to rattle the knob, maybe the workers would think she was escaping and come to check? With grim determination Isaveth began rocking her chair from side to side, twisting her body to shuffle it forward.

There were a few heart-stopping moments when the chair teetered, and one where it almost crashed over. Still Isaveth persisted, inching her chair past the table and along the wall until she reached her goal. Licking her dry lips, she bent to inspect the doorknob. It was too smooth to turn without a hand free, but perhaps she could unlock the thumb-turn with her teeth . . .

She was leaning forward, mouth open to try it, when the knob rattled and the door swung inward. Startled, Isaveth jerked back—and the chair tipped with her, balancing on two legs for one sickening instant before toppling over.

"Miss!" cried a man's voice, but it was the last thing Isaveth heard before she hit the floor.

Chapter Twenty-Five

RUMMAGING THROUGH ISAVETH'S satchel of neatly organized and labeled spells made Esmond feel guilty as a grave robber, but he needed to know what, if anything, she'd taken with her. Had she been at all concerned for her safety when she left the cottage? Or had she gone out unarmed, believing she had nothing to fear?

It was impossible to be certain, but he was leaning toward the latter. The main compartment appeared fully stocked, with at least one of every kind of Common Magic spell Isaveth had made so far. There were even a couple of soap-tablets in case of . . . what? A cleaning emergency?

"What's this?" asked Lilet, plunging a hand past him and seizing a small cloth bag. Before he could stop her she'd dumped Isaveth's sage-charms onto the table.

"Don't touch those," said Esmond, more sharply than

he'd intended, and Lilet gave him an exasperated look.

"I'm not *stupid*," she said. "They're Sagery, aren't they? How do they work?"

Isaveth hadn't taken any charms with her either. He could still see one of every type she'd made so far, including the warding- and sealing-charms he'd crafted for her. Esmond started to pick up the silvery squares, then paused in surprise as his fingers met an unexpected texture. Two of the charms were coated with a rubbery, herb-flecked substance he'd never seen before.

One of Isaveth's experiments? Curious, he pulled out his charm-glass for a closer look.

There was no trace of magic coming from the charms, not even the faintest glow. In fact, if he hadn't known better, he'd have thought they'd never held any power at all. . . .

Lilet eyed him warily. "Why are you grinning?"

She'd done it. Somehow Isaveth had discovered a spell that would cancel out Eryx's charms. Could that be why she'd left the house? Could she be searching for Esmond at this very moment, eager to tell him the good news?

His elation fizzled as he realized that made no sense. If she'd wanted to share her discovery, she'd have brought the charms along to show him. Instead, she'd left the house early that morning (said Lilet), only to return home by the coal lane and enter through the back door (as shown by the melting footprints on the step). She'd stamped the snow off her boots (the mat was still damp), walked to the front (where she'd left the salt-stained ghost of a puddle on the floor), then turned around and went out again. Yet she couldn't have thought she'd be gone long, or she would have left a note. . . .

A note. Esmond dropped the charms into the bag and spun around, staring at the mail slot in the front door.

"Someone sent her a message," he mused aloud. Someone who knew Isaveth had been suspended and wanted to talk to her about it, yet whom Isaveth trusted so completely she hadn't even thought of protecting herself.

Someone like J. J. Wregget.

"Miss! Can you hear me?"

The man spoke softly, but to Isaveth's ringing ears he might as well have shouted. She squirmed against the ropes that bound her, fiery horses galloping through her head.

"That was a nasty crack you gave yourself," said her visitor, easing her chair upright. His square face was lost in shadow, but she could make out his knitted cap and the breadth of his workman's shoulders. "What were you doing right in front of the door?"

"Please," Isaveth mumbled. "I want to go home."

The man straightened up. "Sorry, miss. I got a family to feed, so I do what the boss tells me. I only came to see if you need the toilet."

"Yes," gasped Isaveth, and the workman bent to untie her.

It would have been the perfect chance to bolt, if she'd had the strength. But her head still thundered and her legs felt weak as a baby's. She had to cling to the man's arm as he led her down the corridor to the toilet.

It was scarcely bigger than a broom closet and stank as though no one had cleaned it in weeks. Light filtered through a single vent above her, but it was too high to reach, and so small that even Mimmi would have struggled to get through.

There was no point in lingering, so Isaveth hurried through her business and turned to wash her hands. As she reached for the tap, she noticed the raw marks the ropes had left around her wrists. They didn't hurt much more than a scraped knee, or the burns she'd given herself spell-baking. But they *looked* painful, and maybe . . .

Isaveth grabbed a corner of her woolen overcoat, gritted her teeth, and scrubbed her wrists until they bled. Then she limped out into the corridor, where the workman was waiting. She made no resistance as he steered her back to the room—but when he pointed to the chair again, she held up her hands so he could see them.

"Please," she said in her most pathetic-sounding voice, "could you tie the ropes over my sleeves this time? My wrists hurt."

The man started, then tipped back Isaveth's hat and gazed into her face. "Sages, you're just a kid! What you go snatching the missus's purse for? You oughta be in school."

No wonder no one had come to help her. "I didn't," Isaveth protested. "They kidnapped me—" But a big hand clapped over her mouth before she could finish.

"They said you'd try to talk your way out," the workman muttered. "But I'm not listening. You sit here nice and quiet until the Lawkeepers come to get you, and you can tell them all the stories you like." He covered her mouth until she stopped squealing, then pushed her into the chair and pulled her arms behind her back. Isaveth wilted, feeling more hopeless than ever—but then she felt her coat-sleeves bunch against her wrists and knew she'd gotten through to him after all.

Heart pattering, she sat meekly while he bound her ankles, and waited until he left and shut the door behind him. Then she began to wriggle, trying to pull her arms out of the sleeves.

He'd tied the ropes snug, so it took several minutes

of twisting and flexing to find the right angle. But she managed to slip one hand out, and after that it was easy to release the other. Her ankles came next, and Isaveth was free.

Now for the door, she told herself, and set to work.

"Well, this is an honor." With a gesture Wregget invited Esmond to sit as his secretary retreated, stooped to adjust the carpet, and shut the door. "How can I help you, milord?"

"I'm looking for Isaveth Breck," said Esmond. "Have you seen her?"

The older man blinked. "As a matter of fact, yes. She came to my office this morning."

"At your invitation?"

"Well, that's the odd thing." Wregget scratched his chin. "I hadn't sent for her, but she thought I had. She offered to show me the message, but when Tambor brought her coat it wasn't there."

That was odd. Suspicious, even. "What did you talk about? If I may ask."

Wregget sat down behind the desk, swiveling to face him. "Well, I don't know how much you've heard, but Miss Breck's not the only one who's been having some troubles of late. . . ."

As the president explained about Power-Up's attempt to take over Glow-Mor, Esmond grew restless. Motioning to the other man to keep talking, he rose and strolled about the office. When he reached the entrance he paused, frowning at the carpet, then seized the door and flung it open.

Wregget's secretary leaped up, but Esmond grabbed the man's wrist and pushed his sleeve back, baring the charm-band he wore beneath it. A slender wire ran from the bracelet to the floor, where it ended in a tiny shard of sound-crystal.

"I never wanted to," the man gabbled, poise disintegrating as Esmond dangled the magical listening device in front of him. "They said they'd tell my wife about the money if I didn't—"

"Oh, Tambor," Wregget groaned. "And I thought you were the one man I could trust."

Once Isaveth had her hands free, unlocking the door proved simple: The trick was getting out of the building. The crates were stacked up against the wall, so she couldn't slip behind them, and once she left the shelter of the corridor there was only one way out—straight up the aisle of the warehouse, where a gang of brawny laborers hauled boxes, loaded wheely carts, and wrapped up pallets of freight for transport. She was crouching by the mouth of the hallway, wondering if she could hide somewhere and creep out after everyone had gone home, when a shadow fell over her and a big, hairy hand seized her by the collar.

"Must have forgot your knots, Lanzy," her captor crowed, dragging Isaveth out into the light. "Our little sneak-thief's broke out."

Isaveth stomped on the man's feet, but her boots were no match for his stout ones. He gave her a shake that set her head spinning and shoved her across the floor toward Lanzy.

"Truss her up properly this time," he ordered. "And gag her, too. I'll get a crate ready."

Isaveth yelped as the bigger man seized her sore wrists and started lashing them together. "Let me go, I'm innocent! I haven't stolen anything!"

"If that's so," Lanzy said gruffly, "you've nothing to be afraid of. The Lawkeepers'll sort you out." He lifted Isaveth onto a stack of boxes and tied her ankles.

"Then where are they? The Paskins locked me in that room ages ago, but I don't see any Keepers coming. Do you?"

Lanzy hesitated.

"Ask the clerk at the city records office—that's where I

was when the Paskins kidnapped me. They want to hold me for ransom so they can force the president of Glow-Mor to resign."

The workman snorted. "That's a big story. Who are you supposed to be, then? Old Glow-Britches' darling daughter?"

"No, I'm Isaveth Breck." She was about to explain further, but Lanzy shoved a rag into her mouth.

"Right now, miss, I don't care if you're the Little Queen herself. I've got work to do, and a mug of stout waiting at the end of it." He heaved her over his shoulder and marched out into the aisle. "Got that crate ready, Barto?"

"Esmond?" Civilla stopped halfway across the lobby as he strode in, carrying his bulging school bag over one shoulder and two satchels of Isaveth's on the other. "What's all that for? You look like you're going on an expedition."

She wasn't far wrong, but Esmond had no intention of telling her about it. He had to find Isaveth right away. He started past her, but Civilla caught his arm.

"We need to talk," she said, low and earnest. "I know you don't think I understand, but—"

"Yes, fine, lecture me later!" He shook her off and sprinted up the stairs.

"Esmond, wait!"

Her distress sounded genuine, but he ignored it. Slamming his bedroom door, he dropped the bags onto the carpet, flipped open his knapsack, and started pulling out the clothes he'd bought from a relief shop on the way home.

His father had made him charm-swear that he would never dress up as a street-boy again. But magical oaths only lasted six months at the best of times, and Lord Arvis's death had ended it even sooner. Until Eryx found a new way to compel his obedience, Esmond was free.

He kicked off his school slacks and tugged on the musty-smelling trousers, then traded his linen shirt and waistcoat for a fraying pullover and grease-stained navvy's jacket. The leather eye patch Quiz had worn was long gone, so he combed his hair over his scarred eye with his fingers and tugged on a knitted cap to keep it in place. A handful of soot from the hearth, liberally applied to clothes and skin, and Esmond's disguise was complete.

He was halfway out the window, a float-charm gripped in one hand, when the bedroom door swung open. Blue eyes blazing, Civilla crossed the carpet in three strides and seized him by the collar.

"Not this time, little brother," she said tightly. "I need you to listen to me *now*."

Chapter Twenty-Six

THEY DUMPED ISAVETH into the wooden crate, where she landed on a heap of filthy sacking. She screeched against her gag in protest, but Barto, the shorter and hairier of the two men, only grinned at her before hammering the lid shut.

There was no point in fighting any longer. All the workers knew she was here, but if it troubled them they showed no sign of it. Isaveth gave one last kick at the crate and collapsed, spent.

As she lay there, she caught snatches of what sounded like an argument between Lanzy and his companion. But Barto must have won, because it was his voice she heard giving orders to the other men: "Ziyan! Poyle! Take our little friend down to the *Raider*, and make sure she's loaded before you go. Boss's orders."

The workers tramped over to Isaveth's crate and hefted

it up. They lugged her across the warehouse, arguing good-naturedly about whether the Harbortown Sharks or the Lockland Gaters had the better chances of winning the Cup this year, then shoved Isaveth's crate into the back of a wagon and drove away.

The journey only lasted a few minutes, but by the time they stopped Isaveth had lost all sense of direction. The wagon opened and a chill breeze swirled around her crate. More painful jostles and thumps followed, a rasp and a metallic click, and finally a hoarse shout: *"Take 'er up!"*

With a sickening lurch, Isaveth's crate swung airborne. They were loading her onto a ship—but what kind? If it was one of the short-haul freighters that carried goods across Lake Colonia, Isaveth would have an unpleasant night ahead of her, but at least there'd be a chance of escaping in the morning. If it was one of the great ocean-bound cargoes, though, she'd die of cold and thirst long before they reached port. Even if the Paskins knew she'd lied about her recipe, would they really be as cruel as that?

Two bells later, shivering in the darkness of the ship's hold, Isaveth still had no answer. Every part of her ached, the gag in her mouth was sodden with spit and tears, and she wished with all her heart that she'd told someone where she was going this morning. She'd heard a dock bell clanging a few minutes ago, echoing the peals from the great clock tower at the top of Council House: It was past six now, and Papa and her sisters must be getting anxious. But Tarreton was a huge city, and even if the Lawkeepers cared enough to search for an insignificant Moshite girl whose father was too poor to bribe them, they'd never find Isaveth here.

It was so cold. She still had her coat and boots, but her hat had tumbled off when Lanzy dumped her into the crate, and her gloves were stuffed uselessly into her pocket. She'd curled up as tight as the crate allowed her, but the slats that let her breathe also let in the dank air of the hold, and no matter how she squirmed, she couldn't get warm.

She'd pushed the gag with her tongue, trying to dislodge it. She'd kicked at the crate until every bone in her legs felt bruised. She'd reminded herself of all the stories she knew about Auradia and other brave women like her, and prayed to the All-One to give her courage like theirs. But she hadn't eaten since breakfast, her wrists stung like they'd been wrapped in thorn-wire, and Isaveth was too exhausted to fight any more.

"I'm sorry, Papa," she mumbled, and closed her eyes.

Half dozing, she'd lost track of time when she heard

footsteps above her, and the groan of rusty hinges as a hatch opened and shut. It sounded like a dockhand making the rounds, so Isaveth thought little of it until something thumped into the hold beside her and a voice spoke out of the darkness: "Isaveth?"

Hope blazed up in her like a trodden fire-tablet, and she snapped awake. "Help!" she screamed, though the handkerchief choked it to a feeble moan, surely too weak to carry. She thrashed inside the crate, kicking and pounding the walls with all her might, until with a splintering noise the lid popped open and the blue glow of a light-charm flooded in. Esmond—no, *Quiz*—stooped over her, pry-bar in hand and his blond hair falling over one eye.

"It's all right," he said huskily, pulling Isaveth's gag out and cupping a hand against her cheek. "I'm here, you're safe now. Well, saf*er,* anyway."

"How?" gasped Isaveth. "How did you find me?"

"It's a long story. I'll tell you later." Pulling a knife from his belt, he sawed through Isaveth's bonds, then lifted her from the crate. Her legs wobbled as he set her down, but he kept an arm around her waist, holding her steady until the pins and needles began to fade. "Can you walk? We need to get out of here."

Isaveth nodded, and Esmond helped her across the

near-empty hold to a metal ladder. It was closer than she'd expected; it must be quite a small freighter after all. But her muscles felt watery, her wrists too raw and stiff to bend. How could she climb all the way up to the deck?

"Here," said Esmond, dropping into a crouch. "Get on my back. I'll carry you."

It was even colder on the deck of the freighter, but Isaveth was so glad to be free she didn't care. As they huddled together in the lee of the ship's wheelhouse, waiting for her strength to return, Esmond explained how he'd found her.

"Tambor told us everything he knew about the Paskins, but he wasn't sure where they'd taken you. I wasted a bell or so snooping around the Power-Up factory with a fake parcel under my arm, pretending to be a message-boy, before I realized the warehouse made more sense. It was getting late, so I hitched a ride over on the last delivery wagon and started asking people outright if they'd seen you."

"You're lucky they didn't toss you into the lake." Or rather, onto the ice. What a gobblewit she'd been to worry that the ship might sail away with her: The harbor had been frozen for weeks.

"They almost did," Esmond said. "One big workman

dragged me out of the warehouse with a zeal that was—er—quite convincing." He rubbed his throat ruefully. "I thought I was done for. But once we were out of sight he let go and asked why I wanted you. I told him you were a schoolmate of mine who'd been kidnapped, and that was all it took to win him over."

So she'd gotten through to Lanzy after all. "He told you where to find me?"

"He did, but I had to hang about waiting for the dock-hands to go off shift so I could sneak aboard." Esmond shuffled sideways, peering around the corner of the wheelhouse. "Seems pretty quiet now, though. Think you're feeling up to—"

"Shh." Isaveth grabbed his arm. "I hear something."

Voices echoed across the dockside, rough and indistinct. Then a burly figure staggered out of a laneway, flanked by five brutish-looking workers armed with heavy tools, and Isaveth caught her breath in dismay.

The captive man was Lanzy.

"Boss won't be pleased if his little bird's flown away," growled Barto, prodding Lanzy ahead with his crowbar. "You'll be lucky to keep your hide after this, let alone your job."

"I told you, I didn't—"

"Save it, Lanzy. I don't care." Barto spoke a few curt

words to the other men, who seized Lanzy, dragged him to a bollard, and forced him to sit while they lashed him to it. "Should have known you were too soft to do a real man's work."

"You mean beating on a one-eyed street kid, or tying up a little girl?" Lanzy shot back, and Barto drove the hooked end of the crowbar into his stomach. He groaned and slumped, all defiance gone.

"Get on board," Barto told two of the men, jerking his head at the freighter. "Check the hold and make sure she's still there."

Esmond swore softly. "Time to move," he muttered as he crept back to Isaveth. "It'll be tricky with this thaw, but we'll have to chance it."

Below, the chain-ladder rattled against the ship's side as the two thugs began to climb. "Chance what?" Isaveth whispered, but Esmond touched a finger to his lips for silence. Half-crouching, he held out his hand.

Isaveth took it, trying to ignore the jellylike feeling in her legs, and they crept toward the prow of the freighter. Behind them, the clattering grew louder and the first man landed on the deck with a thump. He flicked on a spell-torch and played it across the deck, its yellow beam sweeping toward them.

Ducking low in the shadow of the wheelhouse,

Esmond scrabbled in his pocket and pressed a charm onto the heels of each of his boots. Then he stood up gingerly on tiptoe and slipped an arm around Isaveth's waist.

"By Sage Trofim," he murmured, and Isaveth clutched him in alarm—but it was too late. Esmond rocked back on his heels, grabbed the rail with his free hand, and vaulted them both over.

Isaveth hid her face against his jacket, half-certain they'd go rocketing off into the sky, then drop like an anchor onto the ice below. But Esmond clearly knew some trick to using charms that she didn't, because they arced smoothly away from the ship's dark prow and landed with barely a crunch on the lake's surface.

"Stand on my boots," he whispered. "The ice here is weak—I'll have to float us both across."

He wasn't exaggerating. Cracks webbed out around them, spidering in all directions. Isaveth stepped onto Esmond's toes and hugged him tight as he skated toward the shoreline, propelling them forward with slow, cautious strokes.

High above, a hatch banged open, and a hoarse voice shouted, "She's gone! He broke her out!"

"Search the ship!" yelled Barto. "We'll check the dockside. They can't have gone far."

Isaveth bit her lip, silently urging Esmond to go faster. They had almost reached the shelter of a neighboring pier when headlamps shone out across the dockside, and a carriage door slammed. Isaveth stood on tiptoe, straining to see over Esmond's shoulder as Mister Paskin strode onto the quay.

Barto rushed to meet him, pointing first to the slumped and silent Lanzy, then the ship. She couldn't hear their conversation, but she didn't need to: Impatience was written in every line of Mister Paskin's silhouette. He waved Barto away and stepped forward, cupping his hands around his mouth as he called up to the ship.

"You may as well give up, kids. There's nowhere for you to run. Why don't you come down, and I'll get you something nice and warm?"

"Like a bullet, no doubt," Esmond muttered, pushing off for another glide. But his boots scraped ice, and it turned into a stumble. The float-charms' magic had worn off.

"Run!" Esmond gasped, shoving Isaveth away, then flailed and fell hard on one knee. The ice crackled—but Isaveth had already skidded into the shadow of the pier, safe from view. She spun and reached out for Esmond.

He hadn't just tripped, as she'd first thought. He'd flopped onto his belly and was crawling toward her on his elbows, a jagged starburst of dark water behind him.

His leg had plunged straight through the ice into the frigid lake below.

She had to get him to safety before Barto's men spotted them. Already their torch-beams were flashing along the shore. Isaveth stretched out flat to grab Esmond's wrists, ignoring the fresh pain in her own, and dragged him beneath the pier.

He was soaked from the hip down. Isaveth pulled off her gloves and tried to undo his bootlace, but the frozen knot refused to budge.

"Leave it," Esmond whispered, but she could feel him shivering. He pushed himself back into the darkness, and she crawled after him as the workmen stalked the wharf above. The deep overhang should make it impossible to spot them, but if their pursuers climbed down . . .

"Just the ice breaking up," said one of the men at last. "Come on, boss's waiting," and they trotted back toward the freighter. Isaveth exhaled and began to slide in the other direction, but Esmond grabbed her shoulder.

"C-can't go," he said through chattering teeth. "G-got to help Lanzy."

Esmond was right: They couldn't just abandon the man. Yet if they stayed here much longer they'd freeze. Isaveth tugged off her knitted scarf and started rolling up Esmond's trouser leg to wrap it around him.

"No, don't. You need it." He shifted onto one hip, digging into his pocket. "Warming-charm in here somewhere."

"We can't, it'll melt the ice." Now she was shivering too.

Esmond blew out a weary breath. "Course not. Stupid of me. Sorry."

Isaveth wound the scarf around his leg and tugged the half-frozen pant leg over it. She could hear the occasional shout from the men searching the freighter and dockside, but they were too far away for her to make out the words. Pulling her knees up against her chest, she squeezed closer to Esmond. *Please let them give up. Please let them go away. . . .*

Esmond put an arm around her. She could feel him trembling and knew she was doing likewise, but she was glad of the extra warmth, however slight. *Please, All-One, keep us safe and bring us home again.*

"Are you praying?"

She must have whispered the words without knowing it. Isaveth nodded, shy.

"Huh. Didn't know it was that easy."

"Really?" She twisted, trying to see his expression, but he was nothing more than an outline in the dark. "You've never prayed?"

Esmond shrugged. "Not like that, just talking. Anyway

we never went to temple much. Father wasn't . . . he didn't . . ." He cleared his throat and fell silent.

Isaveth felt a sudden yearning to comfort him. She reached out, and her fingers brushed his scar.

"Don't." He jerked his head away. "S'ugly."

"It's not," said Isaveth, with a rush of protective anger. "It's *you*." Impulsively she stretched up and kissed his cheek. "Thank you for saving me, Esmond."

He swallowed. "Isaveth . . ."

Whatever he'd meant to say was interrupted by distant shouting, accompanied by the clatter and thump of workers climbing off the ship. An argument broke out on the dockside, Mister Paskin snapping orders while Barto and his men barked and whined in protest. Then came the sound of a gunshot, and an abrupt, horrifying silence.

Isaveth flinched, but Esmond gripped her arm. They stared across the frozen lake as a limp body rolled off the dock by the freighter, hit the ice with a shattering crack, and tumbled into the deadly waters below.

"No," she whimpered. "Please, no, not Lanzy—"

Esmond pressed the scarred side of his face against Isaveth's, his soft hair brushing her cheek. He held her tightly as the workmen yelped and scattered, a carriage door slammed, and with a crackle of tires on gravel, Mister Paskin drove away.

Chapter Twenty-Seven

THE DOCK BY the *Raider* stood empty, silent except for the soft lapping of water against the hole in the ice that had become Lanzy's grave. Like Mister Paskin, Barto and his fellow workmen had vanished; only the sagging loops of rope around the bollard and a dark stain at its base showed that a man had been murdered there.

"He had a family," said Isaveth, her voice thick from crying. "He told me so."

Esmond put his arm around her shoulders. "The Paskins will get what they deserve," he said. "And so will Eryx. I promise."

She scrubbed her eyes with the back of her glove, wishing she had a handkerchief. "You sound confident."

"With good reason, for once. I've got a plan—but we've got to get moving or we'll miss our chance. Come on."

They limped away from the dockside, leaning on each other like a pair of wounded soldiers. All the while Isaveth kept glancing over her shoulder, afraid that Barto or one of his companions would reappear. But they reached the main road in safety, and when Esmond fired off his cab-hailer, a taxi appeared as quickly as though he'd conjured it.

"Rollingdale Court," he said, and flashed a money note at the driver, who lost his skeptical expression at once. Esmond opened the door for Isaveth, and the two of them climbed in.

"I can't take you home yet," he said, pulling a warming-charm from his pocket. "I know your family's worried, but you're not safe there as long as the Paskins are looking for you."

After what she'd seen tonight, Isaveth couldn't argue. She nodded, waiting for Esmond to say the invocation as he broke the charm. But he only held his hand over the pieces a moment, then glanced up and flashed her a smile.

The charm must have been a strong one, because all at once Isaveth felt as flushed as she had on her first visit to J. J. Wregget's office. She slid toward the door and started unbuttoning her coat as Esmond spoke again.

"I've got your satchel of spells back at the mansion,

and I grabbed that old journal Lilet said you'd been using. Do you have any of that sticky stuff left, or do you need to make more?"

Her fingers stilled on the last button. "What sticky stuff?"

As the taxi splashed through the slush-covered streets toward Rollingdale, Esmond explained what he'd discovered about Isaveth's curse-breaking potion, taking the two charms out of his pocket to show her. He was right: The spell had worked after all—as she'd have seen for herself, if she'd only let them dry first.

"I poured it all out," Isaveth groaned. "I thought it was useless. And if I can't go home—"

"That," said Esmond, "is the least of our problems. I brought your spell-baking ingredients, too." He unwound her scarf from his leg and began kneading his chilled muscles. "Now that's settled, let me tell you the plan. . . ."

Isaveth stared into the mirror over the dressing table, amazed at her own transformation. The girl gazing back at her looked years older, and hardly like Urias Breck's daughter at all.

Half a bell ago, Esmond had brought Isaveth into the mansion through the servants' quarters and introduced her to a stern-faced woman named Olina. She'd drawn a hot bath for Isaveth and let her soak while she whisked her dirty clothes away, exchanging them for a long-sleeved maid's dress and white apron.

Once Isaveth was presentable, Olina led her down the corridor to a room with a quilt-covered bed on one side and a dressing table on the other, bandaged her sore wrists so neatly they looked like an extension of her starched cuffs, and sat her in front of the mirror while she pinned Isaveth's wet hair into finger waves. A few disguising strokes of eye paint and lip tint, a white cap to cover her crown, and Isaveth's transformation was complete. As long as she kept her head down and her eyes meekly lowered, she would be just another servant.

"Now," said Olina, handing her a pair of slippers, "I will show you to the kitchen."

It was getting late in the evening, and most of the day-servants had finished up their duties and gone home. A pale-skinned girl washing pots in the great sink glanced up as they walked in, but one look from Olina made her blanch and go back to scrubbing.

Isaveth's satchel waited by the stove for her, as Esmond had promised. He'd run upstairs to make a couple of calls and change his clothing—as he'd said, it would be a pity to alarm their guests. But they'd gone over the plan twice in the taxi, and Isaveth knew what she had to do. She opened the country-mage's journal, unpacked her ingredients, and set to work.

Esmond was pacing the lounge when his sister came downstairs, gowned in violet with a softly gathered bodice and beaded fringes all over the skirt. She looked lovely, but fragile—in fact, very like their mother. That was, until she pursed her lips in displeasure and marched over to smooth Esmond's hair and tug his neck cloth into shape.

"There," she said, appraising him critically. "Almost respectable. Is that the door?"

The first guest to arrive was Eulalie's father, clearly bemused to be invited to drinks at the Sagelord's mansion when the family was still in mourning. But he took the glass Civilla offered him and settled into an armchair as the doorbell chimed again.

J. J. Wregget and his wife came next. The president of Glow-Mor had regained his ruddy color, and he shook Esmond's hand with such vigor that his half glass nearly fell off—but then he and Perline excused themselves and went to join Lady Nessa in her indoor garden.

The third arrival was Delicia Ghataj, looking appropriately grave and concerned for Civilla's welfare, but glowing with an inner radiance that made Esmond want to kick himself for not seeing the truth about her and Eryx at once. She had no idea what was coming, and it almost made him feel sorry for her.

Governor Buldage turned up soon afterward, followed a few minutes later by Su Amaraq, so afire with curiosity it was a wonder she didn't combust. They'd both received their drinks and were sitting down when the front door opened for the last time, and Missus Paskin walked in. She gave her coat to the butler, crossed to the lounge—and stopped, her porcelain features blank. "Where's Lord Eryx?"

"On his way, I believe." Civilla lifted a crystal decanter from the cart. "Would you like a drink while you wait?"

The woman hesitated, clearly discomfited to see so many guests, then pasted on a smile. "Why not?" she said, and sat down.

"Missus Paskin?" asked Esmond earnestly, leaning forward on the sofa. "I heard a rumor today and I'm wondering if it's true. Has Power-Up been trying to buy out Glow-Mor?"

Her smile became fixed. "Really, my Lilord, I had no idea you took an interest in such matters."

"Esmond," said Civilla severely, "don't be rude. No one wants to talk about business right now. Ice with yours, Laraine?"

For a young woman of eighteen she gave a remarkably good impression of being in charge, and Missus Paskin relaxed. "Thank you," she murmured as she accepted the glass.

"Please excuse my brother," said Civilla. "He's studying civics at the college and it's made him terribly opinionated. You know how boys can be." She smiled around at the company, and they smiled wanly back.

"It's just that it seems odd," Esmond went on before anyone else could speak. "I mean, everyone knows Missus Wregget and my mother are friends, and my father—" His voice wavered, and he cleared his throat. "My father took an interest in Glow-Mor's welfare. So I can't help thinking that he might have had an opinion about who ought to be running it. If he hadn't died, I mean."

Laraine Paskin sat rigid as a dressed-up doll. Eulalie's father steepled his fingers, studying Esmond with interest, while Su set her glass down and reached for her purse.

"Oh, I'm sorry," said Esmond. "I'm being rude again, aren't I? Perhaps I'd better change the subject. Good evening, Master Buldage."

The governor looked haunted, as though he'd begun to suspect what was going on. "And to you, milord," he replied.

"It was really quite brave of you, I thought, to accept a

Moshite girl as a student at Tarreton College. One might even say progressive, don't you think? The sort of thing my brother ought to approve of. You know, with his speeches about equality and justice and all that."

Buldage looked positively green now. "Indeed," he croaked.

"Except his speeches have been changing lately, I've noticed. Now it seems to be equality and justice for everyone but Moshites. It almost seems like a grudge of some sort. . . ."

"Speaking of Eryx," began Delicia in a warning tone, but Esmond interrupted her.

"Oh, don't worry, I'll get to him. Or he'll get to us, since I believe that's his spell-carriage coming up the drive. But I'm sure you know the sound of his wheels better than I do, since you've been seeing so much of each other." He got up, crossed to the drinks cart, and poured himself a bubblewater. "Practically engaged, I've heard."

Now it was Delicia's turn to look hunted. She sank back into her chair, avoiding Civilla's gaze.

Esmond turned to Missus Paskin. "Where's your husband, may I ask? He does plan to join us soon, I hope. The party wouldn't be the same without him."

Laraine Paskin set down her glass and stood. "I don't

know what all this is about, milord, but I think there's been a mistake. If you'll excuse me—"

"Ah, there he is!" crowed Esmond as the butler opened the door again and Mister Paskin stepped in. "Do come in; your wife's saved a seat for you."

"I . . . er . . . beg your pardon?" said Mister Paskin, doffing his hat. "We came to see Lord Eryx."

"Yes, I know," said Esmond cheerfully. "I'm told I sound just like him over the ringer, so I thought I'd save him the trouble of inviting you. He's on his way now, though, and I'm sure you'll have plenty to talk about when he arrives." Esmond leaned against the wall, beaming at them. "We might even be able to help. After all, it's not as though you've got anything to *hide*, have you?"

A swift look passed between the Paskins, and for a moment he thought the pair of them might bolt. But then Missus Paskin sat down and her husband walked stiffly to join her.

"My point was, though," Esmond continued in the same bright tone, "doesn't it seem like that Breck girl's had the rottenest luck? First her father gets arrested and charged with murdering the governor of Tarreton College. It turns out he didn't do it, but a lot of people still think he did, which leaves her with a rather unfortunate reputation." He flicked a glance at Su and went back to contemplating his bubblewater. "Then she wins the Glow-Mor scholarship. Hurrah! But she's barely been at the college two weeks before someone leaks her story to the newsrags. And as soon as all the ugliness from that dies down, she gets accused of stealing Betinda Callender's necklace. It's almost like she was *meant* to fail."

He cocked his head at the Paskins. "Speaking of Betinda, isn't your son Tadeus rather friendly with her these days?"

"Esmond!" exclaimed Civilla, clapping a hand to her breast. "Rudeness is one thing, but this is appalling. You can't mean to accuse our friends of deliberately ruining some poor girl's reputation just to weaken Glow-Mor!"

Everyone sat up at that, and Esmond did a little internal dance of glee. But he kept his expression mild as the footsteps in the hallway quickened and Eryx strode in.

"What is this?" he demanded, and everyone began talking at once.

"Oh, Eryx, I'm so glad you're—"

"Milord, I swear I didn't know—"

"Slander, that's what it is! We won't be insulted any—"

Civilla rushed to Eryx, clutching at his arm. "Esmond's been saying the most dreadful things," she gasped. "I think he's gone mad. Please do something—I must tell Mother." She stepped past him and hurried away.

Eryx didn't turn to watch her go. His gaze was on Esmond, dark with reproach. "This is unacceptable. Apologize to our guests at once."

"Why?" asked Esmond. "I haven't said a thing that isn't true. And it would be a shame to stop before the exciting bit." He straightened up to his full height. "There's a kidnapper, an extortioner, and at least two murderers in this room, and I'm not leaving until everyone knows who they are."

When the door to the kitchen swung open, Isaveth was ready. She snatched up the two bottles she'd filled and ran out after Civilla.

"Esmond's going to keep talking as long as he can," Esmond's sister told her as she pulled a key from her waistband. She opened the door to the underground tunnel and locked it behind them, twisting a glow-charm off her bracelet to see by. "But it won't be long before Eryx calls the servants to remove him, and when they don't come he's going to get suspicious. We have to move fast."

Her eyes were glittering, fierce with intent. She looked like a warrior going into battle, and a formidable warrior at that. Isaveth nodded, and the two of them raced for the carriage house.

Eryx's sportster was sitting in the middle bay,

spell-engine ticking as it cooled. Isaveth poured her first bottle over the passenger-side handle while Civilla kindled a warming-charm to help the potion dry.

"Esmond thought you believed Eryx," said Isaveth, watching the decoction ooze around the handle and the charms behind it. *Hurry, hurry* . . . "Why didn't you tell him the truth?"

Civilla sighed. "Because I was afraid. For him, and for myself. The house was full of spies, and Esmond was so young, and so angry . . . I was afraid that if he knew my plan, he might let something slip by accident."

How different things might have been if the two of them had only talked to each other. Yet Civilla had been so anxious to protect Esmond and guard her own secrets that he'd ended up thinking she didn't care. . . .

Much like Isaveth and Annagail.

"You underestimated him," Isaveth said softly. "Like he underestimated you."

"I'm afraid so. But I can't blame him for thinking I was no threat to Eryx when I'd tried so hard to appear that way. Are we ready?"

"Not yet," said Isaveth, squinting through her charm-glass. The aura of power around the door was fading, but the potion wasn't fully dry. "There's still one thing I don't understand, though. If you didn't want Eryx to become

Sagelord, why did you try to stop Esmond investigating your father's death?"

"I thought he might be accusing . . . someone very dear to me. And I couldn't bear that."

"You mean Delicia."

For several heartbeats Civilla was silent. Then she said, "She's been in love with Eryx since we were fifteen. I thought that if she knew what he was like she'd change her mind about him, but . . ." She gave a sad smile. "Perhaps I misjudged her, too."

It was hard to know what to say to that. Isaveth turned back to the door—and her heart leaped. "It's done. You can try it now."

Civilla reached for the handle. Her slim fingers touched it, curled tight . . . and with a click, the door popped open.

The case was on the passenger side, just as Esmond had said. Isaveth examined it carefully to make sure there were no more wards or alert-charms to bypass, then eased it out and laid it on the seat.

"Let me," said Civilla. Before Isaveth could protest, she thumbed up the latches and opened the case.

Dear Isaveth, read the topmost letter—but it was all she saw before the whole pile of documents burst into flame.

Chapter Twenty-Eight

CIVILLA REELED BACK, flinging up an arm to protect herself as Isaveth hurled the last of her potion onto the blaze—but it was useless. Not until Isaveth seized a blanket from the back of the carriage and smothered the case with it did the fire die out, and by then there was nothing left but black ashes and a few crumbling scraps of paper.

Isaveth snatched up the pieces that remained, scanning them desperately. Surely there had to be *something* there that would prove Eryx's guilt. But the few words that were left made no sense to her, so how would they convince anyone else? Letting the papers fall, she sank down on the sportster's running board and buried her face in her hands.

They'd lost everything. There was no way to stop Eryx now.

Civilla's hand brushed Isaveth's shoulder. "I'm so sorry. I should have guessed he'd have one last safeguard inside." She began leafing through the scorched papers, then drew a sharp breath.

"What?" asked Isaveth, twisting around. "What is it?"

Civilla stood unmoving, eyes fixed on something in her palm. A little envelope, rumpled and ash-smudged, but otherwise miraculously intact. "I found it in the pocket," she said slowly—then her lips parted and a gleam came into her eyes. Thrusting the envelope into her bodice, she started for the door.

Isaveth leaped up. "Where are you going?"

"Back to the house," said Civilla. She picked up her skirts, heedless of the black ash staining her fingers, and hurried down the steps to the passage. "Eryx thinks he's beaten us, but he's wrong."

A tiny ember of hope flickered in Isaveth. Had Civilla found something she'd overlooked? She ran after the older girl, then slowed to a discreet walk as they re-entered the mansion.

". . . kidnapped right out of the city records office." Esmond was strolling about the lounge as they entered, talking so rapidly that even Eryx couldn't get a word in. "And the funny thing is, it happened not long after you told Miss Breck that Power-Up had been scheming to buy out Glow-Mor." He turned to the man sitting behind him. "Isn't that right, Mister Wregget?"

Olina had obeyed her mistress well. As soon as Civilla and Isaveth vanished into the tunnel, she'd gone to tell Wregget, and he'd trotted back to rejoin the party—another nasty shock for the Paskins, no doubt.

"Yes, that's—" Wregget began, but Esmond didn't let him finish.

"Or perhaps I should say, right after you told Miss Breck you'd never give up her secret recipe for Resisto-Paper. Which was extremely interesting to the people listening on the other end of this." He reached inside his jacket and pulled out a silver bracelet with a coil of wire and a tiny sound-crystal attached.

"You may as well take this, Mister Paskin," he said, dropping it onto the tea table. "Mister Wregget's secretary won't be spying for you anymore."

Missus Paskin leaped up, quivering with rage. "How dare you! We are respectable business people, and we have every right to make an offer for Glow-Mor if we choose. This trumped-up story about spying and kidnapping is—"

"Trumped-up?" asked Esmond, the last of his humor vanishing. His voice dropped half an octave, and there was nothing silly about it now. "Tell that to the girl you abducted, tied up, and threatened to kill if she wouldn't cooperate. Better yet, tell that to the man your husband shot for daring to help her—oh, wait, you can't. Because his body's at the bottom of Lake Colonia, next to a freighter *your* family owns."

Missus Paskin froze.

"Those are filthy lies," Mister Paskin sputtered. "You have no proof!"

"On the contrary. Miss Breck?"

And here she'd thought Esmond was too busy talking to notice her. Isaveth stepped through the doorway, unwinding her bandages, and held out her rope-burned wrists for all to see.

"Thank you," said Esmond as the Paskins gaped at her. "Mind you, we all know what the word of a Moshite girl is worth in this town, especially one who's just been accused of stealing—so it's a good thing she wasn't the only witness. Remember when Barto rang to tell you about the street-boy who'd been snooping around the warehouse, Mister Paskin? That was me."

Missus Paskin rounded on her husband. "You fool," she snapped, then whirled back to the stone-faced Deputy Fairpont. "I knew nothing about this! If my husband killed someone that was his decision, not mine!"

"You mean Lanzy's murder, Missus Paskin?" Esmond

asked. "Or are you talking about my father's as well?"

Dead silence. Su stopped scribbling in her notebook, and Eryx went so still he might have been made of wax.

"Murder?" The gravelly voice came from Eulalie's father, speaking for the first time. "What makes you think Lord Arvis was murdered?"

"Well, *he* seemed to think so," Esmond told him, "so I thought I'd better look into it. I sent samples of his blood and whatnot for testing, and while I was waiting for the results I found out that the Paskins had stopped by to see Father less than a bell before he collapsed. Seems they weren't happy when they realized he planned to stop them taking over Glow-Mor . . . and since my brother was more sympathetic to their interests, the obvious answer was to get rid of the old Sagelord and set up a new one instead."

"That's a lie!" Mister Paskin burst out, and his wife shrilled, "He died of a bad liver! Everybody knows that! You can't possibly believe that we—"

"Poured him a drink?" Esmond kept his voice light, but there was a tremor in it. "Just a friendly one, while you asked him to reconsider. And when you realized his mind was made up, you gave him another . . . with a little taste of poison to help it go down."

"No!" shouted Mister Paskin. "That's not true!" He turned wildly to Eryx. "Milord, please—"

"This is terrible." Eryx sounded shaken. "How could you do such a thing, Sedric? And Laraine . . . how could you help him?"

The couple stared at Eryx with their mouths open. Then they shrank in on themselves like chastened dogs. "We didn't kill Lord Arvis," Mister Paskin whispered. "I swear it."

Delicia rose and moved to Eryx, folding her fingers into his. They stood together, noble and tragic as two statues in a museum—until Civilla spoke up from behind them.

"Sedric's right, they didn't kill my father. My brother the Sagelord did." She walked into the lounge, pulling the little envelope from her bodice. "In fact, he'd been poisoning him for weeks, with this."

PROPO-SELTZER, read the packet in bold blue letters. It was torn down one side, a white crust clinging to its edge.

"My father took it regularly," Civilla announced, "for headaches and a sour stomach. He almost certainly drank a glass on the night of my ball. If you have this analyzed, Deputy Fairpont, I think you'll find it's been laced with yellow-cap powder—the same toxin found in the samples Esmond sent for testing." She turned accusingly to Eryx. "I found it in my brother's spell-carriage."

"You scheming—" Eryx started toward her, but Esmond stepped into his path.

"One of us is a schemer, all right," he said flatly. "And if you touch Cilla, I'll knock you down."

"You set us up!" shrieked Missus Paskin. "You told us to talk to Lord Arvis and see if he'd change his mind. You murdered your own father so you could become Sage-lord, and then tried to make it look like we'd done it!"

"Don't be a fool, woman!" snapped Eryx. "Can't you see that's what my sister wants you to think?"

Esmond's eyes met Isaveth's, warm with relief and pride—but he also looked puzzled, and she couldn't blame him. He hadn't known about the Propo-Seltzer any more than she had, and he must be wondering why Civilla wasn't showing everyone the documents instead. . . .

The same thought must have occurred to Eryx, because he put a hand to his eyes, his expression shifting to anguish. "Oh, Civilla. Accusing your own brother of murder? I knew you were jealous, but I had no idea you would stoop so low." He drew Delicia close to him again. "No wonder you tried to keep the two of us apart. You knew Delicia would make a better Sagelady than you ever could."

Su Amaraq's lips tightened and her scribbling became so furious that Isaveth half expected to see sparks. But was she angry at Eryx, or indignant on his behalf?

"I was patient with Esmond because he seemed to be making a good case against the Paskins," Eryx continued, "and I know how he feels about Miss Breck. But this allegation is preposterous, and I refuse to dignify it with a rebuttal. Any intelligent person can see it isn't true."

Deputy Fairpont shifted in his armchair. "Milord, it's been a long day, and my wits aren't as sharp as they should be. Perhaps you'd be kind enough to explain."

Eryx sighed. "If I'd been poisoning Father's Propo-Seltzer, why would I keep a packet of the stuff in my sportster where anyone could find it? Why wouldn't I destroy it, and any others that might be left, as soon as I knew he was dying?" He shook his head. "It's obvious what really happened. My sister and Miss Breck plotted together to break into my carriage and plant false evidence against me."

Su frowned at Isaveth. "Really? Had you even met Civilla Ladyship before tonight?"

"No," said Isaveth. Yet Eryx's words troubled her, and she was beginning to wonder if she'd met the real Civilla at all. Was it possible that she'd only pretended to find the packet in Eryx's briefcase? Could she be the murderer, accusing Eryx to avert suspicion from herself?

"I'll admit Miss Breck has motive," Su continued, "seeing as Lord Eryx's been planning to cut her family off relief and leave them all to starve—pardon my bluntness.

But I find this talk of conspiracy a little far-fetched." She turned to Wregget. "You know Miss Breck better than I do. Does she seem like the type of girl to accuse someone she knows to be innocent? Especially after what her own father went through?"

"Not at all," said J. J. Wregget.

"Su!" exclaimed Delicia, but the reporter only shrugged.

"Just doing my job," she said. "Asking the hard questions. What do you think, Governor Buldage? You've been quiet this evening."

"Oh, this is ridiculous," exclaimed Esmond. He turned to Civilla and Isaveth. "Why are we wasting time? Show them the documents."

Buldage shrank back as though trying to blend in to the upholstery. Even Eryx looked uneasy, until Isaveth spoke.

"I'm sorry," she said. "They burned up when we opened the case. There's nothing left."

Esmond staggered as though she'd hit him. He leaned against the drinks cart, his good eye losing focus, and for once he had nothing to say.

"Documents?" asked Su.

Civilla raised her chin. "My brother's secret hoard of blackmail letters and other papers that could destroy his reputation if they became known. Why else would he rig the case to burn them if anyone else opened it?"

"Documents of a sensitive and personal nature," Eryx corrected patiently, "given to me in trust. Naturally I felt it my duty to protect them by any means possible, even if it should result in their destruction." He spread his hands. "Your word against mine, Civilla. The tongue of a petty gossip against the best-loved politician this city's ever known. Who do you think people are going to believe?"

Isaveth wrapped her arms around her stomach, feeling sick. Eryx was right: In such a contest there could be no doubt who would win. But it would never come to that. No ruling Sagelord could be charged with a crime unless there was clear and compelling evidence against him, and they had none. No way to prove that Eryx had poisoned Lord Arvis . . . or that he'd murdered Master Orien, either.

Buldage must have realized the same, because he relaxed as though a burden had rolled off his shoulders. The proof of his guilt was destroyed forever—and with it, the power Eryx held over him.

There was no joy for Isaveth, however. Her last hope had failed, and now she and everyone she loved were at Eryx's mercy. She bowed her head miserably, wishing she could just go home.

"Well," said Deputy Fairpont, "I can't say this has been

a pleasant evening, but it's certainly been an interesting one." He slapped the arms of his chair and rose, his voice turning crisp with authority. "Mister and Missus Paskin, I arrest you for kidnapping, extortion, and the murder of the man known as Lanzy. I'd advise you to come quietly, as I have a squad of Lawkeepers stationed outside."

The Paskins didn't even look at him. They sat listless on the sofa, slumped together like melting candles, as Fairpont picked the packet of Propo-Seltzer from the table and turned to Civilla.

"I'll start an investigation into your father's death. If what you say about the test results and this packet are true, then we'll catch the person who poisoned him, whoever that may be. But I'll need more evidence before I accuse Lord Eryx of murder . . . or your Ladyship of conspiracy, for that matter." He turned to leave.

"Wait." Esmond straightened up, looking pale and very young, and crossed to the doorway. "There's something you ought to see before you go." Then he unhooked his half glass and handed it to Isaveth, revealing his scarred face and milky-blind eye.

Gasps rose from all over the room, and Esmond's cheekbones flamed. But he kept talking. "Eryx did this to me with a fencing sword a year and a half ago," he said. "Right after I refused to help him poison our father."

Eryx opened his mouth to protest, but Civilla spoke first. "He claimed Esmond's injury was an accident," she said. "And my father believed him, so we all had to play along. But it was a lie." Her gaze shifted to Delicia. "Eryx is my brother, and nothing will ever change that. But he is also a murderer, a deceiver, and the foulest hypocrite I have ever known."

Deputy Fairpont looked as though someone had force-fed him a toad. It was a charge too serious to be ignored, yet how to prove it? He still had nothing but Esmond and Civilla's word that Eryx was guilty, and they both stood to gain if their brother lost power. . . .

A throat cleared on the far side of the room. Governor Buldage rose from his seat, shoulders back and graying head held high.

"I have a confession to make," he said. "I am guilty of murdering my predecessor, Governor Orien. A murder that Lord Eryx plotted and helped me to—"

His words ended in a splutter as Eryx grabbed him by the neck. He was shaking Buldage like a puppet, his face twisted to ugliness, when Wregget and Deputy Fairpont leaped to pull him away.

"This is monstrous!" Eryx shouted, struggling so wildly that even Delicia shrank away from him. His hair and clothes were disheveled, his elegance gone. "All the good

I've done for this city—my great plans for reform—and you want to destroy it for the sake of your short-sighted—"

"Eryx?"

Lady Nessa's voice wavered like a frightened child's. She stood in the lobby, Perline Wregget by her side.

"It's all right, Mother." Civilla moved quickly to take her arm, as though fearing the older woman might faint. "Deputy Fairpont has everything under control."

The Sagelady's gaze swept the lounge, taking in all the details—Esmond without his half glass, and Isaveth at his side; Eryx slumped between Wregget and the Deputy Justice, sweating and ashen; the packet of Propo-Seltzer lying on the carpet, where it had tumbled out of Fairpont's pocket in the scuffle. She clapped a hand to her mouth, eyes brimming.

"Mother?" Eryx strained toward her. "Don't tell me you believe them! I didn't poison Father, I swear—"

"It was Eryx, Mother." Civilla held her gaze, reassuring. "It was him all along."

The color eased back into Lady Nessa's face. She laid her hand on Civilla's, gripping it as though drawing on her daughter's strength. "I hoped you would be better, Eryx," she whispered. "But you are your father's son."

Then slowly she turned and let Civilla lead her away.

Chapter Twenty-Nine

THE NEXT FEW DAYS passed like a whirlwind for Isaveth as the city reeled from the shock of Eryx's arrest and the downfall of one of its leading merchant families. At first many people refused to believe Eryx could be guilty, and put forth all sorts of elaborate theories in his defense. But once the Healer-General confirmed that the Propo-Seltzer Lord Arvis had taken was laced with dried yellow-cap, a poisonous mushroom known for its destructive effects on the liver, Deputy Justice Fairpont met with the city council and emerged with their final decision: Eryx would be stripped of his office and tried on several counts of corruption, conspiracy, and murder. Civilla was now the ruling Sagelady of Tarreton.

That same week J. J. Wregget, finding himself head of a smaller and meeker board of directors in the wake of the Power-Up scandal, announced that from now on the Glow-Mor scholarship would be offered only to commoners with a family income of less than fifteen imperials a year. That night he invited Isaveth and her family to dinner at his estate and told her that he and his wife had decided to personally cover all of her college expenses until graduation.

"Th-thank you, sir," stammered Isaveth, too overcome to say more. But she was troubled all the way home, wondering if she could bring herself to accept Wregget's offer.

She knew now that she could never have afforded to patent her own invention even if Esmond had been free to help, so she no longer blamed Wregget for offering her a lump sum instead. But the cruelty, callousness, and deception she'd seen among the wealthy folk of Tarreton haunted her, and she was reluctant to have anything more to do with them. Besides, her sisters were no less needy or deserving than she was, and it seemed unfair for her to have so many privileges they did not.

When she sat down to talk to Papa and Annagail about it, however, her sister was horrified. "You *have* to go back, Vettie," she insisted, reaching across the kitchen table to seize her hand. "You've worked so hard and suffered so much for that scholarship, it would be wicked to ask you to give it up. I'm sorry for the things I said to you—I'm ashamed of them now. You seemed so happy I couldn't help feeling jealous, but if I'd known . . ."

"I don't blame you, Anna," said Isaveth. "I did pretend to be happy, because I thought it was the best way to protect you. But I won't lie to you and Papa again." She turned to their father, sitting quietly by the stove as he smoked his baccy pipe. "Esmond's going to take the tests he missed next week, and Mistress Anandri says I can take mine as well, if I want to. What do you think, Papa?"

"I think, my Vettie, that I'm glad all this sneaking about and keeping secrets from the rest of us is over. I can't blame you for wanting to stand up to Eryx, but I'm not best pleased to find out the trouble my daughters have been getting into behind my back." He frowned at Lilet, who reddened and sank behind her book. "Still, you did it for the right reasons, and that's the main thing. If you want to stick it out at the college, I'll not stand in your way."

So the next Mendday, Isaveth went back to Tarreton College. She'd barely passed the gate before Eulalie came flying to meet her, hugging her so hard the two of them nearly fell over.

"You're back!" she exclaimed. "I missed you terribly. But I've been taking lots of notes in Sagery, and you can borrow them any time. Isn't it splendid about Mistress

Anandri being the new governor, and Paskin and Betinda getting expelled? Nobody will dare bully you now."

Isaveth returned the hug, but part of her was still uncertain. According to Esmond, Eulalie had not only coaxed her father to accept Civilla's last-minute drinks invitation, she'd convinced him to bring a squad of Lawkeepers because a murderer would be revealed that night. It was obvious now that Eulalie hadn't betrayed her—yet there were still a few things Isaveth didn't understand.

"I thought you didn't want to talk about the bullying," she said. "It seemed as though every time I tried, you ran off or changed the subject."

Eulalie's smile faded. "I know," she said. "I hated not being able to do anything to stop it, and I didn't know what to say without hurting you even more. I'm sorry for disappearing on you, but . . ." She raised pleading eyes to Isaveth's. "I didn't always have a choice. I have terrible cramps in my insides nearly every day, and when I'm upset, they get worse."

"Oh, Eulalie! Why didn't you say so?"

"Because I hate talking about it, that's why." She scowled. "I have to sit on the toilet for *ages*, and who wants to hear about that? And every time someone finds out they tell me to try this diet or that exercise or some tonic they heard about on the crystal set, and it makes me want to scream. I don't want people to feel sorry for me or try to fix me. I just want to get on with my life as best as I can."

No wonder Seffania thought Eulalie had been faking. It didn't explain Miss Kehegret's cryptic note, though. "Can I ask one more thing?" asked Isaveth. "Who is DW, and what did you tell him or her about S at the Harvest Dance?"

"That again! I should have known it would get around to you." Eulalie sighed. "Darion Wellman is in third year with Seffania's brother. He asked me if she liked him, and I told him she did, because I thought he meant to ask her to dance. But then he and her brother made fun of Seffania and embarrassed her horribly, and she's never forgiven me. So now I'm the girl who can't keep a secret, and nobody wants to be my friend anymore. Except you." She looked up at Isaveth shyly. "We . . . are still friends, aren't we?"

Isaveth smiled and squeezed the other girl's hand. "Of course we are," she said.

"I still can't believe the council voted Eryx out so quickly," Esmond said as he and Isaveth strolled around the courtyard after school. It felt strange to be talking where anyone could see them, but Civilla had no objection to their friendship, and even Lady Nessa seemed content to overlook it as long as Esmond was happy. "Apparently all those society meetings of Cilla's were a lot more political than I thought."

Isaveth wasn't surprised. From what Eulalie had told her, Civilla's volunteer work had earned her a high reputation among the council ladies and other leading women of the city. They didn't see her as spiteful or prone to gossip, no matter what Eryx had thought.

"You never did tell me exactly what happened between you and Civilla before you came to rescue me," said Isaveth. "What did she say that convinced you she was on our side?"

Esmond raised a hand to adjust his half glass, then smiled ruefully and let it drop. "She told me she'd decided to ruin Eryx as soon as she saw this," he said, gesturing to his new eye patch. "But she couldn't move against him until she came of age to inherit, and she couldn't risk him finding out her plan. So she pretended to believe his story about the accident."

His good eye turned distant. "Then she told me she was sorry, and that she loved me. There . . . was some crying involved."

Not just Civilla's, Isaveth suspected. "So she let you think you were the only one who knew or cared enough to fight Eryx," she said, "while she was quietly stealing his supporters out from under him."

Though she hadn't managed to win over Delicia Ghataj, who remained firmly on Eryx's side. It saddened Isaveth that an intelligent young woman could be so deceived, especially after hearing all the evidence. But according to Mander, Delicia was convinced that the Paskins were the only ones who had done anything criminal, that the fatal packet of Propo-Seltzer had been planted in Eryx's sportster without his knowledge, and that he was wholly innocent of the charges against him.

Civilla had pleaded with her to see reason, reminding her of Governor Buldage's confession and Esmond's ruined eye, but Delicia refused to hear it. She wore Eryx's engagement band openly now, insisting they would be married as soon as the trial was over and his good name restored.

"I thought everyone was fooled by Eryx," said Esmond. "But being charmed by someone and trusting them are two different things, as my mother pointed out. People hoped he'd be a better Sagelord than Father, especially when they didn't think they had any say in the matter. But when the truth came out and they had to make a choice, it was obvious that Civilla was the real politician in the family. Did you know her Women's League has raised nearly a thousand imperials for poverty relief just this year?"

He spoke with pride, and Isaveth felt a surge of happiness for him. He'd been alone so long, it thrilled her to know he finally had a family again—or part of one, at any rate.

"I'm so glad," she said. "She'll make a wonderful Sagelady."

"She will, and I can't believe how I misjudged her. Mother, too. She's not strong, but she's a lot sharper than I realized when my father kept talking over her all the time. It still hurts that he's gone, but I feel like . . . I hardly know how to explain it. Like some great cloud of smog has lifted, and I can breathe again."

Isaveth nodded. She'd seen the change already, at lunchtime: Esmond and Mander Ghataj sitting side by side at the dining table, chatting like old friends. The boy had been crushed to find out Eryx was a murderer—he, at least, didn't share his sister's blindness to the truth. But Esmond knew all too well how it felt to be disappointed by Eryx, so the two of them had much to talk about.

"Do you still miss him?" asked Esmond abruptly, after they'd walked a while in silence. "Quiz, I mean."

Isaveth stopped short. "Oh dear. Was it obvious?"

"A bit. The first few times we met in the bell tower,

you kept looking at me like this." He put on a wistful, slightly tragic expression, and Isaveth had to laugh.

"I did at first," she admitted, "because you seemed so different here than you did when we first met. I didn't know what to make of it, especially when I saw how you behaved with . . . well, everybody but me."

"I thought that might be it. I'm surprised you didn't say so before." He turned to face her, apologetic and a little shy. "I did try to be friendly, when I first came. But people kept saying, 'You're so much like your brother!' and gabbling about how wonderful Eryx was. So I decided the only solution was to act as *un*like him as possible. It wasn't until I became Quiz and met you that I could be myself again."

Until Isaveth heard that, she'd scarcely realized how much the question had troubled her. Now she felt a soaring exhilaration, as though some long-cherished fantasy had turned out to be real after all. "Well, Quiz is a likeable fellow," she said lightly. "I hope more people get to know him."

"What about Esmond Lording? That's my title now, at least until Civilla's got an heir of her own. Do you think you could like him, too?"

"You're the same person," said Isaveth. "I've known that ever since you came to rescue me from the Paskins.

I'm only sorry I didn't trust you enough to believe it before."

Esmond took her gloved hand in both of his. "There's something I've been wanting to ask you. If you say no, I promise I won't ask again." He raised his good eye to hers, searching. "May I?"

It had been so long since they'd played the game that for a moment Isaveth had no idea what he was asking—and then, with a fluttering lurch of her heart, she remembered. Only she couldn't think of any clever retorts for some reason, and the way Esmond was looking at her made her realize it had never really been a joke at all.

The thought made her feel dizzy, like the first time he'd asked her. But back then Isaveth hadn't been sure what she wanted, and she was now. She drew her hand out of the glove, leaving Esmond still holding it, and reached up to touch his face.

"Do you know," she said softly as she rose on tiptoes to kiss him, "this time, I think you may."

Epilogue

LADY NESSA DRIFTED through her indoor garden, trowel and litter bag in hand. She fingered the red-tipped fronds of an Antipodean fern, bent to breathe its fragrance, and passed on, plucking dead blooms and yellow leaves from other plants as she went. Finally she stooped to examine the bed between two of her prized heart-lilies, where a tiny yellow-capped mushroom was just emerging.

The Dowager Sagelady paused, one gloved finger touching the newly regrown fungus in a light, almost tender caress. Then she stabbed her trowel deep into the soil, dug the mushroom out, and continued on her way.

Acknowledgments

Deepest gratitude and appreciation to Reka Simonsen, my editor at Atheneum, who has been a sage advisor, a great help, and a pleasure to work with at every step of the process. I am also indebted to Shannon Vaughan, my wonderful publicist, and the rest of the hard-working team at S&S Canada; to Tom Lintern for the delightful cover art; and to Josh Adams, my superstar agent.

Special thanks for this book are due to my friends in Melbourne: Liz Barr and the staff of Continuum 11, for giving me a much-needed break and change of perspective; Kathryn Andersen, who kindly welcomed me into her home and listened to me ramble about the plot for four days straight; and Amie Kaufman, who is not only a brilliant writer and person but an exceptional zoo guide as well.

Thanks also to all the usual suspects: Deva Fagan and

Peter Anderson for their tireless support and encouragement through the first draft, and E. K. Johnston for loving it even in that disheveled and fledgling state; Stephanie Burgis, Brittany Harrison, and Simon Bohner for guiding and cheering me through the revision phase, and Emily Bytheway for saying lovely things about the manuscript afterward. Meanwhile, Erin Bow, Kel Pero, Judy Williams, Eleanor Jenkins, and Laura McKay kept me fortified with friendly companionship and cups of soothing tea. You're all wonderful and I love you.

Last but never least, to my family: Horst, my ever-patient and caring husband; Nick, Simon, and Paul, my funny, clever, and endlessly delightful sons; and my loving parents Colin and Joan Anderson, who guarded my writing time more zealously than I ever would. I thank God for you every day.